# A TOUCH FOR ALL TIME

## For All Time, Book 3

### by
### Paula Quinn

## ARE YOU SIGNED UP FOR DRAGONBLADE'S BLOG?

You'll get the latest news and information on exclusive giveaways, exclusive excerpts, coming releases, sales, free books, cover reveals and more.

Check out our complete list of authors, too!

No spam, no junk. That's a promise!

### Sign Up Here

www.dragonbladepublishing.com

*Dearest Reader;*

*Thank you for your support of a small press. At Dragonblade Publishing, we strive to bring you the highest quality Historical Romance from some of the best authors in the business. Without your support, there is no 'us', so we sincerely hope you adore these stories and find some new favorite authors along the way.*

*Happy Reading!*

*CEO, Dragonblade Publishing*

# Additional Dragonblade books by Author Paula Quinn

### For All Time Series
A Promise For All Time (Book 1)
A Kiss For All Time (Book 2)
A Touch For All Time (Book 3)

### Hearts of the Conquest Series
The Passionate Heart (Book 1)
The Unchained Heart (Book 2)
The Promised Heart (Book 3)

### Echoes in Time Series
Echo of Roses (Book 1)
Echoes of Abandon (Book 2)
The Warrior's Echo (Book 3)
Echo of a Forbidden Kiss (Novella)

### Rulers of the Sky Series
Scorched (Book 1)
Ember (Book 2)
White Hot (Book 3)

### Hearts of the Highlands Series
Heart of Ashes (Book 1)
Heart of Shadows (Book 2)
Heart of Stone (Book 3)
Lion Heart (Book 4)
Tempest Heart (Book 5)
Forbidden Heart (Book 6)
Heart of Thanks (Novella)

# CHAPTER ONE

*Devon, England*
*Dartmouth Castle*
*1780*

TESSA BLAGDEN HAD to try to remember that the boy was not yet ten summers old. He was squirming in his seat while she spoke because he wanted to go play with his friends. At the thought of him playing, she remembered his father mentioning that since the disappearance of his mother two and a half years ago, the child didn't play all that much. She closed her eyes and gritted her teeth. Now wasn't the time to let pity rule her. The boy had to stay strong.

"Grayson...child, listen to me." She took hold of him by the shoulders and stared into his wide, cerulean eyes—the same color as his great-grandfather, Thoren Ashmore. "I can get into terrible trouble if it is discovered that I gave this to you, though you can probably travel on your own, but just in case, you must keep it hidden. Do you understand?"

"Aye, Grandmother," he said, opening his small hands to receive a master key—the likes of which hadn't been invented yet. This one was fashioned from pure gold.

It was one of many *time-alterers* in Tessa's care since she became a timekeeper over a century or so ago.

"This key will lead you to your heart's desire."

The child nodded and gazed at the door.

"Grayson, are you listening to me? It will help you heal."

His gaze slipped back to hers. He tilted his head slightly as if he was listening to something only he could hear. Then, he spoke in his small voice, "Grandmother, are you going away too?"

She felt her eyes begin to sting with hot tears. He definitely had gifts. As the only living Ashmore male, he potentially had *all* the Ashmore/Blagden gifts. She suspected he could communicate with animals after she saw him sitting at the tree line around Dartmouth Castle with a brown squirrel, a fox and a dozen birds nearby, including a big raven flying above his head on more than one occasion. Animals often stayed close to him, and on several occasions, she had seen him in telepathic communication with them, laughing or teasing a red squirrel or racoon. He'd known his mother would disappear before Tessa had known, but she didn't think he was a seer. When she'd asked him how he'd known about his mother, he told her that he had dreamed about her telling him she had to go away. He was capable of dream communication. Could he travel through time, speak to spirits, see the future? He never spoke of any of it.

"Grayson?" she said instead of answering him and covered the key and his hands in hers. "Did you make any new friends?"

He lowered his gaze and shook his head. "The others do not like me."

"Whyever would they not like you? You are generous and you have a kind heart." He was also the most beautiful of all the children in the castle and the villages surrounding it, but best not to tell him too often.

"They call me names," he confided in his softest voice.

She scowled at his bent head and the glossy black locks falling forward. "What kinds of names?"

"Ballet Gray, Go-away-Gray. They say Mother left because of me."

Tessa stood up with her hands on her hips. "Which children said that to you? Tell me and I will whip their hides with a switch."

He looked up at her and the blue-green facets of his eyes darkened like oceans beneath a thundering sky. "Harry Gable,

2

Timothy Cavendish, Nicholas Rowe, and Alan Stephens. But," he hesitated, looking away again for a moment. "Mother told me not to let the animals hurt them because the animals will suffer." He gave her a worried look. "Will you suffer if you whip their hides?"

She smiled and shook her head, but oh, she had tears to shed for this child. His father kept the boy confined within the castle walls to keep him from being kidnapped by his runaway wife. But the duke was rarely home, and his son escaped often to go play in the forest, where he felt completely at home.

When the duke was at Dartmouth, he didn't know how to raise a boy alone, especially one who was a little odd and had more animal friends than human ones. A boy who snarled, showing his teeth when he was either joyful or angry, and who constantly practiced ballet moves and jumps like the saut de pendu, also known as the 'hanged man's jump' or pirouette basse, or 'low pirouette'.

A time-traveler, Tessa had lived in the twenty-first century long enough to be familiar with classical ballet. Gray's obsession was what, in the eighteenth century, was called comic or grotesque ballet. Grotesque in the sense of the dancer dancing like a dead person, mainly with his head tilted to one side and arms hanging low. The boy was quite good. Even from a springing jump with one toe touching the floor while stretching the other foot well out into the air as high as possible.

"Grandmother, are you going away too?" he asked again.

It was hard to look at him with the truth. Tessa loved him, having been in his life since the moment he entered the world. Her blood flowed through his veins. Gray's mother, Emma, a descendant of Thoren Ashmore, had produced a baby boy but the eighteenth century was not for her. She'd tried to change it but failed.

Tessa held his hands and then lifted them to her cheek. "Yes, Grayson, I have to go away, but I will return to you."

He was silent for three breaths—Tessa Blagden counted them. And then his eyes misted, and the whites reddened, along with his cheeks. But no tears fell. With disdain staining his little face, he yanked his hands free of her grip and stepped back, out of her reach.

"Farewell then," he ground out, then ran from the room.

Tessa took a step to go after him, then stopped. She wiped her eyes, then drew in a deep breath. The coming years were going to be very difficult for him. She wished more than anything that she could remain with him, but it was impossible. In fact, she could feel time changing around her already. Soon, she would be gone, just like his mother, but if Tessa didn't go, the male line of Blagden/Ashmore would cease forever. She had to prepare for her sweet Grayson's future. She would leave Harper to help him when the time came.

She spread her loving gaze around his room, dipping her gaze to his bed, his slippers. She wiped her eyes, then closed them. She would see him again. Someday.

THE BOY OPENED his eyes to his third day of being alone and tried to fight the emptiness inside him from spreading. But his grandmother had left him, and his mother had never returned to his dreams. He lay there in his large bed in a castle that housed over two hundred people and felt lonelier than a boy raised in the wilds of Wales. He realized—far too young—that his mother had left him long before she disappeared. She was never happy with him and his father. Gray had listened behind their bedroom door on nights when she fought with his father. He hadn't wanted to, but he remembered some of the things she said.

*If I had known my life would be like this, I would have rid my body of him when I had the chance. I hate all of you! I hate living here! I hate being your wife. I hate being a mother!*

She hated being his mother.

Abigail, the large Graylag goose from the nearest village, had assured him that adults sometimes told terrible lies. Kitty, the head mouse of the castle, had also promised him that they'd heard his mother say other wonderful things about him on

4

different occasions.

Gray usually believed them, and the things they'd told him helped him not feel so bad. But not this morning.

He kicked his blankets off and climbed out of bed. If his mother never returned to his life or his dreams, why should he care? If his beloved grandmother wanted to leave him the way his mother had, that was fine with him.

The bedroom door opened and Harper, one of the castle musicians, stepped inside and curtsied slightly. "Lord Dartmouth, I was just coming to wake you and help you dress for the day."

He stopped on his way to his wardrobe and stared blankly at her. "Why are you here again instead of the kitchen?"

"I'm not the cook. Your grandmother asked me to serve as your nurse. We discussed this yesterday and the day before that. Don't you remember?"

"Your speech is odd," he noted.

"It's how people speak where I come from."

"*It's*," he repeated with a curious arch of his brow, then shook his head.

"That's right. Mixing two words together. It's called contractions."

He picked up his steps and opened the door to his wardrobe. "I know what it is called. Do I look like a babe to you? But people in the castle do not use contractions."

She smiled at him. "My lord, you're only nine summers old. Here, let me help you dress."

"I am almost ten," he corrected numbly. "I do not need a nurse. Please leave." He didn't speak to her again and began picking out what he would wear. He finished stepping into breeches, dyed red especially for him by Clara, one of the laundresses.

*Gray! Gray help!*

He stopped upon hearing the voice of the goose Abigail in his thoughts. He dropped his shirt and ran out of his bedchamber wearing his nightdress and breeches.

*What is it? Abigail, what is it?!* he begged as he raced down the stairs. She didn't answer.

He ran from the castle without a word to anyone on the way. Barefoot, he sprinted toward the village, calling to her. She usually greeted him at the edge of the road, but she wasn't there now.

"Abigail!" he shouted.

*Gray.* He heard her say his name weakly. He felt ill. Abigail was the first animal he'd ever spoken to. She was his first friend.

*Where are you?* He closed his eyes and thought about her as hard as he could. Then he saw her in his mind. Behind a barn. The Gable's barn. She was laying in the grass, a small arrow protruding from her breast.

*No! No! Abigail, I am coming!*

He knew where the Gables lived and ran to the barn. When he reached Abigail, he fell to his knees beside her and cried, for she was almost gone.

"Who did this to you?" he wept as he gently scooped her up in his arms.

*The boys.*

*Who? Tell me who.*

She made a little sound that broke his heart and made him cry even harder.

*Harry Gable,* she managed, *and...his...friends.* Then there was nothing else.

"Abigail? Please do not go," he wailed. He remembered her chasing Peter, a potbellied pig around and making Gray laugh while he watched. She had also chased Harry Gable on a number of occasions, pecking at his head while he ran away yelping.

Harry Gable.

He wiped his nose and carried Abigail into the barn. He found a shovel and dragged it into the forest to bury his friend.

He wept while he said farewell, and then he didn't cry again.

"Hey, Ballet Gray."

When Gray heard Harry Gable's voice behind him, he turned

slowly and wiped his eyes.

"I was going to eat the fat goose. Dig it back up before I—"

Gray hated him and unable to bear anything more coming from his mouth, leaped at him. But Harry was older and bigger. He also knew how to fight. Still, Gray was able to punch him in the mouth before Harry pelted him with his fists until Gray lay on the ground with blood coming from his nose.

*Help!* he called out, summoning the animals in the forest. *This human boy killed Abigail! Avenge her! Avenge me!*

Immediately, birds swooped down from the branches overhead and began pecking at Harry's head. Groundhogs appeared and nipped at his ankles, seven foxes hurried toward him and bit him repeatedly until Harry screamed in agony.

Watching, Gray smiled. When he saw a black wolf approaching, he motioned with his chin and the wolf approached Harry slowly. The other animals moved aside to give the lone predator space.

The wolf pounced once and tore at Harry's face before a gun sounded in Gray's ears and his smile faded as the majestic wolf fell to the ground with a whimper.

Gray turned to see George Gable, Harry's father holding a smoking flintlock pistol.

Gray rose to his feet. His heart felt as if it had stopped along with Abigail's breath. Or perhaps it had stopped long before that.

He called for more help and within a moment or two, a large raven approached from the north. George Gable didn't have time to reload his weapon before the raven swooped down and plucked him in his eye, and then in his temple.

Gray felt a momentary twinge of guilt over George Gable losing an eye and likely his life, but he deserved to lose it since he shot and killed Davith.

With Harry and his father screaming, Gray left the forest and went home.

It only took a few hours for word to spread and sink into everyone's souls. Grayson Barrington had used animals to kill

George Gable and maul his son. The young lord controlled them through his devilish power. What's more, according to poor, young Harry Gable, that Barrington boy had laughed while the Gables were being attacked.

Gray's father was away in Exeter so he sent word that his son wasn't to be touched or punished as there was no proof of their mad claims. But he allowed the village men to hunt and kill any animals they came upon in the forest.

*You used the animals to hurt others and now they will suffer.*

Gray heard his mother's voice, but it was just a memory. Still, he fought the adults in a heedless attempt to save the animals, but to no avail. When the men were done hunting, they had killed thirty-seven red foxes, a small pack of wolves in the north, six ravens, sixteen rabbits, and even thirteen squirrels. When the last animal was killed, Gray's gift of communicating with them died as well.

Over the years, Gray convinced himself that he had never truly communicated with animals. It had all been just a part of his childish imagination to help him get through the sadness in his life.

Most days, he didn't feel a thing, which made dancing like a hanged man easier.

Most days. But there were others...

*Fifteen years later...*

THE MOST HONORABLE the Marquess of Dartmouth, Lord Grayson Barrington strode into the Ballroom of Dartmouth Castle as if he owned it, which he did.

He was given the castle by his father—much to the contention of Gray's older stepbrother, Timothy Cavendish. Cavendish, the bastard, lived here with his mother.

Gray's father's second wife in the hopes of stealing Gray's birthright. The thought of it brought a sneer to Gray's lips and murder to his gaze.

Of course, Gray wouldn't murder Cavendish. He'd killed on the battlefield, and even then, only when he had to. He was sick of the sight and the smell of blood and was discharged two years ago for medical reasons after he was found sitting among a dead regimen of French soldiers. A time of his life he would prefer to forget.

From the corner of his eye, he could see the flushed, smiling faces of the younger women—daughters of his father's noble guests fawning over the sight of him in his green silk-velvet three-piece suit, edged in bronze embroidery. His snug, matching breeches and tight hose drew their eyes to his strong thighs and shapely calves. His raven hair, kept shorter than was the fashion because it was easier to wear it disheveled or spiky, as it was tonight, was waxed and powdered white just beyond his dark roots.

He was the only man at court who wore his natural hair powdered instead of a wig. But Lord Dartmouth was known to be odd and a bit off. He did what he wanted, dressed however he liked, whether his style was in fashion or not. As for his hair, why should he force a tight wig onto his head when he had a perfectly thick head of hair? Sometimes he left it as black as the waters of the Dart Estuary outside the castle, and slicked back, displaying his stark beauty.

He cast the younger ladies a sensual, come-hither look and bit his bottom lip. He beckoned them to him, but none had the courage to step forward. He laughed softly, turning his attention to the disapproving glares of the duke and duchess of Milford, Earl Bixley and his wife, and Earl Swatington. Swatington's wife was sizing him up like a juicy slab of beef and she had not enjoyed any meat in years.

He was mad. Rebellious. Obsessed with the macabre. Poor duke to have such an heir.

He'd heard it all before and let it bounce off his armor. Two things would happen before this, his stepmother's first ball of the early spring season was over tonight. First, he would anger and embarrass his father and his father's wife, and the second, he would enjoy doing it.

He wished the enjoyment would last, but it never did. It was always temporary, momentary, and then the anger and the misery returned. These people had no idea how his dancing kept him sane and all of them unharmed.

No one here would be able to stop him if drew his sword. After years of training for war and then actually fighting one against the French, he knew how to kill, and he knew how to be merciless if necessary.

He spotted Elspeth Gable pretending to find no interest in him while he strode forward. He let his gaze rake over the hall until he found Elspeth's husband, Harry Gable.

Gray had often thought about killing him. But...he slid his warm gaze back to Elspeth...making Harry's wife desire him was a far more satisfying revenge.

And so, he kept his eyes on her while he cued the musicians to play the music he had chosen from an Italian composer Francesco Molino. Gray took the liberty of changing the tempo. When the musicians picked up their instruments, the guests gave him the dance floor and he took it.

He leaped high, extending his legs and landing as if he broke all his bones. He stood and bent his arms, swinging them at the elbows. He stepped forward, keeping time with the tempo, hips thrust out, toes pointed. He bent lower and spun on one foot while holding his face in his hands and turning his head as if he might twist it off. His body moved in perfect synchronicity with the music, and while some—including Elspeth Gable—watched him in spellbound awe, most looked away from the grotesque sight.

He caught his father's eye from where the duke sat at the dais with his wife, Eloise Cavendish, Duchess of Devonshire. Gray liked his stepmother as much as he liked her son.

His father glared at him across the empty floor. Gray chuckled silently. Was it anything new? No. Every time Gray danced his father cast him murderous looks. Gray didn't remember a time when he hoped his father would watch him with pride and perhaps a little admiration for his son's expertise on the dance floor.

Gray had learned every dance there was and practiced the steps until he didn't have to think about them. But knowing how to dance was one thing; being the best dancer, according to everyone who'd seen him, was another. Even those who didn't like his unconventional style had to admit Grayson possessed a natural flair that made his body move differently and better than anyone else.

But Thomas Barrington, His Grace the Duke of Devonshire, didn't agree. He continued to glare.

Gray didn't care. He continued dancing until his breath came hard, raising his shoulders around his ears. When the musicians began to play an English folk song about a man shooting his neighbor over a spilled drink, Gray danced his sometimes-comedic style of ballet. When the lyrics told of a villain aiming his gun at his neighbor, Gray found Harry Gable again in the crowd. He lifted his index and middle fingers and closed one eye to aim, then fired.

Surrounded by gasps and whispers, Gray lowered his hand and grinned at Harry.

# CHAPTER TWO

*New York City*
*Summer 2024*

ARIA STUDIED THREE of her best students while they practiced. Michael's isolations and gestures were almost perfect, Jake's lifts and contributions to the choreography were unparalleled, and Brenda—well, she was already the star of the show. The top in her dance class, Brenda Louise Peacock was Blagden's School of Contemporary Dance's prima ballerina. But which of the men would Aria send to the next round of auditions? Both were extremely talented, and they shared great potential. Together they were perfect, but individually, they lacked in certain areas. One area was passion. Their facial expressions were wooden.

"Michael," Aria said sternly, walking toward him, her dance slippers silent on the polished wooden floor, "your breath is off. Fix it. The best of the best will all be there tomorrow, vying for the chance to be Romeo in this production. If you're content to remain off-Broadway, then don't do your best."

He had the gall to smile at her, as if all this was a joke.

"Michael, I wouldn't mind your arrogance if you had what it took to back it up," she said wryly. "But you don't. I'm going to show you." She cast her cool, blue gaze at Jake and Brenda. "Take five. Not you," she told Michael when he moved to sit with them. She called to Alexa to play her playlist. She looked in the wall-length mirror, loving this side of it, missing it as if it were her last breath.

She'd rather be dancing than teaching...than anything. But

her dancing days were over. She'd had to accept it after the car accident left her close to being unable to walk again, let alone dance. Still, she'd been spared more than her older brother, Connall. More than her father. The money from teaching paid the rent where she lived with her family. She also worked a night job and would get a third job if she had to. They didn't receive money from the accident since they claimed it was her father's fault. She would do whatever was needed to help her mother, since her father could no longer do anything but lie in his sickbed.

She pulled her ponytail free, and locks of glossy, chestnut hair cascaded over her shoulders almost to her waist.

"I'd rather watch you dance, Ms. Darling," Michael said dreamily.

She looked at him standing beside her in the mirror. "Keep up with me, or you're out."

"C'mon, Ms. Darling," Michael lamented, sounding younger than his nineteen years. "That's not fair. No one can keep up with you."

She bit her lip. Maybe that had been true before the car accident that left her with broken bones everywhere, including a compound break of her tibia that stopped her from pursuing her professional dance career.

The memory of that fateful night a little over a year ago brought tears to her eyes and made her throat burn. She didn't try to subdue her emotions but let them lead her. The music started.

She had been dancing since she was a little girl. She'd worked harder than any in her class and always gave one hundred percent. It had earned her the lead in a Broadway production. Her dream had come true. To celebrate, her parents and brother had taken her out to dinner. She remembered how proud they were of her. Her father even bought an expensive bottle of wine so they could toast her. He'd had one glass.

One glass.

For the first few seconds, she kept her steps simple, but she soon grew lost in the dance, a blend of ballet and lyrical dance.

She'd trained in jazz and three different forms of ballet, lyrical and contemporary.

They crashed trying to avoid another car that ran a red light.

Her push and pull were clearly defined as she pumped her chest toward the lights on the ceiling—or in her mind, the starry night she had opened her eyes to, trapped upside down in her parents' car.

While she danced, she kept her breath steady as she spun her head, fanning her tresses outward. She bent into a penché then straightened with the perfect grace of a cat stretching under the sun. She didn't jump or leap. She never would again. She spun on the heels of her feet, knees bent, head thrown back spilling her hair to the floor.

Why would she care what Michael thought was fair? Was it fair that her father had worked hard all his life, only to get charged with a DUI, lose his pension, and gain a head injury that left him unresponsive but clinging to life, and a prognosis that left his family devastated. Or her brother, whose dream it was to be a police officer, now confined for life to a wheelchair or prosthetic legs. Everyone's dream had ended on a night of celebration. The world wasn't fair. A lesson Michael hadn't yet learned.

She changed the dynamic of the dance to something more emotionally charged, complete with running her palm over the side of her face and temple, tears streaming down her cheeks as she gazed in the mirror, bringing more interest to her most miniscule gestures. One didn't need perfect pirouettes and grand jetés to compete. Her form down to her fingertips was more fluid than Michael's, while at the same time her moves were more powerful, more expressive, and conveyed a more passionate love of what she was doing.

At some point, Michael gave up and stopped dancing to watch her. When she finished, she heard some sniffling. She may have made them cry but she was being careful, afraid to break again.

Her students clapped, including Michael. He hadn't been able to keep up. "Class is over."

"Miss Darling—" Michael began.

"Jake, I'll see you tomorrow at the audition."

"Seriously?" Michael snorted and shook his head at her.

"You're making my decision easier," she warned him. "You know as well as I do that you're not ready for a full length production. Practice until you're at your best."

He looked as if he could punch her in the jaw. He murmured something Aria was sure she wouldn't like if she bothered to listen and stormed out.

After Jake thanked her profusely, he left with Brenda. It wasn't because he was better than Michael that she chose him. He wasn't her ideal to play the role of Romeo, in Shakespeare's Romeo and Juliet. But then, she'd never met a Romeo she actually liked. It wasn't what they lacked in dancing, but rather what they lacked in emotion. It was as if they were all afraid of being too vulnerable, of going deep and letting true passion take over. Shame, it was part of what made a good dancer great.

She was about to shut the lights and leave the studio when the door opened, and Mrs. Blagden of Blagden's School of Contemporary Dance stepped into the studio.

"Oh, I'm so glad I caught you before you left, Aria," the older woman said, coming to her. She wore a long cream-colored dress made of thin linen fabric with tiny brown leaves sewn down the side. Low brown heels clicked on the floor as she approached. Her gray hair was drawn back in a loose bun low on her nape. Pearl stud earrings added to her ethereal appearance.

Aria had known the older, eccentric woman since she was seven. Mrs. Blagden had invited Aria's mother to bring her daughter to the dance school she'd just opened. For free. Of course, her mother had agreed, since Aria had already shown interest in becoming a ballerina. Over the years, Aria discovered that Mrs. Blagden had money coming out of her ears and she showered Aria with a lot of it for some reason Aria never questioned. Even paying the hospital bills after the accident. She would have opened an art school if Aria had wanted to paint, a photography school if Aria had shown interest in taking pictures. But Aria had wanted to dance.

She gave Aria every opportunity she needed to be a professional dancer if Aria put the work in, and of course, Aria had. After the accident, she even offered to pay for a nurse to care for her father and brother. Aria's mother had refused.

"I got a call from my daughter in England," Mrs. Blagden told her now. "There was an offer on some property I own over there. I must meet with the buyer the day after next."

"I didn't know you had property across the pond," Aria said, surprised. There was so much she didn't know about her benefactor. "Is it a castle or something?" she asked with a playful smile.

"No, no," Mrs. Blagden laughed. "It's nothing so grand."

Aria narrowed her gray-blue eyes on the attractive old woman. Aria often imagined Mrs. Hester Blagden had been a pretty woman in her day. "I have a feeling it has at least twenty rooms."

"It's missing more than half the roof."

Aria laughed and pulled off her dancing shoes. "When are you leaving?"

"Tonight," Mrs. B. informed her while Aria slipped into leather flats and straightened.

"Take this." She handed Aria a key.

It was an old-fashioned looking thing. A skeleton key if Aria remembered correctly. It had a pretty, filigree-shaped bow with a long stem and a folded bit that shined under light.

"It's the building key. I just need you to lock the doors in the evening and unlock them in the morning."

"Of course." Aria took the key and then held it up to the light. "It's so shiny and golden."

"Yes, it's made of gold."

Aria's eyes opened wider. "*Real* gold?"

"Yes, dear, and it's one of a kind so don't lose it. I'll leave it with you tonight and let you practice locking up. The key can be a little tricky."

Aria nodded and clutched the key in both hands.

"Is that what you're going to wear to go home?" Mrs. B. looked her over in her sleeveless top and short, flowy skirt and leotard with a worried frown creasing her brow. "Don't you have anything to cover up your legs a bit more? Also, it's dangerous out there, dearest. That skimpy top you're wearing might be taken the wrong way by unethical men."

Aria looked down at herself. "It's ninety degrees outside," she muttered quickly. In a louder voice she looked up apologetically. "Mrs. B., you know I can take care of myself out there. You're the one who paid for my self-defense lessons. Besides, I don't have anything here to change into."

Mrs. Blagden sucked her teeth and shook her head. "What's that pink shirt hanging over there? And I know I saw a blanket in your office the day before last. Bring them."

Aria blinked at her. "Bring my sweatshirt and a blanket? Why do you want me to take a blanket? Are you sure you're okay?"

"Of course, my dear girl. Just humor me and wear the shirt over the top you're wearing." She took a little breath and shook her head slightly. "It doesn't even have sleeves. Take the blanket, hmm?"

Aria bit her bottom lip, then did as she was bid. Was her friend ill? Should Aria insist on taking her to the hospital? Why would she need to wear a sweatshirt and have a blanket? It was hot and humid out in the middle of August.

Nevertheless, she slipped on the sweatshirt, gathered the folded blanket in her small office, then returned to her Mrs. B.

"Isn't today your brother's birthday?" Mrs. Blagden remarked after Aria shut off the lights and they left the studio together.

"Yes," Aria answered, not surprised that her dear friend re-membered Connall's birthday. "Twenty-five."

"Oh, maybe I should give you the key for another night."

"Nonsense," Aria said, refusing to give it back. "What does Conn's birthday have to do with anything?"

Mrs. B. looked to be thinking about the question, then she sighed softly. "How is the poor dear doing?"

"He'd love it if you came by," Aria told her.

"Oh, I'd love to, but my flight is in a few hours. I'll bring something back for him."

Aria smiled lovingly. Mrs. Blagden claimed to be eighty-three, but her skin was peachy smooth with very few wrinkles.

"He'll be happy just to see you," Aria told her, taking her hand as they walked together to the exit of the building. The sad truth was that Conn wasn't happy about anything anymore. "Mom will make your favorite, her beloved crock-pot beef stew."

"You know I do love her beef stew."

Aria looked at her as they came to the building doors. "You sound melancholy, as if you won't eat it again. Is everything alright?"

"Yes, yes. I was just remembering all the flavors and how tender the meat is. Perfect for my old teeth."

Aria pulled her a little closer. "I've been practicing the recipe so I can make it for you."

Mrs. Blagden pulled Aria's hand to her cheek. "You are my dear girl."

Aria smiled, knowing how much Mrs. B. cared for her. She'd already written Aria into her will to inherit the building. Aria couldn't express her gratitude enough. Bills were beginning to get paid off and there was money for her parent's rent.

They left the building, and Aria slipped the key into the key-hole.

"Aria, my dear," she heard Mrs. Blagden say. Her voice sounded different—weaker, distant. "I saw you dance."

Aria lifted her gaze from the keyhole to her friend. She blinked, and then her heart began to race. The vision of Mrs. Blagden was fading.

"I want you to... always... dance."

One second. Less than that and she was gone.

She vanished before Aria's astonished eyes. "Mrs. B?" She

reached out her hand, but no one was there. In fact, everything had changed. There were no buildings anywhere her eyes could see. There were trees—bare, snow-covered trees everywhere. Snow? What? She closed her eyes and shook her head. Maybe it was she who needed to go to the hospital. None of this was real. It couldn't be. "Mrs. B?" she tried again. "If you can hear me, call an ambulance right away."

She waited a second, then opened her eyes. Nothing had changed. Trees as far as her eyes could see. A white fog appeared before her face until she realized what it was and stopped breathing. It was cold out. Really cold. How? How could that possibly be? It couldn't be. She let out her breath and watched the swirling wisps rise from her mouth.

She wrapped the blanket around her shoulders. How had Mrs. B. known she'd need to stay warm?

"Mrs. B., something terrible has happened to me? It must be from the accident. I...I can't see you and there's snow everywhere."

But her friend didn't answer her. In fact, silence echoed around her. And the booming sound of a twig snapping.

Had dancing triggered some abnormality in her brain?

"Hello? Someone help."

She heard movement to her right. She looked that way, her heart pounding so hard, it hurt. Her head felt as if it was spinning. She closed her eyes as a wave of nausea washed over her. She had to try to relax. How? How does one find rest when the whole world just changed before their eyes? She took a tentative step, wrapped in her throw. What was she going to do? Where was she supposed to go?

"Miss?"

She spun around. A man stood behind her. He looked to be about the same age as she. He wore...he wore an overcoat of brown leather that reached his ankles and flared out into two tails behind him. He carried a shovel.

"Stay away from me!" Aria warned. She didn't care what he

looked like. He either wasn't real; she'd made him up in her mind—or he was real, and if that was the case, why did he have a shovel? She didn't want to wait around for answers. She turned again to leave and tripped over her numb feet.

She felt his fingers clamp around her upper arm. She flailed and the blanket fell into the snow. Snow. Her feet were so cold.

The man pulled her to her feet and smiled again. "Are you hurt?"

"No!" She stepped back and readied herself to kick him in the throat if he moved. "Where am I?"

"Hmm?" he asked, giving her a curious look. "On our land."

"Whose is 'our'?"

"My family. The Gables."

"Where though? What's the name of this place? All of it, not just your land? Where are we?"

"We are in Dartmouth in Devon," he told her, his expression turning to pity. "In England."

Yes! He had a British accent! No. No. It couldn't be! England? She laughed holding her palm to her head. "Is this a joke? Please, tell me it's a joke."

He shook his head, looking confused.

"I was in New York. This is New York." She closed her eyes and said it over again. "This is New York. This is New York."

"You should come inside before you freeze to death. Odd that we had such a heavy snowfall in May, but—"

"May?" she asked, feeling dizzy. "But it's August."

"Come, Miss. Come inside. I fear the cold has already—"

"Come inside where? What do you intend to do? I'll tear out your eyes."

He stared at her for a minute, looking more serious. "I intend to bring you to my mother and to our table so you can fill your belly. Mayhap, my sister will let you share her bed so you can sleep under the shelter of our roof."

A tempting offer. But...he could be a rapist, a maniac who went around killing women with a shovel. "No thanks."

"Where will you sleep?" he asked.

She looked around. There was nothing but trees. She thought she saw a movement within the trunks. What...

"Miss. You will die if you do not find shelter."

She looked at the guy again. "You said you have a sister. Bring her here."

He hesitated for a moment and then turned and hurried away.

Aria watched him go. Should she go home with him? Was she crazy even considering going home with some stranger? She was a New Yorker. Trust no one.

While she waited, she played over and over in her head what had happened. She was talking and walking with Mrs. B. They'd left the building, and Aria had turned to lock...the key. The key. The more she thought about it, the more it warmed her...hand. She looked down at it still in her palm. Had it brought her to some field within a forest in England? She should laugh. It was impossible. Then she heard something. Aria turned her chattering teeth and frozen toes to the trees. Could it be a bear? Her mouth went dry and her heart pounded again. There it was again! The slightest movement deep in the shadows, then a flash of red! She narrowed her eyes on the shadows. "Hello?"

Only silence met her ears. A twig cracked, booming in the wind.

Should she run?

She wiped the cold sweat from her brow and narrowed her eyes on the forest. Seconds passed with her searching, ready to flee.

"Miss? Here's my sister, Sarah."

Aria turned, her heart still racing, and faced the man who had returned with a younger woman with dark chestnut hair, like her alleged brother's. Hers was long and braided down her back. Her smile was shy.

"You can come home with us and get warm. Will will not hurt you."

"Will?"

"My brother," Sarah let her know, motioning to him.

Aria sighed with deep relief and looked over her shoulder again where she'd seen...something. Finally, she nodded and took a step closer to the girl.

"By the way?" Aria asked them as they walked in the snow. "What kind of clothes are you wearing? They don't look anything like what I've seen where I live."

"I was going to ask you the same thing," Sarah admitted with a shy smile. "You must be freezing without an overcoat."

"It was sum—I wasn't prepared for this."

Will flashed his smile at her. She looked away. There was a reason she was single at twenty-three without a guy for miles. Oh, there were plenty around her, but no one appealed to her. Mrs. B. used to say it was because the right man hadn't come into her life yet. When he did, Aria would know it.

And then what was she supposed to do? Date someone who made her belly flip for a second—until she got to know him better. Men, especially the few dancers she knew, were basically alike, dead, dispassionate, wet fish who knew nothing about real love.

"You mentioned New York earlier," Will brought up. "Where is that?"

"In America."

Will and Sarah stopped.

"You come from the colonies?"

"Is that not where all the miscreants are sent?" Sarah asked, bringing her hands to her chest.

Will put his hand on his sister's shoulder. "I am sure this lady is no miscreant."

How did he know? How could he make such a declaration? "You're right, I'm not."

"How did you get here?" Sarah asked.

Aria swallowed and closed her hand tighter around the key. She didn't think she should tell these two strangers any more than she already had.

She saw the house nestled within a stand of trees. It was made from timber and stone. Smoke rose from the chimney and candles lit the windows. It looked warm. She needed warmth.

"Are you sure it's okay with your mother to take in a stranger?"

Will nodded, then glanced down at her hopping feet. "May I carry you before your feet get frostbitten?"

If he wasn't a killer, he had a nice voice, soft and laced with concern and kindness.

"I think I can make it to the door," she reassured him—and then tripped over her numb feet and headed straight for the ground.

Will's hands came to her rescue. He caught her in the cradle of his arms before she hit the cold, hard ground. He stared down at her as if nothing else existed in the world but her.

She looked away, flushed by a possible killer!

Before she had time to tell him to put her down, he scooped her off her feet and carried her the rest of the way to the house.

"This may sound a little crazy," Aria began, avoiding his gaze, "but what year is this supposed to be? Is it still 2024?"

He dipped his dark brow giving her a look that said exactly what she would have said if someone asked her what she just asked. "It is 1795, Miss."

She didn't move. She didn't breathe. "17—no. Impossible." She felt as if something inside her was rumbling, making her whole body shake. "No. It can't be. It's impossible. My family—" Her eyes filled with tears. "If this is real, how will I get back to the twenty-first century? My family needs me! Oh, I need to wake up. Sarah! Pinch me!"

"Miss, you need to remain calm," Will reasoned. "No one is going to pinch you. We will find your family."

Aria wanted to believe him—but she couldn't. She didn't know him. He'd never ever believe what had happened to her. She didn't believe it. Best not to come off as a raving lunatic claiming unearthly things. "So cold."

She felt Will draw her closer. She closed her eyes, safe for the first time since this madness began. And then a sword came down hard on Will's blade. Will had a sword? She hadn't noticed it before. She wanted to stay awake, but the world she didn't know began to fade. Was she going somewhere else? Home?

She caught sight of something red before she fell unconscious from the freezing air. It was a man, though she couldn't see his face. High on horseback, his shoulders under his woolen, red overcoat wide and straight. He'd been watching her from the trees. Now he was fighting Will. For her? He turned and for the briefest of moments he settled his gaze on her in Will's arms. His eyes were the color of Caribbean waters filled with deadly creatures and fathomless secrets. He reached behind his back for a red feather-tipped arrow and then, bringing his bow up, he nocked his arrow, pulled his bowstring taut, and began to turn to someone to their left. He fired before his gaze reached whoever he was about to shoot.

Aria heard someone's body thump on the ground, and then she didn't see or hear anything else.

# CHAPTER THREE

A RIA SAT PROPPED up against a pillow in Sarah Gable's bed. By the light in the window on the east wall, she could see that it was the day. She had opened her eyes to pain in her feet and fear in her heart. They wanted her to believe that what happened wasn't a dream. She had somehow—no—she covered her head and shook it. Somehow, she had traveled back in time to 1795. She wanted to laugh but the urge to cry was stronger. Before she began to obsess again on how all this could even be possible, the bedroom door opened and a pretty young woman...Sarah, she remembered, stepped inside carrying a tray in both hands.

"Good morning, Miss," Sarah greeted with a bright smile. "We were so happy to see you awake earlier.

"I was awake earlier?" She didn't remem—oh, yes, she did remember. She tried to leave the bed and run away. This couldn't be real. It had to be a cruel joke.

"My mother has never treated anyone with the cold sickness like yours. Your toes were slightly frost-bitten."

Aria shivered. How long would it take for her insides to warm up? "You and your mother have my thanks for all your trouble."

"You were no trouble, Miss. Mum's only sorry that there's no fruit to offer you."

"Please call me Aria," Aria offered as she accepted the tray from Will's sister. There was what Aria suspected was porridge, along with slices of freshly baked bread and two small jars beside the plate. One with honey and the other with soft butter.

"Aria is a beautiful name."

"So is Sarah," Aria said, biting into her bread, slathered with both butter and honey.

"I've never heard of your name."

"It means lion of God." Aria stopped chewing and cast the younger hostess a slight side-smile. "It also means song or melody."

Sarah smiled and then turned to the door when a knock came from the other side. "Come."

Will opened the door and stepped inside. A vision of a different man dressed in a beautiful red coat and a fur wreath around his face, blacker than night, invaded her thoughts. He'd shot someone with an arrow. Her eyes opened wider as she looked at Will.

"You're okay?"

"Okay?" Will asked with a smile of confusion on his lips.

Right, Aria remembered. This was supposed to be the eighteenth century. They didn't use words like okay. Did they?

"I thought—"

"It is good to see you awake." He came to the bed and stood at the edge looking down at her. "My mother will arrive in a moment or two to greet you."

Had she been that sick? "That's very nice of her. Um…" She paused and closed her eyes. She had to ask. She had to know. "Do I still have all my toes? No! Wait!" she commanded when he opened his mouth to answer. "Don't tell me."

She opened her eyes to look for herself, but she saw Will offer her a reassuring smile. She breathed a deep sigh of relief. Then, "Was there a man in a red coat here last night? I saw him shoot an arrow at someone."

"Yes, the marquess," Will answered, his smile fading.

"The marquess?" Aria asked him.

He nodded. "The Marquess of Dartmouth, son of the Duke

of Devonshire.

"He arrived just in time to stop the thieves about to rob us and God knows what else," Sarah let her know between dreamy sighs and slight, fearful cries.

"Apparently," Will picked up the explanation, "the marquess had been following them after whispers had reached him that there were thieves who had been robbing the people in Dartmouth's three villages."

"Did he kill them?" Aria asked, horrified that it had happened right in front of her. She didn't like this world. No. Not at all.

"No, he shot them all in the leg and then bound their wrists to his horse and made them walk at a brisk pace to the castle."

"There's a castle?" Why was she really surprised? This seemed more and more to be Mrs. B.'s fantasy.

"Dartmouth Castle," Will told her.

She lifted her hand to her sweatshirt and the word sewn across her chest. *Dartmouth*. She had attended Princeton University, but she loved the pale pink of Dartmouth's shirt. Coincidence that Mrs. B. told her to wear it?

She resumed eating. She was hungry after all.

"The marquess returned the next day," Will went on. "He said he wished to speak to you the moment you woke up. We have not sent word to him yet.

He wanted to speak with her? Her thoughts stopped. All but one. "What do you mean he returned the next day. How long have I been asleep?"

"It has been four days, lady—?" He waited for her to supply the rest.

"Darling." she supplied, numbly, then shook her head at him seeing that his gaze had gone warm. "It's my last name. Aria Darling."

Sarah made a little sound like another dreamy sigh. Her brother stared at her for a moment, then coughed into his hand.

"Tell me what do you mean four days?" she demanded quietly. "I feel as if I've been asleep for hours not days."

"Ah, but is that not how sleep distorts time?" An older version of Sarah remarked, entering the room. "I am Mary Gable. You've met my son and daughter already. I hope they have been hospitable to you?"

They spoke for another ten minutes. There were moments in their conversation when Aria had to bite her lip to keep from crying. Will's sibling reminded her of her brother. She'd missed his birthday. If she didn't find a way home, who would help Conn learn how to live again? She missed her mother, always trying to appear unruffled but, in truth, she was exhausted. How would she get on without Aria?

Finally with chores to see done, the Gables left her alone. Will lingered behind.

"Lady, you are welcome to stay here for as long as you need. It is dangerous out there, but I will keep you safe."

Someone snorted behind Will at the door. Will turned and went still. It was the man in the red coat. The marquess. Will didn't question his mocking smirk but faced him straight on.

"She needs rest, my lord."

"Step aside, Gable."

The marquess' voice was throaty and deep, with a musical British accent. It held the command of a confident king and Will obeyed and moved out of his path.

Aria's blood burned, coursing through her veins. She met Will's gaze and then tossed the marquess a distasteful glare.

In truth, she could hardly breathe. Her thoughts ended and all her clarity of mind went into soaking up his appearance, beginning with his face when he pushed back his fur-lined hood. She'd never seen such a starkly handsome man before. Much as she wanted to, she couldn't look away. He belonged on the cover of GQ or something devoted to ruggedly handsome noblemen.

He moved with a grace and masculinity that made her knees shake. Good thing she was in bed, or she would have been on her backside. He was lean and about six feet tall in his red overcoat that tapered slightly at his waist and then fanned outward, reaching his boots. Up close, she could see the beautiful, full roses and green leaves sewn into the left breast of the outside. His hair was black, cut shorter in the back and left to fall over his brow and eclipse his turquoise-colored eyes.

"Where did you come from?"

Her mouth went dry at the husky depth of his voice and his lips that formed his words.

They were full—both top and bottom—to the degree of being luscious and spellbindingly inviting.

"Are you going to answer me or lay there as if the sight before you has made you go dull."

She blinked. Dull? Son of a—"The sight before me being you?"

He shifted on his feet and gave her an impatient look. "I saw you come into the forest that day," he let her know, leaning in a bit closer so that only she would hear. "Where did you come from?"

She imagined she must have appeared as if she'd been spit out of time's mouth. He had seen her. Did that mean it was all real, provided he was telling her the truth? What was she supposed to tell him now? "I...I don't remember."

"Of course you do," he countered smoothly. Then, "Why do you wear the clothes of Dartmouth? Do you belong to me?"

"What?" she demanded with a tight laugh. "I don't belong to anyone. Understand?"

"Alright, little lion," he mused, but there was nothing soft or warm in the steel of his eyes or the unyielding cut of his jawline.

Now she was sure none of this was real. Men that looked like him didn't exist and if they did, it was thanks to lots of makeup. He was close enough to see he wore no makeup.

"Forget the shirt you wear with my name scribed across it. Just tell me the truth about how you appeared out of thin air."

Was it real then? Was it real?

"I don't have to tell you anything. I don't even know who you are. You're very threatening, all big and brooding, and...cold." She almost said sinfully attractive.

He ground his teeth, making his jawline twitch. "Very well. I'll return every day to ask you again." He flicked his gaze, along with a smirk out of the corner of his mouth, to Will. "I'm certain the Gables won't mind having me visit their home on a more regular basis."

Aria looked past him at Will. He was pale. His eyes were squeezed shut. He appeared extremely unhappy about the prospect of having the marquess here.

"Listen here," she commanded again, "You're not going to march into my life and start making demands. I don't care what century this is. I don't belong to you. Understand? The Gables have been very kind to me. You don't get to threaten people who help me. If you wanted to make the point that you're a crappy human, you succeeded. But you still don't get to threaten me. You can come here until you've wasted a year of your life—I'll tell you nothing."

He didn't move but simply stared at her. He didn't look angry or impatient, nor did he appear to be amused. For a second, she thought she saw something glint across his penetrating gaze. What was it? Something roiling within, churning just beyond the veil.

"Are you finished?" he asked calmly.

Oh, how she wished she was on her feet and not helpless in a stranger's bed. "That depends on if you are."

His expression didn't change. In fact, he barely revealed any emotion at all. If "deadpan" was a person, it would be the Marquess of Dartmouth. It wasn't that he didn't care about getting answers. The lackadaisical intensity of his gaze proved that he did. Just another guy unable to express his emotions. Aria scoffed and was about to roll her eyes at him when he began to turn away from her without another word. Except that she caught the faint smile forming on his lips.

So then, he did feel something.

She watched him walk away, toward the outside where his

pale gray horse waited. He was fascinating to look at, even from behind. The red tails of his coat snapped out around his boots; his hood, lined in black fur, fell between his broad shoulders, along with his bow and quiver of red feathered arrows, but it was his gait that trumpeted his virility.

He didn't return the next day as he'd threatened, or the day after that. Mrs. Gable, Will's mother, wouldn't hear of Aria leaving in her condition—which was no longer dangerous. Her feet were almost completely healed, and she hadn't had the chills in two nights. But she had to find a way home and stop infringing on this poor family. And poor, they were.

She learned one night after dinner, when Mrs. Gable had left the table, that Will was just nine when his father was killed, leaving his family with nothing. He'd been attacked by a raven that plucked and tore at his eyes and temples until it killed him.

Will's older brother, Harry, had been mauled by a wolf and other forest animals that same day after he had killed a goose from the village. A goose that the young marquess of Dartmouth had considered his "dearest friend". Will and Sarah had told her how the villagers believed the marquess had the power to control the animals.

"According to my brother," Will had told her. "He is a madman who was snarling while the raven killed our father."

"He was more likely smiling," Sarah corrected. "He used to crinkle his nose when he smiled. One of his eyes would close from the intensity of it. But I doubt he was snarling."

"So?" Will turned to his sister, who possibly had a crush on the marquess. "It is alright with you then that he was smiling while he watched animals kill our father, as long as we know he was not snarling like the animals he claimed to be friends with?"

She gave him a horrified stare. "No! Of course not! That is not what I meant, William, and you know it! I am just saying he was a boy. Think about what he witnessed that day. Has anyone ever asked him?"

Will gave his sister an indulgent sigh and then returned his attention to Aria. "He is considered mad to this day."

"He is not mad," Sarah brooded.

"Very well, odd and eccentric then."

"If anyone considered him beyond rumors," Sarah went on, "they would know he would have no desire to control animals. He wishes to live in freedom and would wish the same for his friends."

"Freedom from what?" Aria asked her.

"I'm not sure, the responsibilities of being the duke's son, I presume?"

Aria bristled. So, he rebuked his responsibilities. His type sickened her. He was likely a playboy without a conscience. He certainly had the face and physique for it.

"Perhaps the animals needed his permission to harm the man who killed their friend. I heard Father killed the wolf that attacked Harry."

"Then," Aria said, "you believe he can communicate with animals?"

"I had been sent to gather the lord's soiled linens," Sarah told her. "Though I was only six, I often helped my mother. I practically grew up with the marquess. One day soon after my father died, I was back to gathering linens and I heard the marquess weeping in his bed. The young lord thought he was alone, but he kept saying words between his sobs. Words like, 'sorry', and 'my fault', and 'but I told them...they listened to me'." Sarah shrugged her shoulders, "He was young. He has admitted to imagining it all."

"You know much about him," Aria said with a soft smile.

She found herself wondering if the marquess reciprocated Sarah's feelings. After meeting him and finding that he offered Sarah neither a word nor a nod before he rode off on his horse, Aria didn't think Sarah's feelings were shared.

Will's younger sister plucked her serviette from the dinner table and covered her chuckle.

Will looked away.

"Do you blame him for your father's death?" Aria asked him.

"Harry does," Will let her know. "He blames the marquess for what happened to our father and to him. There is hatred between them, and I fear it will only be satisfied by death. You would do best to stay away from both of them."

Aria felt another chill go up her spine and concealed it lest they send her back to bed.

She thought of a warrior clothed in red, who had backed down from a bed-ridden woman. She didn't realize she was smiling until Will leaned down and grinned at her.

"What are you thinking about?"

"Me?" she asked, wide-eyed, then swallowed hard when he nodded. "Nothing really...the warm weather in New York." Yes. She'd welcome the humid, hot steam over the freezing cold seeping in through cracks in the walls.

When Will slipped his gaze to his sister, as if thinking about the way she too smiled when she thought of...No! Aria denied. She wasn't that obvious.

She met Harry and his wife, Elspeth, the next morning at breakfast. The oldest of the Gable offspring was over six feet tall. He might have been handsome like his younger brother at one time, but not since he was eleven and forest animals had attacked him. His face was scarred from his forehead to his chin in one place and across his cheek. He didn't greet her but scowled.

"I understand Dartmouth is interested in her. He has stationed thirty of his men to guard the perimeter of this house."

The marquess did that? Aria wondered. Why? Was it because of the thieves?

"Let him take her," Harry Gable muttered.

Aria's mouth fell open. Right, she had to keep in mind *when* she was. This was the way things were.

"I do not want him coming here again over her."

"Mr. Gable—" Aria began, but Will covered her elbow from where he sat beside her.

"What is it?" The scarred head of the Gable family didn't

meet her gaze. "Say what you were going to say."

"I don't care for the marquess." Aria saw Harry's interest peek right away.

"Prove it," he said simply.

"Why should I prove anything to you?"

"If you do not," he said from across the table, "I will see you thrown out and unable to find a room for yourself."

She was certain by now that she'd die if she was thrown out of the Gable home. She couldn't die. She had to help her mother. Without Aria's pay her family would be thrown out or go hungry.

"What do you want me to do?"

He pulled out a small poster-like paper and held it up. "The Duchess of Devonshire requests our attendance at her next ball in three days."

"That woman does love spending her husband's money," said the pretty young woman with pale blonde hair piled high on her head and half-covered with a veil. Harry's wife, Elspeth.

"What happens at a ball?" Aria asked, "I've never been to one."

Harry and Elspeth gave her a smirk that said she was the dumbest human on the planet.

"Everyone dances," Sarah informed her, "including Lord Dartmouth. He's known for being the best dancer in all of Devonshire and beyond."

Was Aria hearing things? Things she'd love to hear about anyone. He was known to be the best? What was considered best here in the eighteenth century? Should she attend? Should she let this unpleasant man sitting in front of her boss her around?

"Sure, I'll go. But you still haven't told me how to prove to you that I don't like him.

Harry stared at her as if considering her for something, and then looked away, dismissing her. "People will clear the floor for Dartmouth. He will dance and you may even be a bit beguiled by him, but remain strong and when he is finished, laugh at him. No matter how well he did. You will mock and deride him in front of everyone."

"That seems a bit immature," she commented.

"You will have two hours to pluck this proud peacock's feathers so I can stick them in my hat."

"Harry," Sarah said, frustrated with her brother. "You know how the marquess feels about dancing. Why provoke him?"

How did the marquess feel about dancing? Aria wished she knew. How could she ask Sarah without them growing suspicious of her?

"William," his older brother's voice pierced the peace. "If she brings any trouble upon this family, I will hold you responsible since you carelessly brought her into Mother's home."

Aria gave him a slight glare. "I won't bring any trouble."

She ate the same thing she'd eaten every morning at the Gable household, porridge with cream or eggs, and fresh bread with butter and honey, but it tasted better today—maybe because she had been invited to eat at their table and be a part of their conversation.

She didn't mention that she could dance.

She enjoyed her breakfast and didn't bother anymore with Harry or his snooty wife, or if she would really mock the marquess' dancing skill. When they were done eating, she stayed behind and helped Mrs. Gable clean up. Will stayed behind as well, sweeping the floor. She was surprised and saddened that it took her traveling back in time over two hundred years to find a nice guy. And the more time that passed, the more she believed she might actually have travelled into the past. Things like not a single plane in the air, no lights outside at night, no cars or tire tracks anywhere, convinced her. Or having to walk or ride a horse wherever she wanted to go, or the way Harry had spoken to his wife. Most women in 2024 wouldn't have put up with it.

She still didn't know how it could possibly be real but she was beginning to believe it.

And yet, she couldn't get the arrogant rich guy out of her

head. She'd agreed to attend his family's ball, but would she be here three days from now? What about finding a way home in the meantime?

"I think I'll go for a walk," she told Will and his mother while she reached for the thick coat Sarah had loaned her hanging on a peg by the back door.

"A walk to where?" Will asked, coming to stand near her while she slipped into the boots his mother gave her.

"I need to find a door."

"A door in the forest?" He looked on the verge of laughter, but he held back.

"Yes, something like that. The way I came."

His smile faded. "You are trying to find your way home."

"Yes. My family needs me."

He nodded, likely understanding since he lived with his family and helped pay their debts. He walked her to the tree line and to the guarded perimeter, but there was no door.

"I do not think you are going to find a door in the middle of the woods," Will insisted. "But Dartmouth Castle has seventy-two rooms. They all have doors."

"Seven-two doors?" Aria echoed in astonishment. "How will I...?"

"The ball. I will escort you and we will find your door."

Yes, the castle. Was it the same castle Mrs. B. was returning to England to sell? Of course, the door would be there. All of this somehow had to do with Mrs. B. Aria would have to wait three days for the ball before she could get home.

"Did the marquess really station his men around your house?" she asked Will as they walked back to the Gable's residence.

"He did."

"Your brother made it sound as if he did it for me."

"It seems that way, but before you extend your mercies to the marquess, I would have you understand that it is more likely that he did it to keep you from leaving than to stop others from

36

getting in."

"Why would he want to keep me from leaving?"

Will shrugged a shoulder. "He seems very curious about how you came here."

He saw her appear *out of thin air*, and now he wasn't going to let her leave. No wonder he hadn't bothered returning to the house as he'd threatened. Even if there was a door somewhere beyond the perimeter of the house, she wouldn't be able to get to it.

"Who does he think he is anyway?" she murmured more to herself than to Will.

"He is the duke's son," Will answered anyway.

"He's not my duke," Aria reminded him with a huff.

Will slowed and stared at her. "You are very bold." Instead of smiling at her though, he scowled. "I do not know from where or when you came—"

She had already told him. She guessed she didn't blame him for not believing her, but it still stung.

—"but if you do not want to be punished, then you will obey the duke."

"And his son," she added through tight lips, then without waiting for Will's response, she spun on her heel and headed for the perimeter.

# CHAPTER FOUR

G RAY SAT ALONE on a cushioned bench high above the Dart Estuary and, having taken in the stunning beauty around him, closed his eyes, letting the sounds of nature fill the rest of his senses. The rolling waves blended with the waves slapping against the rocks below, creating a melody more profound than any man had ever written. Every so often flocks of birds took off from the bare branches around him and on the other side of the estuary, adding to the percussion with their flapping wings. The wind on its journey here or there moved over his ears and through the trees like woodwinds.

Ever since he was a little boy he heard music in almost everything. Even in the thunderous sounds of horse's hooves shaking the earth or musket balls firing from guns—

He rose to his feet to escape the sounds of war.

The moment he was on his feet his back arched until his hand touched the ground behind him, stretching his belly taut. He swayed, then cranked himself back up and jerked his movements like a marionette controlled by strings.

He'd gone mad, alone on a battlefield of pointing fingers, whispers, and laughter. He'd had nothing to fight the emptiness within. It was so much worse than the loneliness outside of him. He understood that he'd lost his mother and grandmother, but there were other things. He couldn't remember any of them.

Dreams of his mother's dulcet voice changed the melody to

one of haunting beauty that made his smile deepen and match. He brought his arms together as if to hold someone close, but there was no one there, and his smile began to fade. The serene sound of her began to echo his loneliness. Why had she left him, in life and in his dreams? She wasn't the only one who had abandoned him.

How could anyone blame him for resenting them all and making him hate who he was?

With a pained expression, he beat his fist against his breast, then he pushed out his chest and sank it with a groan.

He'd gone off to fight France when he was eighteen, hoping to get killed quickly. He killed instead—with his pistol, his sword, and his hands. He never found a moment of comfort or peace.

He leaped high doing a double pirouette, then a grand jeté that felt as if he could reach heaven if he stretched just a bit more.

"Grayson!"

Harper's screech rang through Gray's ears, and he landed a few inches from the short wall. He shook his head, then set his eyes on her. "I would have landed before leaping over the wall."

"Really?" she asked doubtfully. "For whom?"

"What?" he asked, running his fingers through his hair to clear it from his eyes.

His grandmother had left Harper Black to take care of him when she was twenty-three. No matter how much he'd defied her or how hard he worked at ignoring her, she never left his side. She played the violin, and she played it well. When he was twelve, he began letting her play for him while he practiced. After that, she became his friend. When he returned from battle two years ago, she was there to welcome him home.

The only one.

"For whom would you be keeping yourself here?" she clarified and tossed his coat to him. "You were close, Grayson," she said, softening her voice. "If I hadn't stopped you, who would have?"

He couldn't think of anyone. Not a single lady who'd ever

occupied a thought of his. He didn't have a friend besides Harper. He didn't want any. He had saved the lives of the men he fought with so many times because it was his duty to keep them alive.

"Not who, Harper. What." He put on his coat and took a step closer to the door, and her. "Dancing saves me. It always has."

He watched her sigh with resolve. She knew he was speaking the truth. More than anyone, she knew.

"Why didn't you send for me to play for you?" she asked.

"It was spontaneous," he told her, leaving the rooftop. Then, "What brings you up here?"

"Your guardsman Ector was looking for you to report that the woman staying with the Gables left the perimeter."

Now Gray stopped and turned to her.

"What?" she asked. "Who is she?"

"A woman who is lost and alone. She turned up here..." in a blur like a wrinkle in the way the world was supposed to work.

"Yes?" Harper asked, her interest piqued. "She turned up here...?"

"She turned up out of nowhere. That is, nowhere that I know of."

"I see," she said after a moment and a slight breath. "Well, according to Ector, when your men tried to stop her, she kicked two of them in the jaw and sped away before the others reached her.

He felt the insane urge to laugh. In the jaw? She wouldn't be constrained. Very well.

"She's quite a delicate looking creature," he mused on a soft breath. "More like a feral cat."

"You like cats," Harper remarked.

"I like all animals," he countered with a playful smirk.

"Who is she?" Harper's question brought him back to the present. "And why did you tell thirty of your men to make sure she doesn't leave?"

"It wasn't that," he defended with a pout and started walking again. "The forest is a dangerous place. Are Mrs. Gable and her daughter not my tenants? Shouldn't I protect them?"

"Yes. Yes, you should," Harper agreed. "But Mrs. Gable and Sarah have been here for years, yet you never put your men around their holding. Why now?"

"In case you haven't noticed," he said, "there are more and more thieves in the woods every year."

"Does the stranger staying with them have something to do with it?"

He stopped and turned to her again. "Let me find her and then I'll answer you."

Gray knew Harper wouldn't stop him when he went in search of the girl. As he made his way to the stables, he wondered how a slight veil like her could kick two of his men in the jaw? How did she even gain that much height?

He didn't wait for Ghost, his horse to be saddled but leaped onto her back, grabbed fistfuls of her mane, and took off. He'd ridden bareback many times before. In fact, he preferred it to the bulkiness of a saddle. He had a feeling Ghost preferred it as well. The mare ran faster and longer unsaddled.

He broke through the woods as if he knew where every tree was and didn't come close to barreling into any of them.

He hoped he found the girl. She piqued his interest. Besides appearing in the gossamer fog as if God Himself had dropped her down to earth, her eyes were as vast and as stormy blue as the sky from which she'd fallen. When he'd spoken to her at the Gable's, her eyes had bore into him, challenging him, unafraid. He'd never met a woman like her. She wasn't demure. There didn't seem to be a prudish bone in her body. She wore her silky sun-streaked hair loose around her pretty face. Her cheeks had been red from the cold. Her clothes were out of the ordinary to be sure. She'd worn hose covering her shapely legs under a little skirt in one layer of sheer silk. It was quite indecent. Gray couldn't say he was opposed to it.

It didn't take him long to reach the village. The Gable's homestead was about a mile farther away. But this was the first village she would have come to, so he decided to look here first.

When he didn't find her, he asked if anyone else had seen her. Old Beatrice Herderson told him a pretty, young stranger came through earlier asking how to get to Dartmouth Castle.

"My castle?" he asked, not sure he heard her right.

"Yes, as a matter of fact," she said, staring at him as if she just remembered something, "she was looking for you in particular, my lord."

"Me?" he repeated, looking surprised. "Did she say why?"

Old Beatrice blushed. "Now, my lord, who needs a reason to want to see you?"

"She does, Beatrice." He pouted, curling his lower lip. "She doesn't like me."

He was in the habit of doing one of two things—either remaining utterly detached or wearing his heart on his sleeve to anyone who would listen. Besides, almost everyone in the first village of Dartmouth liked Gray. Many of the older tenants, like Beatrice, remembered his mother and his grandmother, and how he was treated when the animals killed George Gable. After everyone had time to think about the accusations against the duke's odd son, they realized how mad it was to believe that he had ordered the animals to do it, and that they obeyed him.

"Why wouldn't she like you, child?"

Listening to her, Gray was reminded of the many times she or one of the other elders had tried to convince him that he was wrong about the other children not liking him. He looked at the dirt beneath his boots and put on a slight smile. He wasn't a child anymore.

"She has every reason to find you appealing," Beatrice defended him. "You are kind and generous. Edward the butcher told us how you made a deal with cattle farmers to supply Edward with all his meat at substantially less than what he paid elsewhere, saving his business. You are the most handsome young man in the castle and the three villages! You are not haughty, despite being the duke's only son, a Barrington, and dripping in power and prestige. You do a good job appearing as if you do not care about much—but some of us know better."

Now he settled his gaze on her and let a warm smile shine on her from the corner of his mouth. He didn't say anything. He didn't believe words had the same impact as a well-timed, earnest smile.

Why was the girl looking for him? Despite Beatrice's reassurances, he didn't think the stranger cared much what he looked like. From the way she argued with him, it was clear she didn't care about his power or prestige.

She kicked two of his guardsmen in the jaw to get away. And where was she headed? His castle! Where in the blazes was Will Gable? If he couldn't stop her, why hadn't he gone with her?

Should he go to the Gable's or to his castle?

He decided on the latter and took the shortcut along Castle Road. He'd almost made it back to the castle when he saw her walking up ahead, alone. He slowed his mount, watching her.

She moved at a slow pace, her arms dangling at her sides. She wore a coat, likely belonging to Elspeth or the youngest Gable, Sarah, and today she wore a petticoat beneath her skirts, most likely belonging to one of the other women in the Gable household.

Madly, Gray felt grateful that her hosts were taking care of her, and that today was noticeably warmer than the day she arrived.

He was happy to see her hair falling down her back, free to snap around her when a breeze blew by. Sizing her up, he decided he liked her gait. It was feminine and unhurried, confident and—the thing he liked best—graceful. Even brushing away a strand of her hair from across her eyes captivated him. He barely realized in time that she was turning. She must have heard him behind—

"Are you following me?" she demanded.

Her eyes were large and so very—

"Hello?" she asked with a sharp snap of her tongue when he didn't answer her. "What are you doing sneaking up behind me?

And didn't you think I'd hear and *smell* your horse?" He opened his mouth to speak but her eyes, like storm-filled skies growing darker and more menacing as they bore into him, quieted him.

"How long have you been back there, following me? What are you, a creep?"

*Creep?*

"A stalker?" she went on. "Because let me warn you right now, I'm not like the other girls here. I'll fight you."

He felt a stirring to smile, but even this beautiful woman couldn't lure him on a path he didn't want to travel. Nothing ever made him happy for long. Half the women he knew wanted to mother him, the other half wanted to tame him. A mother was the one thing he *didn't* want. And taming him…well, he wouldn't be tamed by anyone. His father knew it well enough. So did anyone else who tried to mold him into someone he wasn't.

He let any traces of humor or softness fade from his expression. "The same way you fought my men?"

He thought he saw tendrils of smoke puff out of her nose. "Yes."

"I can assure you," he warned with thunder in his own eyes, "I won't be so easily defeated."

"Good," she told him. "I like a challenge."

He quirked his mouth. It wasn't really a smile, but more like a mocking smirk. "You have courage, little lion. Is that why you're walking out here alone? If so, you're a fool if you think you can fight against a man and his sword."

"What's my alternative, Marquess? Lay back and let some—"

He leaped out of the saddle, landing like a lithe cat and took a step toward her. "I am not some scoundrel," he replied calmly, though inside the seas were stirring. This conversation with her felt familiar with him trying to defend himself. He would find out what she wanted and then leave and forget her. "Why were you looking for me?"

"What?" She blinked and the storms were swept away leaving clear, blue eyes. Then her cheeks slowly grew pink in the cold—

or her temper. "Oh, right. I wanted to tell you that I won't be a prisoner here. I'll come and go as I please until I find my way home. Release your men from their station. Yes, I know it's dangerous here, so I'll ask Will to come with me next time."

Gray looked around for Gable, then cast her a doubtful look.

"I told him not to follow me. I was angry about you trying to keep me here."

"Why were you angry about that? Even though that's not why I stationed the men there. But if I had, wouldn't it simply mean I know what kind of world it is and I would keep you safe?"

"I would appreciate that, but I don't need you to watch my back. So, I would have to decline your protection."

"Why?"

"For a lot of reasons. I don't know you, for one. I can protect myself. I grew up in New York City."

At this, he gave her a confused look. She didn't clarify.

"Mostly because your protection feels like you're keeping me in, not keeping the bad guys out. As I've said, I don't like that."

He stared at her. Damnation, she was stubborn. He didn't particularly care for stubborn people, women especially. This one insulted him every time she opened her mouth. He also knew she was lying about where she came from. *New* York *City?* Gray's father knew the duke of York. It would be simple for Gray to do a little investigating. But why should he? Did he really care where she came from? Still, he should prove to her that she, in fact, did need protection.

While she was still speaking, he drew his sword. He was quick, intending to grab her and hold the blade's edge to her throat.

But in one fluid movement, she snapped her coat off and swept her foot across his ankles.

He sat there in the grass on the road, on his arse. He looked up at her with a silken side smirk and he came up gracefully, using only his feet. Facing her, he tossed away his sword and reached for her. She kicked his hands away, fascinating him with her skillfully evasive maneuvers. He grabbed. She kicked. He smacked her boots away. She tried to kick him in his groin. He stepped back just in time and glared at her. But he wasn't angry. He was impressed and curious about her.

"Where did you learn to fight?" he asked, staying back.

"I took classes with my brother."

Who taught women how to fight, because it was clear that someone had indeed taught her. "Are you going to tell me where you came from?" he pressed. "Are you a witch?" When she gasped, he was quick to hold up his hands and correct her. "I don't care if you're a witch."

"I'm not!" she snapped. "And you could get me killed with that kind of question."

"Not in Dartmouth. My word stands firm here."

She stepped closer to him and leaned in conspiratorially. "Fair or not fair?"

He knew what she was doing—trying to figure him out. Was he a tyrant, a man of decency, a charmer whose promises were as frivolous as his heart?

He chuckled in her face. "I'm fairer than any man in the castle or the three villages because I have no favorites. I feel the same way about everyone."

Her pretty smile returned, tempting him to stare at it. "The people who spoke to me in the village seem very fond of you."

He thought of Old Beatrice. "Some have been acquainted with me since my childhood," he told her quietly. "Their opinions of me have no bearing on how I feel in return."

She became quiet for a moment, then. "Who hurt you?"

He raised his gaze to her. "What?"

She appeared as if she wanted to say more. She didn't.

"I'll let the men who are protecting the Gable holding know that you are to have access to anywhere you wish to go, as long as you have an escort."

She nodded, still looking at him as if she were trying to see inside him.

Not wanting anyone to see that deeply, he turned away and went to his horse.

"Hey—" she stopped, and then, "My lord, thank you for the invitation to the ball. I—"

"I didn't send it." he said, mounting his horse and chuckling, though he was angry at whoever gave her the invitation. He didn't want her at the castle with his stepmother and her son.

"Oh, I assumed you did."

"Why would you assume that?" he asked lightly.

Her lips tightened. "Because I don't know your stepmother, and she doesn't know me. Since you're the only Barrington I *do* know, I thought it was you."

He thought it was amusing that she lost her temper so fast. Despite being nothing but a pain in his neck, and reviling him every chance she got, she was amusing.

"What are you called, little lion?"

"Aria."

Damn him. He was tempted to smile. "Aria, as in a solo performance in an opera. Your name is musical."

"Do you like music?" she asked him.

"Yes. Yes, I do." he told her. Then, "What family are you from?"

"The Darlings."

"Aria Darling?" he repeated, well-practiced at keeping any emotion from his heart, or his expression. Most of the time.

He'd already been ready to smile, so it came more easily when he spoke her name. He suddenly felt as if he couldn't breathe. His belly also knotted and made him feel ill.

"Miss Aria Darling from New York City. You might not feel welcome at the castle, so it's best if you don't attend. It's probably something you wouldn't like anyway."

Her expression hardened, and he was sorry that it had.

"Oh, of course I was about to decline before you began talking," she let him know icily and tucked her hair behind her ear. "Well, it was...interesting. Goodbye, or farewell, whatever you people say in this century."

Her voice faded into a mumble as she turned.

In this century? It was the second time she mentioned it as if she didn't come from the one they were in. What did she mean? He watched her walk off. He didn't call her back or go after her. He'd head home and find out who sent her the invitation. Who at the castle knew her? Commoners were rarely on the invitation list. So, why was Aria Darling's name on it? Was the invitation to one or both of Gable's children? Sarah and Elspeth were maids for his stepmother. The duchess sometimes invited them to her balls. Yes, that had to be it.

Miss Aria Darling was unusual.

He rode off and didn't realize he was smiling until he was halfway home.

Harper was the first person he met once he left Ghost to his stable hand and returned to the castle.

"Where have you been?" she asked, following him into his rooms. Basically, the entire west wing was his.

"You know your father wants you to take your guard when you ride off."

"I fought a war, but I need guardsmen to protect me now?"

"Even in war, you had a regiment at your back." Harper defended his father.

At your back. An odd thing to say. Where had he heard it before? He stopped so suddenly, she walked into his back. He turned to stare at her. "She speaks like you."

"Who?"

"The woman staying with the Gables. Do you know who sent her an invitation to my stepmother's ball?"

"Are you saying she received one?" Harper asked. "Who is she?"

"Aria Darling from *New* York *City*."

Harper looked as if she stopped breathing.

"A pretty name, I agree," Gray told her, continuing through his rooms in the castle.

"Yes, it is," Harper said. "Did you go out to find her?"

"Yes."

"And did you?"

"Uh huh," he replied, using her words.

"What happened?"

"We sparred," he told her while she followed him into his bedchamber.

"You sparred with a woman?" Harper asked with a doubtful smirk.

"She was well-trained. She bested me."

Harper stared at him, open-mouthed, when he turned to her.

"Harper?"

"Mmmh?" she mumbled.

"Are you from *New* York *City*?"

She snapped to attention and shook her head. "Just because someone speaks like another person doesn't mean they came from the same place."

"It usually does."

"You speak like me," she pointed out. "That doesn't mean you come from the north, like me. You picked up my words and some of my accent because I raised you."

She was clever, reminding him what she was to him. A replacement mother for the one who left him. A father for the one who preferred to work from dusk until dawn rather than spend time with his son. And lastly, Harper was a friend for the ones who laughed at him and then bullied him his whole life. If someone asked him who he cared for the most, he would say Harper Black. He trusted her.

"Harper, I don't think she comes from here—or the north. I saw her as if she fell from the stars. Will Gable got to her before I did."

"Oh..." Harper lamented. "You mustn't speak of this to anyone. They will say you're mad."

"They already say that," he reminded her. "Anyway, who would I tell? I just want to sleep before we eat."

Harper nodded and left him without another word. Something wasn't right about her behavior, but Gray wouldn't ponder it. If Harper knew something and had never told him, it would be difficult to trust her again—so he wouldn't ponder that.

He'd much rather ponder Miss Aria Darling. *Aria-music, Darling-beloved. Music beloved. Yes, music was his beloved.*

# CHAPTER FIVE

Aria finished plucking the feathers from a dead chicken, set it on the chopping block and rushed to the bucket of water in the Gable's kitchen to scrub her hands clean. God help her she had to pluck a dead chicken! She never appreciated a grocery store so much in her life. Everything here had to be either grown or killed. Umm, no thank you.

If not for the memory of Lord Grayson Barrington, Marquess of Dartmouth dancing on his castle rooftop while she had watched him from the woods yesterday, she would have been sick all over these nice people's dinner. Twice. The images of him didn't leave her when she sneezed for the tenth time. They just went fuzzy for a moment but then returned, as they had all night and all morning.

She wiped her nose and went to her coat hanging on a peg inside the front door. Mrs. Gable had asked her if after plucking the chicken she could shovel the yard a bit since it snowed again last night.

Would he dance in the snow?

She had gone to Dartmouth Castle yesterday to rebuke him, but she had ended up spotting him. She had watched him with breath held and her heart flipping somersaults until she ran off without telling him off. But he'd come looking for her on the road…

She opened the door now and was blinded for a moment by

the late snow glistening beneath the bright sun. She opened her eyes more as they grew used to the color and beheld a world without skyscrapers, billboards, smog, smoke, concrete. For a minute she just breathed in the fresh air and soaked in the view of snow-capped trees and the white hills beyond them. It was like a winter wonderland, but even though it was radiant and glorious, it was also dangerous.

Like a magnificent panther.

She thought of the way the marquess' hair had fallen over his marred brow, adding shadows to his eyes, or how it flung each way as his body jerked and bounced when he began his dance. He used inhalations and exhalations to perfection, bringing emotion, hurt, betrayal, sadness to the watcher—in that case, her, while his body was pulled this way or that. She'd watched his fingers gracefully slide across his vision and then he'd snapped his wrists back, melding them together over his head.

He was Romeo, Othello, anyone she could think of. How could such virility become so graceful, and then with a few hard moves or pops masculine again?

Where did all that beautiful emotion that she'd longed to see on a dancer's face, come from? The few times she met him, he barely cracked a smile, a frown, or even appeared surprised.

He did have a weird habit of staring intensely and not looking away when caught.

As a dancer, she was acquainted with people who had two completely different personalities, one on stage and one off. One usually protected the other. She guessed the marquess had some life issues that shaped him—as everyone did. But a huge part of who he was, was buried somewhere beneath anger, sorrow, betrayal, joy, loss. And only in dance could he express them.

She had breathed, not realizing she'd stopped. Watching him made her long to dance again—to leap again.

She replayed yesterday in her mind a thousand times already. She'd taken Castle Road like Beatrice from the village had advised. The road brought her to a hill overlooking the castle, which was built above the coves Will had told her about. She could see the rooftop within the parapets. She could see him there, alone and seemingly in terrible pain.

He had danced without the need of music. Or...was there music? The more she'd listened, the more she heard: the howl of the wind above the water, the swoosh of waves, and then the sound they made when they crashed into the rocks, birds, treetops...there was music in everything.

She used to hear it all, like a symphony in her ears. She'd even, on a few occasions, heard music in the blaring honks of cars. She had stopped hearing the music of the earth and of life when she had to stop dancing.

But she heard it again when she saw the Marquess of Dartmouth dancing on the roof of a castle overlooking the sea. She was sure that if she lived a hundred more lifetimes, she would never forget his beautiful lines and the way he stretched his lean body over backwards until one hand touched the floor and the other reached toward Heaven. He straightened with spasmodic movements. His expressions were as erratic as the rest of him. One instant he was grinning and the next, he sneered with vengeful purpose. Yanking at his hair, he'd compelled her to get closer, to help him. He expressed his open, raw emotions, emotions most men had a very difficult time putting out there. He was profoundly moving as he uncovered bits of himself in his tempo, choreography, and gestures.

She had intended to tell him what she thought of a man in power using it to imprison her in gates made of brawny flesh and bone. Flesh and bone that could be taken down with a spinning back kick to the jaw, or a knee or front kick to the groin, solar plexus, kidneys, whatever the case was.

She wanted him to know she wasn't like Elspeth...or even Sarah—or any eighteenth century woman. She ended up running away instead before he finished his dance.

But the memory of him had begun to haunt her even while she ran back up the hill. She'd been sure his dance would haunt her for a long time to come. He was a true dancer, moving with his heart, muscles, bones, traces of joy for dancing—despite it all—either in a glint in his eyes, the tilt of his smile, or his lighter tempo. It made her not want them to be enemies.

Still, she didn't want to have to fight every time she wanted to check the forest for doors—and she'd have to check even more now that she'd been uninvited to the ball in the castle with seventy-two doors. She kicked the snow under her foot. What exactly had he meant when he said she might not feel welcome at the castle, so it was best if she didn't attend? How rude could a guy get?

She had found the road by tracing her steps backwards. She was excellent with directions. One had to be if one lived in a busy city with several different forms of transportation. She'd continued onward with the dancer leaping into her thoughts. His clean lines and stunning features shot across her mind like stars in a moonlit sky.

She shoveled and swore quietly under her breath while she remembered that he'd been following her. She had had to keep her head on straight, but when he pulled out his sword with a bit of a macabre grin, she instinctively swept him. And then, oddly enough he tossed his blade away and sparred with her. She wondered if he would have struck her if she hadn't evaded or blocked his blows. He seemed to enjoy it.

What did she care anyway? He was a jerk. A jerk who could dance better in a minute than any man could in her future.

She spotted Will on his brown and white horse approaching in the snow from the opposite direction. He was too far away to see her. She knew where he'd been thanks to Sarah. He'd been chopping wood for his uncle Edward, his father's brother. Will's job was mostly physical labor and to fix everything for his mother and the rest of his family. Sarah helped. Harry did not.

Aria heard a sound to her left. But when she turned toward it there was nothing there but fog. Soon though, like an apparition coming to life, the marquess appeared on his gray horse. He was watching her like some wild predator with shining blue-green eyes eclipsed by raven strands of hair. He wore his red coat with the fur-lined hood over his head. He reached her before Will did.

"My lord."

He blinked and seemed to come awake. He looked uncomfortable in his own skin. "I was just making certain there was no trouble here."

"Thank you. There isn't."

He tipped his head toward the sun as he passed her in his saddle. His hood slipped back and fell to his shoulders.

Aria caught her breath at the shape of his face. Why was the angle of his jaw so perfectly crafted, the square tip of his chin so able to support all the emotions and reactions a dancer should be able to support?

Refusing to ponder him the way he had clearly been pondering her when she'd seen him, she pushed the shovel into the snowy path and heaved the snow out of the way.

She heard boots hit the snow and then move toward her. She picked up her head to see the marquess standing over her. He pulled the shovel out of her hand. "Let me."

"No, that's fine." She tried to get the shovel back. "You're a marquess. I'm sure you've never shoveled a day in your life."

He paused to pout. "I feel as if you're insulting me."

"I can see why," Aria agreed, hating how quickly he'd gone from looking like a wolf that had just found breakfast to boyishly adorable. "I'm basically calling you lazy."

He squared his gaze on hers and tore away every barrier she'd ever built, as if they were made of wisps of smoke. "Fine," he said, without giving away what he saw. "You want to know what kind of man I am."

"Ha! Why would I care what kind of man you are?"

"I'll shovel this entire yard. For you."

She couldn't break away from his gaze for a second. "Why would you talk like that? Are you trying to get me to like you? If so, you can forget it right now."

"Why?" he asked with the slightest hint of a smile. "Am I so bad that you can't like me?"

She saw right through his practiced smile to that poignant dancer and lowered her eyes.

"My lord!" Will's voice broke through every haunting thought. "Why are you—here, give me that!" He bounced from his saddle when he reached them and reached for the shovel.

The marquess wouldn't give it up and finally, in a stern voice, ordered Will to let go.

"I'll stay while he shovels," Aria said, still staring at the snowy ground.

"What? Why?" Will asked her.

"Because he's doing it for me."

The marquess nodded and shoveled some more.

"What do you mean, he's doing it for you?" Will asked. "Come inside with me."

She sighed quietly. She found it difficult to ask Will not to push her around. He had done so much for her. He'd become her well-needed friend. But she didn't like how indebted she felt to him.

"Will," she said. She felt the marquess' eyes on her and turned to find him blatantly staring at her, waiting for the rest of her response.

He didn't say a word and gave away nothing about what he wanted—for her to stay with him or go.

"I'll...I'll be in shortly."

The marquess smiled, then shoved his silver tongue into his cheek.

She narrowed her eyes on him, then shook her head. "It was a small victory," she said softly, leaning in toward him as Will returned to the house, stomping his feet every few steps.

"A victory nonetheless," the marquess expressed and kept shoveling.

"Is it just about being the victor?"

He glanced at her, then tossed a shovelful of snow away.

"What else is there for it to be about?"

"Well, it would depend on what you're fighting for." A moment of sanity drifted over her and she wondered how crazy she was to stand outside, freezing her fingers off to talk to a guy she claimed not to like because he'd pushed his weight around with Will. "If you're fighting because of your pride, then I think the victory shouldn't be celebrated.

"You think pride was driving me?" he asked and pushed the shovel into the snow.

"Yes," she told him honestly. "Whether I stayed with you or left you was my decision."

"That's why I remained quiet," he pointed out.

She gave him the slightest smile. "You did something right."

"I'll astonish you," he teased.

She wanted to tell him he already had. What he had was rare. She had a thousand questions for him, but she didn't want him to know that she'd watched him dance while he was alone. It was weird to spy and do exactly what she accused him of doing.

He was about to push the shovel into the snow when he stopped. He said nothing but inclined his ear and knelt. The next instant he used his hands to shovel the snow away. He suddenly stopped. Aria thought she heard him groan. He scooped something up in his hands and stared at it.

Looking over his shoulder, Aria saw a sparrow in his hand.

"Is it..."

"It's gone."

Aria liked sparrows but she didn't know she liked them enough to cry when she saw a little dead one. Her eyes burned and her tears were icy cold slipping down her cheeks. Looking up, she saw the marquess watching her tears as they fell from her face.

Then, he straightened, still holding the sparrow. "Will you hold it while I dig?"

She nodded without hesitation, and they exchanged the sparrow in their hands. Aria held its icy body while the marquess dug a proper little place for the bird to rest.

Who was this man? A crazy person who found the death of his enemy amusing, a magnificent dancer who could convey an emotional range from madness and despair to rapture.

"How did you know its body was under the snow?" she asked him when he stepped back.

He didn't answer and then shook his head and looked away. "I don't know. I just did."

"Can you really talk to animals?"

He returned his harder gaze to her. "You shouldn't listen to ridiculous rumors spread by people who don't know anything."

"So, it's not true then?" she pressed.

His gaze intensified for a moment. He didn't answer her, then continued shoveling.

Well, he really didn't deny it. He didn't admit it either. Why was she even entertaining this nonsense? No one could communicate with animals.

Right, and no one could travel through time either.

She watched the marquess of Dartmouth shovel the Gable's front yard. For her. She blurted out a short laugh. She certainly wasn't going to fall for his silver tongue.

"Hmm?" the marquess urged, hearing her laughter.

"I was thinking of your silver tongue."

He lifted his brows slightly.

"When you said you were shoveling for me," she clarified. His expression didn't change at all.

"What?" she insisted.

"What?" He stopped shoveling.

"You're not saying anything."

"What would you have me say?"

Goodness, his gaze was so intense. She hated herself for being overcome by something so shallow, but his eyes spoke for him, and they were telling her that he found her amusing. "What did you mean when you said you were shoveling for me?

"I think it's quite clear, Miss Darling." He said her name with the slightest trace of a smile, then seemed to catch himself and grew serious again. In fact, he appeared a little impatient. "If someone tells you they are doing something for you, what more do you need to know?"

How was it that the honey tone of his voice could seep so deeply to cover her bones?

"I need to know why. Why would you do any hard work for me? You don't even know me. Do I have you all wrong and you do this for all your tenants? Or is this your way of trying to seduce me?"

He chuckled but dipped his head and blew a breath out of his nostrils, reminding Aria of some kind of animal getting ready to attack.

"I already answered your question," he said, heaving snow aside. "I'm doing this to show you what kind of man I am."

"Why do you care what I think of you?" she pressed.

"Because I saw you, Miss Darling. I saw you appear in an instant, standing in a place you weren't standing a moment before. Your clothes were like garments I've never seen. They were scant and thin and not appropriate for the last week of April. It was if you were somewhere warm and then dropped here."

Yes. She wanted to tell him. He seemed as if he would somehow understand and maybe help her. Would he believe her because he saw her appear?

"All of this makes me curious about you," he continued. "I just want to know where you came from and if you know someone I used to know. I assure you I am in no way trying to seduce you."

He looked a little sick to his stomach. Aria took offense. Was the thought of seducing her sickening to him? What a jerk! What was so revolting about her? Alright then, since he wanted to know so bad, she would tell him, and then she'd never bother thinking about him again.

"Fine! You saw me coming from another century in time. To be more exact, summer, New York City 2024 where I lived my life with my parents and my disabled brother, who I miss enough to scream. I missed his birthday!"

He looked like he was going to say something. She wasn't finished. "I miss where I worked with Mrs. B. I miss my students." She stopped to sniff. "I don't even know how Jake did at the audition!"

Was she really crying in front of this jerk? She swiped her tears away and set her jaw. "Thanks for shoveling. Bye."

She turned around and took a step. His fingers closing around her wrist stopped her.

"Don't go," he beckoned softly, like a melancholy wish—which was why she didn't kick him. "What power brought you here?"

What? That's what he chose to say? No compassion for her. Not a mention of her missing anyone and crying.

Jerk!

She yanked her arm free. "There's nothing else I'm telling you."

He didn't stop her again as she headed to the house. And it was a good thing. She would have fought him.

Before she reached the house, a large raven flew across the pale gray sky and screeched above the marquess. He didn't look up but turned to his horse.

Above him, the raven followed him, swooping low behind him, flying from side to side, but not too close.

Aria's blood ran cold. Didn't the Gables tell her a raven killed their father? What possible reason could there be for a raven to want the marquess' attention—which it didn't get?

How had the marquess known where the dead sparrow was under the snow? Could he truly communicate with animals? She now knew that anything was possible.

# CHAPTER SIX

2024?

Gray would have laughed but something in his belly twisted and knotted. It wasn't just a random number, but *summer* 2024. It was a date. A year. She claimed she came from the twenty-first century.

He would have thought her mad, but didn't he used to believe that his mother had disappeared into the future?

He'd seen Miss Darling appear out of nothing, just as he'd seen his mother do a number of times. If Miss Darling came from the future, then his mother might be there. Yes, he would have laughed at such a preposterous notion as time-travel, adding it to what was so unusual about Miss Darling, but her tears were convincing. Tears she shed for a bird.

She was convincing for certain. She wept over a family she believed she'd left in the future. A brother whose birthday she'd missed. Her students—she was a teacher. She'd mentioned an audition. Did she teach the deaf?

He didn't care. He'd refused to care. It hadn't been easy. He'd felt unfamiliar stirrings of pity, perhaps even traces of compassion and threw water on that fire quickly. He wouldn't allow such damaging emotions to infect him.

Chasing Will Gable's guest from his thoughts, Gray glanced up at the raven again. The creature was difficult to ignore.

A raven had followed him for two years after the Gable incident and then disappeared, until today. Gray wasn't certain it was the same raven that had pecked George Gable in the temple until he died. They all looked the same, though the one that killed Mr. Gable was bigger than the others. The one flying above him now was large and loud, swooping low and cawing almost in Gray's ear. Gray reached out at one point and practically pushed the creature out of his way. He wouldn't take a swing at it. He didn't hurt animals.

Why was it following him though? What did it want? If it was the one that killed Mr. Gable, he'd rather it didn't follow him.

He ignored it as best he could and finally reached the castle. He wanted to find Harper and ask her if she knew anything about people traveling back in time, back from, say, the year 2024? Harper had denied any knowledge of a place called New York City. But the more he'd brought it up, the less he believed her. What did it all mean? Why would Harper lie to him? He hoped she wasn't lying to him about this.

He nodded to the stable hand, then gave Ghost a pet between the eyes. *Thank you for carrying me around all day.* He didn't express his gratitude out loud. No reason to set tongues flapping about him speaking to the animals again. He wasn't expecting an answer from the horse, and he didn't get one. He wasn't a child anymore with childhood fancies. He looked up as he strode for the doors. The raven was gone. He wondered if Miss Darling had seen the huge bird following him.

He felt a flush of warmth flow through him at the thought of her name. Would just thinking her name forever bring color to his face? Was he a cat beguiled by a shiny object? He scoffed at himself and pulled the castle door open. Inside, he shrugged out of his coat, then took it by the shoulders and snapped it. Scattered snowflakes and cold air hit Timothy Cavendish in the face. Gray's older stepbrother glared at him.

"Thankfully, it's nothing that can kill you," Gray remarked as he passed him.

"Grayson!" his stepbrother screeched. Gray stopped and

turned to him with impatience slouching his shoulders. "What?"

"Father is looking for you."

Gray really hated this ant calling the duke his father. He tried to tell himself that he didn't hate Timothy Cavendish, but he couldn't deny the rage he always had to fight back when Cavendish was around.

"You're always the bearer of bad news, aren't you?" Gray asked in a knowing drawl and gave him a stiff half-smile. "Where is the old boy?"

Cavendish gaped at the way Gray addressed his father. "I'm going to tell him exactly what a miscreant his son is until I've convinced him enough for him to strip you of everything—and then I'm going to sit in your chair."

Gray looked heavenward and stopped listening. "I'll find him myself."

He left the babbling dullard and headed for the stairs. He knew if his father was in Dartmouth, he could be found in his private study. When Gray reached the study door, he took a breath to steady his heart and knocked.

"Come," his father called out from inside.

Gray knew exactly where he'd find the Duke of Devonshire— at his desk behind the window, his gaze fastened on one of the many papers on his desk.

"You wanted to see me." Gray stepped inside and sat in one of the two chairs on the other side of the duke's desk. The other chair was Cavendish's. It was the first thing Gray was going to burn when his father left this earth and the castle became completely his. Just seeing the chair, a place for someone who should not be there, darkened Gray's mood.

"What is the meaning of placing thirty men around the Gable's holding?" the duke asked without looking up.

*What is the meaning of seating your second wife's son in the chair beside the son of your loins?* Gray wanted to ask him in return.

"The Gable holding is in the direct line of the band of thieves who have been raiding the three villages," Gray said instead. "The three men I caught confessed to there being a group of at least twenty—the highest they could count—men in the band of thieves. Our villages are ripe for picking without any shield from us, the ones they pay for protection."

There, Gray mused as the duke set his fiery gaze on him. That got his father's attention.

"The ones who give them land on which to live," the duke snarled.

"Land they must farm by the sweat of their brow. One bad season and they go hungry." Very few knew about Gray's stash of grain deep in the cellars of Dartmouth Castle. There were about eleven tons of it, collected over the years and brought in secretly with only himself and Harper accepting the sacks and having them transported to the cellars.

"Son."

Gray grinned, but it was something more macabre than warm. He'd never been a son to this man. Not a true son who could go to his father when the world, and his own young mind, beat him up. He'd never been a son who was chastised out of love. The duke never cared enough to get involved in Gray's life.

"Anyway," he said before the duke spoke further, "they're my men, and that's where I want them."

He didn't move from the chair but waited a moment, then two.

"Very well, do as you like," the duke acquiesced. "But Grayson," he said as his son stood from his chair, "if you would continue to have your way while I live, I want you to try to get along with your brother."

The fire felt as if it were blazing in his belly, searing and scorching as it rose to his chest. "No."

"Son—"

"He's not my brother. He's a worm and you know it. How could you ask me to get along with one of the boys who used to kick me while I lay curled up in a corner? Who made my life hell with Harry Gable and the others?" He paused and let the smoke leave him with a deep exhalation.

"All those things happened long ago, Son. You must forget them. You were boys. Boys fight."

Gray let out a short laugh and then left the study. He shut the door behind him and ground his jaw. He stopped the first servant who passed him in the hall and bid her to find Harper and send her and her violin to his dance hall. No one stopped him while he made his way to the private hall he'd built above the cliffs on the side of the castle.

*Boys fight.*

He hadn't fought. He'd lost. But what did his father know? The duke spewed his orders from afar, and Gray had been expected to follow them. One of his orders was that Gray leave ballet. It would stop the boys from mocking him, his father had said without an ounce of empathy in his voice. "And besides," the duke had continued while his new wife sat watching him, smiling, "a boy should be learning academics and weaponry. Not art."

Gray hadn't agreed but had no choice. None of his dance instructors would teach him a single step. They were the worst years of Gray's life. He'd vowed he'd never follow another order in his life. Even when he joined the Royal Army, he'd gone in to die. Following orders was last on his list. He still wasn't sure how he'd survived. But he had, and not only that, he survived with a hero's honor among his men. As for the duke, Gray would never obey him again.

Stepping into the hall, he removed his waistcoat and unraveled the lace and loosened it around his neck. He paced while he waited for Harper. He felt taut, all wound up. He rubbed the back of his neck and ran his hand through his hair. He listened to the click of his boots against the floor and walked faster, picking up the tempo he was hearing in his head. He walked to the center of the floor, swaying and bending his legs outward while he went.

By the time Harper arrived, he was engrossed in his dance, dancing to music only he could hear.

Without disturbing him, Harper took her seat in a small chair in the corner. She watched him for a moment, taking in the speed of his movements. She placed her violin under her chin and, still watching him, began to play.

Gray heard the music of her violin and smiled as the sound filled his bones. He spun and twirled in two pirouettes and a grand-jeté and landed running and leaping, arching his back and letting his arms fall at his sides. He looked to be running out of stamina, but Harper kept playing, knowing better that it took much more strenuous, longer routines to tire him to the point where he couldn't continue.

All the years of him being forced to study the sciences and almost everything under God's blue skies when all he thought about was dancing. Now, no one would stop him. Here. This was what he wanted, dreamed about since he was six, moving with rhythm to music, soaring in leaps and spins, being free and unhindered by the tethers of life.

He danced and practiced a new dance for the ball. He knew most of the stately, stuffy nobles attended to get a look at him so they would have something to talk about at their dull tables. He didn't care. Let them talk. He'd wasted enough years trying to please others.

He wished he hadn't uninvited Miss Darling. Damnation, hers was a sweet name. But he knew his family and he knew he'd done the right thing. The Cavendishes would ask her endless questions about her family line until they discovered if she was rich or poor. If she was poor, she'd be promptly abandoned and never addressed again. How was he supposed to dance and take pleasure in his family's disgrace of him if he was worrying about her?

He wondered which, if any, dances Miss Darling knew? She believed she came from the future. What would dancing be like in the twenty-first century?

The things she had told him chipped at the thick shell he'd created around himself. His heart wasn't the only thing repeatedly broken as a child. His body had been broken on so many occasions he'd stopped counting. Though he'd remained outwardly aloof and detached toward Harper, he was grateful for the times she stitched him up and put him back together. The bullying eased up a bit after the Gable incident. Gray guessed the boys were afraid he'd get the animals after them. Gray laughed. Yes, he was a 'special child' who could speak to animals and his dead mother. The whispers made him feel removed from society. When he first danced his marionette piece he'd simply called 'Broken', Harper wept and sobbed watching.

It was because of her that the boys left him alone once and for all. He wasn't sure what she'd said or done to them, but they were afraid of her, and they left Gray alone. He never planned revenge on them for all they'd done. He thought Harry Gable almost losing his face and losing his father was enough. He tried to bury his hatred toward Cavendish.

Most of the hatred.

Dancing gave him relief about it all. Nothing was bad enough that it stayed on his mind while he danced. It was his shield, able to deflect the worst arrows shot at him.

He liked to dance with stiff white hair. What Harper liked to call his *mad scientist* look. He'd even used lavender or red powder on a few occasions, and fragranced it with rosewood oil and nutmeg or orange. The powder, made with dried white clay and a bit of lard worked perfectly to give his hair a spiny, jagged look. He'd refused to wear a wig, powered or not. He had his own hair, black as it was. If he was feeling particularly gloomy, he lightly powdered it, stopping when it was gray. If the ball was tonight, he would attend with ice blue powdered hair. Thanks to his father earlier, he felt particularly detached and merciless.

When he finished practicing, he barely spoke to Harper, except to thank her for playing her violin for him.

"What has set your expression to stone, little brother?" she asked, following him out of the dancing hall.

"My father requested that I try to get along with Cavendish, who only moments before I spoke with the duke, threatened my seat and title." He wasn't finished. What he just told her was only a small bit of what he was feeling. But he was ready to admit that the roiling turmoil within him was because of Miss Aria Darling, and he didn't know how to stop it. He hated it. He hated feeling anything. It was too dangerous. Oh, too dangerous.

He could never express his gratitude to Harper for her silence. She didn't make little of what his father had said, nor did she give it more worth than it deserved. He offered her a side glance and a smile.

"You can stop following me," he muttered, striding to his rooms.

"It's my duty to be at your side," she reminded him, striving to keep up.

He turned to look at her and stopped as a question popped into his mind that he'd foolishly never considered. "Who gave you this duty? Surely not my father. If it was my grandmother, why didn't she ever introduce me to you? And who is she that you've kept your word and did your duty for fifteen years?"

"Why are you suddenly asking these cryptic questions?"

"Harper."

She nodded, swallowing.

"Why am I so important to you that you gave up the best part of your life?"

Her gray eyes misted with tears, and she reached out her hand to his cheek. Her touch was as light as a feather and as brief as a summer breeze. He moved his head back enough for her to understand. That was enough touching.

"You are the best part of my life, Grayson," she told him, unaffected by his cool demeanor.

He remembered the way Miss Darling questioned him. She was relentless. He tried it on Harper. "Why? What makes me the best part of your life? When you barely knew me and I did nothing to help that, was I worth missing events with your friends, dates with your suitors?"

"Yes."

"Why, Harper?"

"Grayson, now look—"

"What am I to you?"

She said nothing for a moment and then gritted her teeth. "Alright, let's go to your rooms. I can't speak of these things in the open."

Ah, finally some answers—and was he really surprised Harper had them? No. What else had his only friend, whom he trusted, kept from him? He brought her to his rooms and sat with her in his parlor, though he was aching to stand and keep moving.

"Your mother was an Ashmore," she began, taking him by surprise. What did this have to do with his mother?

"Ashley," he corrected with pout plumping his lips. "Her name was Emma Ashley."

"Yes, daughter of Adam Ashley and Claire Hawke. Claire was the daughter of Sarah, granddaughter of Thoren Ashmore, first and only son born of Josiah Ashmore and Mercy Blagden—"

"Grandmother Blagden," he said softly. He almost didn't hear himself over his thrashing heartbeat.

Harper nodded. "Mercy was her great granddaughter give or take a few generations."

Gray quickly did the math in his head. One good thing that had come from his academic studies. He was very good at mathematics. "That's impossible. Your dates are incorrect."

She shook her head giving him a pitying look.

Then it dawned on him. He scoffed at first, but he remembered what Miss Darling had told him. *Summer, New York City 2024.* "Is it possible?" he whispered more to his own unbelieving mind. "Harper," he said, giving her a serious look, "what is this about?"

"Grayson—"

He looked up at the ceiling with frustration.

"This is quite a lot to take in," she explained in a calming tone.

He knew she was protecting him from whatever it was. But

he wanted answers. What did this have to do with his mother? Who was Thoren Ashmore and why was it notable that he was the only son of Josiah Ashmore and Mercy Blagden? "What does my mother have to do with Miss Darling?"

He could pirouette a total of nine times, sometimes ten, and he'd never felt as dizzy as he did now.

"Your mother and Miss Darling are not related in any way," Harper told him. "All of this is about you, Grayson. You're the last Ashmore. Miss Darling has the potential to give you sons. Seven to be exact. Seven Ashmore/Blagden males to break some curse. I'm not sure of its origin. Of course, Lady Rose Planc de'Vere also has the same potential. There's a possibility of having them with Sarah Gable—"

"Harper," he snarled through clenched lips. "Don't say another word. Sons with Sarah Gable? Have you gone mad? And how in damnation would you know about how many sons I could have with these women? Is this real, Harper? Are you from the future? Have you seen my entire life played out?" He didn't realize it but tears were glistening at the rims of his eyes. "Have you been lying to me since I was ten years old? Because keeping a truth like you come from the future is a series betrayal! Is my mother in the future?"

She opened her mouth to speak but he cut her off.

"Are you going to tell me that my grandmother made you keep this from me and in the fifteen years that you've known me, you never cared for me enough to go against her and tell me the truth?"

"I'm telling you now," she tried.

"And since you're so gifted a liar, I'll consider it another lie that Miss Darling has nothing to do with this since she *obviously* comes from your future."

"Grayson, listen—"

He shook his head. "I'm finished listening. I don't know what is going on, or who to trust. I don't even know if I can trust my own eyes. I thought I could trust you. Whatever the reason for all this is... Whatever you and my grandmother—and possibly the woman who gave birth to me had planned, won't work. I may dance like a puppet, but I don't do anyone else's bidding. My purpose here is not to father seven sons to break a curse. Tell my grandmother I'll choose my own wife and my own path."

He left the parlor and the main door to his rooms. He strode back to his dance hall and didn't come out for the next two days.

# CHAPTER SEVEN

GRAY STOOD IN front of his Baroque wall mirror while his personal butler Jonathan tied a lavish bow made of expensive cream-colored lace at Gray's nape. The loops were small and the tails long, pulling the back of his shirt down. Jonathan never questioned Gray's fashion statements, trusting that his lord would always look his best. And he did, even with his hair powdered gray and slicked back with two thin tendrils waxed with pomade, one curled against his forehead in the shape of an S and one down his temple. He wore a dark turquoise coat with cream edging and strips hanging down his arms. A matching shirt with lace ruffles at his cuffs and down his chest and beige breeches with polished boots.

"My lord," Jonathan said, stepping back to examine his work, "may I say you will have every tongue wagging at the ball tonight."

Gray shifted his gaze, made all the more colorful by his suit, all the slyer by the chiseled cut of his shaved jaw and sleek hair.

"I heard that the Duke of Hamilton and his daughter will be in attendance."

"Yes, my lord. He has accepted his invitation."

Gray nodded and returned his hard gaze to his reflection. Gray had been told that Duke Hamilton had suggested to Gray's father that he should consider sending Gray back to the battlefield instead of constantly letting his son bring shame upon them.

He felt like he might smile for the first time in days, but it wouldn't form on his lips. He looked away and refused the cup of wine offered to him by Clifford, one of the servants.

He went to the door and opened it. Music wafted up the stairs, drawing him out of his rooms. Harper would be downstairs. He hadn't seen or spoken to her in two days. He didn't know if he ever wanted to speak to her again. He didn't want to hear any more about Thoren Ashmore, the Blagdens, time-travelers, trust, or anything else. He wouldn't send Harper away or stop her from marrying, but her duty to him was over.

Miss Darling wouldn't be there. Good. That was how he wanted it. He didn't want her to see him dance. Especially not the ones he'd practiced for the last pair of days. For the most part, he had put her out of his mind while he practiced—which was day and night. There were a few times he was tempted to ride around the perimeter of the Gable holding and watch out for her. Spirited, saucy, hell witch.

"My lord, are you feeling unwell?" Jonathan said, keeping pace beside him and gaping at Gray's flushed cheeks.

"Go away," Gray warned quietly. "Go find Mae in the kitchen and take her out to look at the stars."

"My thanks, my lord," Jonathan hurried on ahead without argument and raced down the stairs. Gray watched Jonathan leap down the last four steps and run toward the kitchen.

Without pausing to smile, Gray's gaze warmed on the servants and guests as he kept going. As he approached the main ballroom, his icy expression returned. He hated facing his father and the disappointment and anger in the duke's eyes. But it didn't hurt anymore that his father found his replacement. Now, while his father lived in Dartmouth, Gray would bring him more "shame". Gray didn't expect his father to find pride in his son's dancing and interpretation skills. The Duke of Devonshire had not been a father to him. Gray felt little or no loyalty toward him or his new family.

But he did like making an entrance and watching everyone's

gaze turn in unison to his father.

Now, he descended the stairs and strode toward the open doors and the people dancing on the other side.

"My lord."

Gray turned before he entered the ballroom to the woman coming toward him. He tried to remember her name, then gave up.

"I was hoping to see you tonight." She reached him and gave him her most radiant smile.

"Why is that?" he asked, slipping his gaze to the people dancing just beyond the doors.

"You are an interesting man, unlike the others here. You do what you like and to hell with what the rest of us think."

He paused another moment to look at her. "This is a trait you appreciate?"

"Yes, of course!"

He curled one side of his lips. "Then you'll understand when I request that you wait here while I enter the ballroom before you."

She looked surprised and then ashamed when she nodded and stepped back.

"There's nothing to be ashamed of, my lady. I'm simply saving your reputation."

Without waiting for her reply, he stepped inside the ballroom. The musicians stopped playing. People stopped dancing. He barely noticed them as he turned to his father and bowed. His father and his stepmother were staring at him when he straightened. They wouldn't say a word to him here, but their eyes lingered on his hair and the lacy bow hanging down his back.

Was that the slightest hint of a warm smile on his father's face?

Of course not, Gray thought. His father never smiled at him.

Granting it no further attention, he turned to his father's guest. Gray knew where Duke Hamilton stood. He'd spotted the oversized duke the moment he'd entered the ballroom. When his eyes met the duke's, he thought he should have powdered his hair red. Red for war. But silver gray was the next best thing. He didn't care enough to go to war. Well, maybe a bit of a fight. Gray grinned and winked at the duke with cold eyes.

He turned his gaze to the musicians and gave them a silent warning to play the music brought to them or risk disobeying the duke of Devon's son, and lord of this castle.

The violin picked up and drew Gray's attention to the musician. It was a man. He blew out a breath. That was the end of Harper harping on his thoughts.

He tapped his foot on the freshly polished floor when the other musicians blended their sound together. He liked this new composer Ludwig van Beethoven's music. He let the music seep into him. He didn't need a special score to dance the way he did. He just needed to feel. And when he danced, he did.

The moment he stepped onto the dance floor, the other guests made way for him until he stood alone in the center of the floor.

Though they all heard the same music in their ears, Gray moved to it differently. He thought it silly that folks thought he could speak with animals. No, it was music that spoke to him. He was able to isolate his movements so that they moved exactly as the sound directed. He made eye-contact with everyone as he turned his knees outward and then bent them low. He came back up rolling his chest and shoulders, smiling and drawing in his bottom lip. He watched wives and daughters swoon on their feet but none of them held his attention for longer than a breath.

He hung his lifeless arms down for a moment of impact. He moved around the floor on quick, light feet, stretching his arms and legs as the music freed him.

When he stopped, he stood before Duke Hamilton. Gray's slight grin was more intimidating than the most fearsome scowl. He shook his head and his finger at the man whose jowls trembled. Fascinating how pale a man could become.

"Your Grace," Gray said over the music. Almost immediately

after, it stopped. "We all heard what your son Reginald did to the women who were left alive when their small town in Anjou was attacked by Reginald's regiment. Does it not shame you?"

The duke looked around nervously at the people listening. Gray knew if he denied it—or that it shamed him, the other nobles would look down on him. "My son was already brought before the king and has paid a hefty fine."

"That was not what I asked you. Let me ask again. Does it not shame you that your son attacked women after he killed their husbands, and they had no one to defend them?"

The duke looked pleadingly toward Gray's father, then lowered his gaze.

"Poor duke, you should see your miscreant son sent to the front lines. Better that he die than shame your family any further, hmm? I'll write to the king on your behalf about reinstating him to his regiment."

While the duke stammered and shook in his chair, Gray made his way back to the center of the floor and bent his knees apart and outward again, but this time accompanied by his arms lifted at his sides with his forearms hanging limp. He danced, letting the strips hanging from his coat insinuate that he was being moved. But then, in a burst of fury clearly played out on his face, he spun like a destructive whirlwind. His thoughts of knocking some of the guests into Harper's future made him want to laugh. Cavendish, Gable, Hamilton—

Gable? Not Harry, but William. The younger Gable never came to the castle. For an instant Gray flicked his murderous gaze to his stepmother. She constantly invited the Gables to her balls.

He returned his gaze to Will—and then did his best not to respond when he saw Miss Darling standing close by in the crowd, watching him.

Not skipping a beat, Gray performed six pirouettes and finished with a graceful penché.

He left the dance floor, swearing in his head. He strode directly to Miss Darling.

Damnation, but her eyes were deep oceans of fathomless blue. If one wasn't careful, one could drown in them.

"I thought we agreed that you weren't coming."

Her breathless smile faded, leaving a stormy, cold expression in its wake. "I changed my mind."

Gray shifted his gaze to Will Gable. "And what are you doing here?"

"I came as Miss Darling's escort," Will advised him.

Gray glanced at her and caught her studying his hair. He waited an instant until her eyes widened on his when she realized she'd been caught. Gray was displeased with himself for letting her stir something in his belly. He looked away quickly, forgetting what he'd wanted to say.

"Keep her away from Cavendish," he warned Will Gable instead. "If I see him speaking with her, I'll hold you responsible."

He walked off before either of them could say a word. He didn't feel like dancing anymore. In fact, he felt like tearing something apart. His gaze drifted to Duke Hamilton, still sitting in the seat he'd fallen into at one of Gray's tables, shoving a spoonful of food into his big mouth, where he had suggested to his father that Grayson be sent to the front lines.

Gray started for him, walking between the guests like a wolf stalking its prey from within the trees. The duke was too busy chewing and laughing at something the duke of Nottingham, sitting on the other side of him, said.

When Gray slipped into the empty chair beside Hamilton, he said nothing for a moment. He boldly took in the sight of him with the hint of a mocking smile on his lips. When Hamilton turned to see him, he stopped chewing.

Good, now that Gray had his attention, he smiled slightly and motioned to his father across the floor. "For wanting me dead, when he dies, you'll die too."

He leaned in closer, and closer still until the strength and power in his gaze made the duke whimper. "Depending on what else you tell the duke of Devon..." he paused and set his hungry gaze on the duke's dimple-cheeked daughter… "you will or won't go alone."

Judging by Hamilton choking on his air, he got Gray's meaning. Good, Gray hated having to explain himself. Before he left the table he turned to Hamilton's daughter and let his gaze rove over her dark tresses piled in curls over her ears. She smiled slightly and gave her hair a prim pat. Gray knew he had her—and after he'd threatened her father, no less.

"Catherine," he said, using her familiar name, "I'll call on you for…tea. I hope you will accept."

She blushed to her roots and nodded. "Of course, my lord."

His eyes didn't leave the duke's, even when he nodded.

He started for Cavendish next, when he saw his stepmother standing over Miss Darling. He cut a path for them and arrived in time to hear his father's wife flap her tongue.

"There is not much known about you, Miss Darling. Where did you say is the city of your birth? Might we be acquainted with your father?"

"I doubt it, Eloise. Excuse us." He cupped Miss Darling's elbow in his palm and led her away, flashing a dark look at Will.

"You did not say anything about the duchess," Will defended, catching up.

Gray ignored him and kept walking with Miss Darling. When she realized he was escorting her out, she yanked her elbow out of his hand.

"Are you throwing me out?" she demanded.

"Yes!" he said, refusing to be moved by a mere wisp of a woman. "You have no idea—"

She folded her arms across her chest. "I'm not leaving."

Did she just say—"What? What do you mean? When someone throws you out—"

"I said I'm not going," she repeated. "The whispers about you are true, I see. You are dim-witted."

He stood there staring at her, lips parted, caught on a breath and on an oath trapped in his throat. He looked at Will for a moment, but the carpenter gave no answers, though he'd lived with her for days now.

"Fine," he relented reluctantly. "Stay then. But don't leave my side." He took her by the wrist and pulled her toward the tables. Gable followed them and Gray was reminded of the time he had a thistle in his boot while he fought a battle.

"Sit. Eat," he grumbled when they reached a rectangular table with four couples already sitting and eating while the musicians played.

When Miss Darling looked down at his feet, he followed her gaze with a curious look.

"Oh, sorry," she said, "just checking to see if your knuckles reached the floor."

Gable sat on the other side of her and also gave Gray's boots a curious look. Harper, on the other hand, giggled as she finally showed up in the ballroom and passed their table with a glance Gray's way.

And then at Miss Darling.

Gray let her pass without stopping her, then turned to Miss Darling. "Do you know her?"

"No. Why?"

"She comes from your future."

On the other side of her Gable coughed into his cup. So, she had already told Gable.

"What do you know about my future?" she asked him.

What did he know? Not much. He knew more about the past, at this point. About the Ashmores and the Blagdens...and only about their lines and male heirs. Miss Darling would think him mad if he told her such things. But what if she already knew? He didn't trust anyone, not even Harper, anymore. Not even Harper...his eyes found her picking up her strings and sitting with the other musicians.

Her betrayal cut like the deepest knife. She'd had fifteen years to tell him things weren't as they seemed, that he wasn't mad in the head, and that for some reason his grandmother could travel through time.

Feeling his gaze on her, Harper looked at him. He turned away and looked into Miss Darling's watchful gaze.

"She seems a bit old for you," his guest pointed out.

"She raised me," he corrected without anger. Indeed, he was beginning to feel nothing again. It was how he wanted it. It was his shield against Harper and everyone else.

"She raised you? Did your mother…"

"She disappeared," Gray told her, then tossed her a careless smile. "Maybe she ran away from me to your 2024? Emma Ashley. Ever hear of her?"

"No, I'm afraid not," Miss Darling told him, her voice softer than it was a moment ago. "But where I come from is much more crowded than it is now."

"I see."

"So, you believe her?" Will Gable asked in a hushed voice.

He'd seen her appear out of thin air. If nothing else, there was that. It was no trick of the light. There was no excuse to be made. She wasn't there and then she was, looking as confused and terrified as anyone who had just traveled through time would.

Gray stared at her long enough to make anyone else twitch. She merely smiled and clearly won the battle when he felt as if he needed to scoop his heart up off the floor and bury it deeper into his chest.

"Do you?" she asked, giving his ruffled sleeve a tug. "Do you believe me?"

"Yes. I do," he said, ignoring the way her smile deepened. "But don't tell another soul or they'll make your life hell. Do you understand?"

She nodded at him.

"Good." He set his hard gaze on Gable. "Then, if I hear a rumor of this, I'll know it was you who spread it."

"You will not hear a word of it from me," Will let him know with a bit of a bite in his tone.

Did Gable care for her? Gray clenched his cheek. Why did it

have to be a Gable who'd come upon her first? A Gable who was likely stealing her heart? Will was handsome, with eyes the color of strong cedars and a deep dimple in his left cheek. He didn't seem as insufferable as his brother, Harry. Miss Darling likely already cared for him.

"You dance really...um...well."

He slid his gaze to Miss Darling. Was she mocking him? Really well? Or something else she decided not to say?

"Where did you go to school?"

"I didn't go to school. I learned here at Dartmouth as a child. I had the best ballet teachers for a while, and then afterward...I taught myself."

"Really?" she asked, doubting what he told her. "After what?"

He sat back in his chair and looked her over. What were these questions she was asking him? No one had ever asked him before.

"After my father forbade me to dance."

She blinked and her eyes turned red and bright blue. "You weren't allowed to dance?"

He shook his head. "But it didn't stop me."

"It's in your blood," she said quietly.

He heard her. What did she know of what was in his blood? Even though she was correct. Dancing flowed through his veins, and it was pleasant to speak to someone about it.

"You tell a story with your body," she went on, "and with your heart baring itself on your face."

He stared at her. "How do you understand these things?" he asked so quietly she moved closer to hear him. The scent of jasmine wafted through his nostrils and went to his head.

"I teach dancing at home," he heard her silken voice in his ears, his head.

She taught dancing?

"Do you dance?"

She didn't answer but sipped from her cup of wine. He waited, then finally pinched the sleeve of her white top beneath her pretty saffron colored stays.

"No!" she pulled away with a short laugh. "Don't even *think* about dragging me to the dance floor. After the car accident my body doesn't like to move that way."

"Car… accident?" he asked seemingly confused. "Yes. My leg was broken in four places along with my pelvis, collarbone, six ribs, and my ankle."

His face drained of color. "How did you live through it?"

"Broken bones are easy to mend though sometimes they can break again. It's better than what my poor father and brother are suffering."

*Broken.* She'd been broken, even worse than he. She knew what it was like not to be able to dance. She also had a father…a poor father and brother who suffered with her. More than her. What a hell she must be a prisoner to. He could barely think of it. "You cannot dance so you teach it instead."

"Right!" she smiled as though it weren't the worst punishment in the world.

"Perhaps you could teach me," he said quietly.

"I really don't think there's much I could teach you. You're better than anyone at my school."

"Even Jake?"

She laughed and nodded.

"Who's Jake?" Will Gable asked.

"One of her students," they both answered together. It made Gray want to smile—so he did. Slightly. His gaze settled on Harper and then away again when she gave him a stunned look.

"Are you going to dance again?" Miss Darling asked him.

"Perhaps," he teased. "But now I'll feel as if I'm being judged."

"By me?" she asked with a playful smile. She laughed when he nodded. "My lord, really, you're outstanding. You're Romeo."

At this he grinned and that broke into a quick, short laugh that felt as if it shook his entire body.

"Then I think I will." He rose up and with one last look at her, he stepped out onto the dance floor. He danced the minuet alone and with his own special spin that made the onlookers either burst into applause or scandalous gasps that left his father slumped in his chair.

Gray couldn't care less if he was applauded or reviled. He danced because he enjoyed—no, he loved it. It was in his blood. He swept across the dance floor, spinning and flying in the air in perfect grand jetés. He didn't know how long he'd been dancing before he looked toward his table. Miss Darling and Will Gable were gone. He looked around, casting his well-practiced smile at Miss Clementine, daughter of the earl of Aimsley, when he met her gaze. He only spared her a brief instant before his eyes searched the ballroom for Miss Darling.

When the dance was over, he walked to his table and looked around again. Harper was also gone. Were they together? He cast his stepbrother and Cavendish's mother a steely glance. Miss Darling was not with them. He moved through the guests, searching their faces. Miss Darling was no longer in attendance. He strode toward the doors. Would she just leave without a farewell? His belly burned. What did she owe him that he should expect a farewell? He swallowed a short laugh bubbling upward. When had he become such a pathetic creature?

If she left, good riddance, he thought, making his way upstairs to his rooms. He hadn't wanted her there in the first place. His dances were ugly. That's how he intended them. Especially tonight's dances. But she'd shown up. She changed her mind, and that lowly creature Gable had followed her.

She'd called him Romeo. Everyone knew who Romeo Montague was—the male protagonist in William Shakespeare's masterpiece *Romeo & Juliet*. Gray smiled to himself, liking the compliment. It was the first he'd received that he believed was sincere.

When he reached the top of the stairs, he heard the muffled speech of a familiar voice. He turned the corner and then leaped back behind the wall.

Peeking around the wall, he watched Miss Darling shove a

key into his stepbrother's door. He almost stepped out, revealing himself. What was she doing? None of the doors were locked. What was Gable doing here with her? Were they trying to rob the place?

When she opened Cavendish's door and looked inside, while Gable kept an eye out, Gray had had enough.

"What are you two doing?"

At the sound of his voice, Will Gable jumped backward and looked about to fall faint. But Gray barely noticed him. His hooded eyes were fastened on Miss Darling.

"Did you ask me to dance to get rid of me?" If she answered yes, he would have known that he was wrong about her. Her kind words about him being like Romeo weren't sincere.

"No, and I don't want you thinking that of me. I would never disrespect talent like yours. I watched until my opportunity almost slipped away."

"What opportunity?" he asked, stepping closer, without looking away.

She stared at him for a moment before she answered. "To check your seventy-two doors."

"Check them for what?"

"My home."

# CHAPTER EIGHT

ARIA FOLLOWED THE marquess to a small terrace on the third landing. At his insistence she sat in one of the two delicate wooden chairs overlooking the crashing waves below. The heavy woolen blanket the marquess spread over her didn't warm her as much as the blood rushing through her veins at his closeness when he leaned down to tuck her in. She worried that he could hear her heartbeat through her flesh and bone. It was all his dancing. It had gone straight to her head.

She looked up at Will to get her thoughts off the marquess above her against the backdrop of a starry, velvety sky. There was room for a third chair to be carried in for Will. But no offer was made by the marquess.

"Again, I would caution you not to speak of this so freely—and especially don't go running around the halls checking doors or I might not be able to save you from the stake."

The stake? Aria ran the back of her hand across her forehead. Did he mean, like, her *burning* at the stake? Oh, she really didn't like the eighteenth century.

"You can speak freely to me out here," the marquess offered.

Could she? What choice did she have? From the beginning, he claimed to have seen her arrival.

"Was there a door on your side?" he asked. It didn't take a brain surgeon to put that together since she'd been checking doors for a way back. But in all the days she'd known Will, he hadn't asked her. In fact, he didn't ask her anything about the future or how she'd gone back through time. Because he didn't believe her? Could she blame him?

"Yes," she answered. "The door to the building. I was locking it."

"So, there's a key?" he asked.

Did he really believe her? It was such a huge relief that she relaxed in her chair, despite the turbulent waters below.

"Yes," she told him. Then caught her breath at the magnificent beauty before her. The marquess was the most handsome man she'd ever seen. She wasn't usually moved by such a thing, but she remembered the myriad expressions that painted him into masterpieces when he danced. He was trained in ballet. Yes, it showed. She hadn't lied, she'd watched him spin and perform the immensely difficult grand jeté three times in the ballroom downstairs. In her future, he'd get every audition and would wind up on Broadway in no time.

"Miss Darling would like to keep the key in her possession, my lord," Gable said.

"Who is discussing taking it from her?" the marquess asked coolly, sparing him a glance. Without waiting for an answer, he returned his attention to her. "I have no intention of taking your key, Miss Darling."

She nodded, believing him and pulled the key from a pocket in her sleeve. "It's one of those—"

"Master keys," he finished for her, not remembering where he had heard the term. He reached for it.

"I'm told it's made of real gold," she told him while he examined it.

He blinked his somber gaze from the key to her. "Who told you that?"

Aria looked at him. His tone had changed. He sounded slicker, more doubtful. "The owner of the key, Mrs. B...Blagden, my—"

"Blagden?" His voice shook, his eyebrows rose over his cerulean eyes and revealed such innocence, such...betrayal, Aria almost recoiled. His expression had changed in an instant from some kind of revelation. "She sent you here," he breathed out. He turned to Gable. "Go find Harper and bring her to me."

"With respect, my lord, I think I should remain with—"

"You're insulting me by not trusting me with her. Do you really want to make me your enemy as your brother has?"

Will didn't protest again but turned and hurried off the terrace in search of Harper.

"Why are you so nasty to people?"

The marquess stared at her and then at the key. "People deserve it."

Goodness, something had really broken him and changed his life. She'd seen hints of it in his dances. Had it been the death of Will and Sarah's father, or was it something else? The loss of his mother? Wait. He'd fallen apart before her eyes when she mentioned Mrs. B. Or more specifically, the name Blagden. But it didn't pardon him from being mean.

"Why does Will deserve it?" she asked him.

"Because he's a Gable."

"Ridiculous!" She tried to snatch the key from his hand, but he held it over his shoulder, about to hurl it into the sea.

"No!" She stepped up on her chair and leaped at him to grab his wrist. "Please! Please, I need it to go home."

He looked into her eyes level with his as he caught her in one arm. "I'm a puppet."

It was more like a groan than a statement. They were close enough to share breath. He hadn't moved to give her the key so that she would back off, so she didn't. "Please don't throw it away."

Finally, he lowered his arm and handed her the key. "Try the front doors on your way out."

He left her alone on the terrace and disappeared inside the castle. Did he just throw her out...again? She was almost glad that he didn't wear his heart on his sleeve when he wasn't dancing.

His sadness was too palpable. He was angry, as well. The kind of anger that seeps deep into your bones and begins to shape you. Aria sat back down and looked at the key in her hand. This stupid thing caused more trouble than it was worth. What did it have to do with him? Why had he looked as if he recognized it? How would that be possible? Why had he wanted to hurl it into the estuary?

*I'm a puppet.*

Images of him dancing with his elbows up and his forearms dangling, a mad gleam in his eyes, and a macabre grin on his lips, assailed her. No. This really wasn't her problem.

Aria rose to her feet to leave. She would check the main castle doors as the marquess suggested. He probably hoped she disappeared the way she'd come. Why would he want her around? He didn't seem to like her very much—or anyone else for that matter.

She took a step toward the door when Will returned. The woman who was playing the violin earlier was with him. She looked around, scowling when she didn't see the marquees. This was the woman he believed also came from the future and the woman who raised him after his mother disappeared.

"He left," Aria let her know. "He was angry," she told her quickly when the woman turned to leave them.

The woman returned her attention to Aria. "What happened? Why was he angry?"

"He said he was a puppet."

The woman—Harper—looked as if Aria had slapped her. She stumbled into one of the chairs. Will hurried to her aid, but she waved him away. "I don't know why they don't just explain things to him."

"Explain what?" Aria asked, taking the seat beside her. "Who do you mean?"

Harper stared at her. She was pretty, Aria thought, mid to late thirties.

"Tell me about yourself," Harper invited in a suddenly curious tone.

"Since the marquess mentioned that you're from my future," Aria informed, "why don't you tell me about *yourself* instead?"

"He told you... I see. Just how close are you to him? I know you've spent time with him."

"How do I get home?" Aria asked her. "That's all I care about."

"How did you get here?"

"A key. A gold skeleton-type key. What do I do with it? How do I get it to take me home? I believe him about you coming from the future. You speak differently than the others. So does he. None of this is a coincidence—and he knows it."

"He spent eight years in my care before he joined the fight against the French."

"Eight years of being forbidden to dance?"

Harper raised an eyebrow at her. "That's right. As for the key, you must find the right door."

Obviously, Aria scoffed to herself while her teeth chattered.

"Why don't we go inside where it's warm," Will suggested.

Aria thought about a burning stake with her tied to it. "A few more minutes, Will," she said and turned back to Harper. It was cold up here above the sea. She'd have to hurry. "Do you have any idea why the surname Blagden would affect him?"

Harper's pretty features froze up before she slipped her gaze to Will. "I'm afraid I won't be able to answer your questions if we aren't alone."

Aria tried to protest. She trusted Will not to betray her. He'd done a lot for her, and she wouldn't stand by while he was mistreated. "But he's—"

"He's unfortunately the brother of Gray—the marquess' worst enemy," the woman who raised the marquess said. "He would consider it a betrayal if I were to speak of him to a Gable." She shook her head and sucked her teeth. "It's really a pity that you met a Gable first—and the kind brother, no less. Now, I can't confide in you because you'll confide—" She flicked her gaze to

Will—"in him."

Aria gaped at her as Harper spoke and then headed for the castle door. Did everyone here specialize in rudeness?

She'd forgotten that there was a reason that the marquess didn't like the Gables—and a reason the Gables didn't like the marquess. No matter what Will said to the contrary, she knew it would have been hard—maybe impossible—to forgive the person accused of being responsible for his father's death. She imagined that every time Will witnessed his mother with less than enough on the table, he hated the marquess as much as his brother did.

She followed Will inside and back downstairs. While he was helping her into her coat, the castle doors opened, and Harry Gable stepped inside bringing the cold with him. "Ahh, Miss Darling," he drawled, heading for her. Will tried to head him off but was too late. The marquess was not.

"Show Harry Gable out," he called to the guards who hurried to his side.

"No need," Harry chuckled. "I have come to bring my brother and his guest home. She insisted on attending to see you dance. Well, lady, what did you think of the spectacle?"

Aria could feel the marquess' piercing eyes on her. He stared so obviously at her, not caring about the whispers around them. Aria knew what Harry was doing here. They'd made a deal. She was supposed to laugh at the marquess' dancing abilities or risk being thrown out of Mrs. Gable's warm house.

She turned her head to meet his seafoam gaze. She smiled, but she couldn't laugh—not at something so important in someone's life.

"I think he's quite astounding and original," she said truthfully, then shared a hint of a smile with him. "In fact, he's Romeo in every girl's dreams."

She closed her eyes and swallowed when Harry's face went red, all except his scars. She hoped Will defended her and kept her from sleeping outside.

"Miss Darling," Harry ground out through clenched teeth.

"I'm afraid a wild animal broke through your window and tore your bed to shreds for some strange reason. Who knows why stupid animals do what they do, eh?" He set his disgusted expression on the marquess.

"Miss Darling can stay here until she returns home." The marquess stunned the crowd and seemingly himself when he spoke. "I have many beds."

"My lord," Will seemed the most surprised, "for the good of Miss Darling's reputation, I cannot agree to her remaining here with you without any escort."

"Very well," the marquess allowed. "Your sister, Sarah may stay and see to her and make certain I remain an honorable man."

"I can see to that myself," Aria huffed, "But I'll stay if Sarah can stay with me." She looked around for the Gable's sister.

The marquess nodded, then motioned for his guards to escort Harry out. Will reluctantly followed his brother, looking over his shoulder at Aria while he went.

"He cares for you," the marquess stated, turning to her.

"No." She leaned in closer to him and lifted her lips to his ear. "He'd be a fool to lose his heart to me. He knows I'm not staying in this time."

The marquess stared sedately at her. "What if he makes you want to stay?"

She gave the short laugh his suggestion deserved. But...when her gaze met his, she saw something in their blue-green fathoms. A great disturbance in the depths. Turmoil so deeply ingrained that it was almost impossible to read on his face. She'd only seen it two other times. When he danced, and when she mentioned the name Blagden.

Why was he asking her such a question? What did he care if Will tried to change her mind about staying? What did he care about? What could stir his guarded emotions? Suddenly she wanted to know.

"What's wrong?" she asked him, all traces of humor gone from her face.

He blinked. "What?"

"Something's bothering you."

He offered her a practiced smile, but then pushed his tongue into his cheek and looked away. Was he uncomfortable because she'd looked so deep? Or was this one of his ways of seducing women? Hit her with an adorable, boyish charm?

"What did Harry Gable want from you?" he asked her.

She wouldn't lie to him. "He wanted me to laugh at your dancing in front of everyone."

Instead of getting angry, he smiled at her, then started walking away.

"Why do you hate him?" she asked, following him. Will had told her the marquess and Harry hated each other. She knew why Harry Gable would hate the marquess, but what reason did the marquess have for hating Harry?

"The Gables didn't tell you, then?"

"What really happened?"

"I commanded the forest animals to kill their father and maul their brother."

She shook her head, then scoffed. "Surely no one believed that."

"They all did," he countered. "My mother had been rumored to be a witch; they thought I was the same."

"I thought they burned witches at the stake."

"Twice, they tried to burn her. Twice, she disappeared from her bindings—and two men on the council disappeared with her. When she returned alone days later, I saw her appear from the air, as you had. After that, the rest of the council was too afraid of her to approach her again. No one knew exactly what she had done or if she was in any way responsible for the disappearance of men who had tried to burn her. I think I know now." He bowed his head and chuckled. Then he shook his head, as if it was all too difficult to relive.

"You think your mother took those men to the future?"

He nodded.

"You believe me then."

"Yes."

"So, your mother—were you there when they—"

"I was four and then five years the last time they tried."

"I'm sorry you went through that. It must have been extremely difficult."

He stopped and turned to look at her. She almost tripped over her feet. He didn't move to catch her. She held herself up, though she wasn't sure how she did while his eyes searched hers, probed like a soft breath, reaching...everywhere, until she felt utterly consumed by him. But as he assailed her senses, she saw him stripped of his own guard.

"It wasn't," he confessed softly and without concern, "extremely difficult."

He was lying. It was part of his armor.

"How old were you when she disappeared for good?"

"Seven," he said, pulling at his backward collar. "After she left, my father kept me locked behind the castle's walls until I escaped to the Royal Army. I returned to find him and his new family living here, in the castle he'd given me. I took ownership of Dartmouth and moved in with them. When my father dies, I can throw the Cavendishes out."

He sounded completely unaffected by speaking of his father's death or of throwing out a mother and her son. But he didn't look at her.

She followed him up the stairs and down the long corridor to one of the seven doors in the hall. She didn't know where her chaperone, Sarah Gable was, or what was behind that door. Did she trust this stranger to follow him into his—he opened the door—*dance studio?* It was huge! Twice the size of hers at the school. The floor was made of wood and there were wooden horizontal bars around the perimeter. Perfect for someone studying ballet.

"It's quiet here," he said.

She spun around to find his eyes closed and breathing the

place in. "Is this where you practice?"

"Yes, or other places."

Like on the roof of the castle. "You said you escaped and went into the army." She wanted to know what made him dance the way he did. "What did you escape?"

He looked at her, then laughed softly. "You say what you're thinking."

"Not always," she countered cryptically, then smiled. "But really, what did you escape? Can you talk about it? We can talk about something else. I don't know why I'm acting so comfortably with you. I don't usually intrude on people's private lives. You don't have—"

"I escaped the defenses that kept me alive, like my father's power when words like magic, witch, and murderer were being flung around, and Harper's temper against bullies who left me as a pile of broken bones. If I had the animals at my command," he mumbled under his breath. "Harry Gable, Timothy Cavendish, and the others would find living very difficult."

Wasn't Timothy Cavendish his stepbrother?

Wait—"What do you mean you escaped the defenses that kept you alive? Are you saying that you went away to fight so that..." she paled and felt ill. "So, you would die?"

"It didn't work out that way," he laughed and pulled off his boots.

He left the protection of his hell, seeking...

Aria folded her legs, sat on the floor, and covered her mouth with her hands.

He'd wanted to die. It had been so bad he had wanted to die. And now, he lived with some of them who'd made him feel that way.

"What do you think of living now?" she asked, watching him sit on the floor beside her.

He turned his head to look at her and she was sure he was smiling—it was slight, hardly noticeable. But she noticed.

"It's much better with dancing in it."

Yes, it was a way to let all that steam out. Better than to take revenge on the people who hurt him. When she sighed though, he turned to face her. "What is a car?" She smiled at him. "What?"

"You said a car accident caused you to break your bones. What does that mean?" Did she want to talk about this with him? She hadn't spoken to anyone but Mrs. B. And really, was this the time? She looked around at the soft golden candle lit studio…er, hall, with the aroma of polished wood soothing her nerves. This was a place to dance, to be free, and she was sitting here with a man who felt every instant of music and became one with it. There was no better place to open up than here. Before she could stop herself, she opened up to him.

First, she captivated him with descriptions of cars and how they operate, then she told him about her family's celebration and the car crashing. Twice, when he asked her what it was like to crash, her explanation drained his face of color.

"My mother walked away unscathed. She insisted on sitting in the rear seats with me so my brother could sit near my dad in the passenger seat. She blamed herself for Connall losing his legs instead of it happening to her."

"Your brother lost his legs?" he asked, horrified with her.

She nodded and wiped her eyes but kept going. "He was so active. He was always camping or hiking or practicing self-defense. He was a black belt—"

He put his arm around her while she wept silently.

"My dad never woke up, but he was alive. Maybe he heard them saying that the accident was all his fault, that he destroyed his children's lives. But my mother never blamed him. I don't know about Conn. He stopped speaking to anyone."

After a while, when the marquess spoke again, it was to tell her that he understood now why she wanted to get back home so urgently.

"You do understand?" she asked, unable to stop her smile from forming.

"Of course."

And here she had thought he tried to shirk his responsibilities. She was wrong about him.

"But dancing helps."

She slipped him a repentant side-glance. "Do you want to dance right now?"

He didn't laugh, but a sound came out of him, and he stared at her with shining eyes. "No, I don't want to. I was hoping you would."

Her eyes filled with tears yet again. She wished she could. She wanted to dance every day. Not a single day passed when she wasn't wishing she was dancing. "I can't. If I fall the wrong way, I could shatter my ankle and then I won't even be able to practice."

"You won't fall, Miss Darling," he promised.

She scoffed lightly. "How do you know that?"

"Because I'll catch you."

# CHAPTER NINE

FROSTY SWIRLS ROSE from Ghost's huge nostrils, but the horse made no sound nor moved an inch in the brisk morning air. Gray wondered, while they waited in the stillness of the forest, if his horse cursed him for bringing him out into the cold. Gray doubted she did, since Ghost, a splendid war horse, had been with him in the army. Thanks to Ghost's color, on foggy mornings, like this one, Gray went unseen until he was on top of his enemy.

He'd left the castle on the pretext of finding more thieves from the band that had been raiding the villages. But he wanted to be away from the woman who brought him to the edge of a precipice with her smiles behind a saucy mouth and her fierce courage even in the face of a brute like Harry Gable.

The bastard. Gray knew Harry had threatened to toss Miss Darling out into the cold if she didn't laugh at him. She'd risked it for Gray and lost. He'd had no choice but to offer her a bed. It was one more thing to hate Harry for.

Aria Darling was turning his insides to warm honey. He wanted...no, he needed to be away from her, so he came out here, where the cold felt familiar.

He pulled his hood farther up on his darker, wet head. He'd bathed and washed the lard and powder from his hair on the beach along Castle Cove. His body had dried, but his hair hadn't. He felt a chill from deep within and blamed Miss Aria Darling.

He'd wanted her to dance. He'd even considered dancing

with her, but she'd refused. In the cold light of day, he was glad she had refused. He must have been out of his mind. Why did he want to get closer to her? She was already in trouble. He thought of her too often. He even thought of her family now. He fell, lost in the memory of the blue depths of her eyes. His blood sizzled in his veins at the thought of touching her. He'd promised to catch her if she fell.

He heard a twig snap to his left and inched his ear toward the sound. His thighs tightened around Ghost. *Easy, my lady. Not yet.*

The horse didn't move.

Something running through the bare bramble. Something big.

*Now!*

Ghost leaped forward and took off running. Sitting low on her back, Gray barely had to guide her. She knew what they were after.

Gray saw the rider, the first of three more. They rode up beside and behind Gray, swinging their swords. He ducked and blocked with his sword, but he didn't want to kill them.

"I'm the Marquess of Dartmouth. Stop, and your head won't be impaled on a pike in front of my castle."

Two of them slowed and lowered their swords. Gray pulled on the bow behind him, then plucked an arrow from his quiver. He aimed upward and let the arrow fly. Before it landed, he loosened the rope tied to his thigh, leaped from Ghost, and tied the two men to Ghost's waist.

"If you try to escape, she will kick your face off."

The thieves paled and swore they wouldn't try. Gray ran to the third thief felled by his arrow. The thief was hit in the shoulder. It had been a risky shot. Gray couldn't aim for the culprit's leg. The arrow would have gone through flesh and blood and landed on the horse. He checked the horse just to make sure the creature wasn't injured, then dragged the thief to his two friends. The thieves' horses, though untethered, remained close to Gray.

"What's goin' to happen to us?" one of the first two asked.

"That's up to my father," Gray let them know and moved toward Ghost. He gave the horse a scratch down her long nose. "It was worth getting out of bed for, hmm, old friend?"

"So then," said the thief with the arrow through his shoulder and a sneer on his face, "the rumors are true, you do speak to animals."

"Mostly just this one," Gray smirked at him, then leaped onto Ghost's back.

"My lord?" the other of the first two called out.

Gray half turned to him, tied to Ghost behind them.

"Will we be killed? You said we wouldn't be."

"I said you wouldn't be impaled on a pike in front of my castle. Do you remember?"

The thief, a young man of about eighteen years, lowered his gaze and nodded. "My father will never forgive me, but I had no choice. My mother already perished from lack of food. My father suffers constant ailments, and there's no food for him to get well."

Gray had little compassion for those he knew and none for strangers. Spending almost six years in the military had done nothing to nurture such a wasteful emotion. "Better if you had considered all you've told me *before* you robbed what you needed from others who need it as well. The life of someone else's father means little compared to yours?"

"To me, it does," the young thief cried. "Forgive me for saying, my lord, but no one's father means more to me than mine."

Gray looked him over in his tattered breeches and a coat in even worse condition. Was the boy's story true? He guessed there were many more similar stories out there. His father was still in control of laws and the punishment for breaking them, money collected from his vassals for land and agriculture, and more. The full bellies of his people had never been a priority to the duke of Devon. They wouldn't be important to Timothy Cavendish either. That's why Gray didn't have the luxury of just leaving the way his mother had. What did he really care about rules and the selfish men who made them? But when his father died, Gray had to make certain Cavendish didn't take his title.

"Please, my lord, if you would just check on my father occasionally. His name is Nate Somner."

The first thief scoffed. "You think the marquess will do anything for you but deliver you to his father for the noose? You are a fool boy!"

The young thief closed his eyes to keep his tears from spilling over.

Gray cast the first thief a murderous glare. "What do you think you deserve for stealing from the mouths of children?"

"Forgive me," the young thief cried without opening his eyes.

Gray stared at him for a moment, then turned and flicked his reins. Ghost trotted along at a slow pace, while the wounded thief and his unrepentant companion went back and forth from complaining to begging for their lives. Gray listened to some of it, but he was mostly immune to begging. He'd heard it often in battle.

A raven gave out a shrill cry above his head. Gray and the other three men looked up, for the bird was flying low.

It was big, the same one that had followed him the last time Gray had been out. He scowled at it. What did the creature want? He felt an elusive memory pass through his head of being young—perhaps five or six—and laughing while he ran through his mother's garden with a raven pecking softly at his sides and back.

A large raven killing George Gable.

He put the memories out of his head. Miss Darling made it easier to do, since she constantly plagued his thoughts.

She had accused him of being nasty to the Gables and she even defended Will Gable. Part of him was the slightest bit bothered by it. It didn't matter what she felt for Will. She was going to leave if she found the correct door. The thought of going with her to perhaps find his mother, crossed his mind. But he didn't want to find her and he wasn't about to let Cavendish have Dartmouth.

He simply had to guard himself extra hard against Miss Darling and all the things about her that tempted him to tear off his armor and compel her to stay. He didn't find her half as irritating as everyone else he knew. She was dangerous—so dangerous, he thought, shaking his head at himself. He could almost feel himself falling to every useless emotion that had a name.

But she drew him the way music did. After checking and finding it gone, Gray was certain the key his grandmother had given him was the object that brought Miss Darling here—to the past. Miss Darling was a dance teacher and a dancer herself. It was as if she were handpicked and sent back to him all wrapped in a pretty bow. Yes, he believed it all. It made sense to his poor head that his mother had gone *ahead*. That grandmother had gone next and had given the key to Miss Darling. The questions were why and how much did Miss Darling know? Was she in on the grand plan? Or was she too a victim of the Blagdens?

She'd been broken, like him, and it had cost her what she loved most.

He scowled at himself as a wave of warmth, like the deepest caress, flowed through him. Empathy. The first of the curses. Mother to sympathy and compassion, they wreaked havoc on the heart and if he wasn't careful, he could find himself torn to bits, not by any forest animal, but by the people around him.

Not him. Not ever again.

He ignored the young thief's quiet cries and handed the three men over to his guardsmen to be brought to the dungeon. But when his men turned for the stairs, Gray followed them. He reached the young thief's coat and yanked him around to face him.

"We're going to validate your story." He didn't give the boy the opportunity to reply but dragged him in the opposite direction.

He practically flung the thief into the saddle of one the three horses that had followed him home.

"Take me to your father," Gray demanded, leaping onto Ghost's back.

"Thank you, my lord. You have my loyalty above my own life."

Gray shook his head. "Don't die for a sentiment. Always do what you can to protect your life."

They traveled north to Norton and reached the small hovel where the young thief, who was called Robin, claimed to live.

Nate Somner was blinded with age and extraordinarily thankful that the marquess of Dartmouth would deign to take such care of his son. "He is a good boy," Mr. Somner said of his son.

Gray nodded. He hadn't told the boy's father the real reason he brought him home. "Yes. I believe he is."

Gray warned Robin never to rob again and left him to care for his father. He returned to the castle alone. When he set foot beyond the castle doors, he sensed Harper in the shadows, watching to make certain he came home safely. He kept up his pace to his room, though twice he almost turned to order her out of the shadows.

He was glad no one else—like Miss Darling for instance—met him in the halls. He wondered, for the briefest of moments, where she was.

Without considering what it meant, he allowed himself to wonder what it was like in the future. What was dancing like? Miss Darling stirred something in him. He was curious about her dancing.

Curiosity. Another curse that gives birth to temptation. He couldn't be tempted by her. He wouldn't allow it. No lady at court had ever tempted him. The years he fought for the king were spent in celibacy. He didn't mind. He was with a woman once and it wasn't what he'd imagined it to be. Sexual intimacy hadn't been intimate for him. It had been quick. He didn't have the heart for it, so he stopped doing it. But on more than one occasion while in the company of Miss Darling, the memory of the first time he'd seen her in a scandalously short skirt and her legs encased in some sort of hose, as tight as her skin, stirred his blood. The sound of her voice, her laughter, even when she reviled him, sent tremors deep into where his heart and soul slept.

She had the courage to stand up to him, and to Harry Gable, as well. She'd reached out her hand to Gray, unafraid of being bitten, and touched him. How long before she discovered the wolf she stroked had been locked away for a reason? Only...he couldn't remember what it was.

He heard footsteps coming toward him and looked up, away from his thoughts.

It was as if she stepped out of his head and landed in front of him, just her clothes were different. Unfortunately, she looked no less beguiling in her pale blue eighteenth century robe over layers of muslin, cinched at her small waist. Her long, chestnut tresses were loose, tied back at the temples. He half-turned to hurry back the other way, then realized how pathetic he must appear and straightened.

He counted how many of her footfalls echoed within him— or was it his heartbeat?

She was smiling.

He dipped his gaze to her lips when she reached him.

"Lord Dartmouth, have you been avoiding me all day?"

Had she noticed his absence? What did it mean? Why did he care? This veil of a woman seemed to have the power to demolish the great fortress he'd built around himself, where even animals dared not go.

"I had more thieves to catch, Miss Darling," he told her woodenly.

"Did you catch any?"

He refused to let himself fall captivated by her shining, sapphire eyes and breathless smile. "Two. Now, if you will excuse me—"

"So then, you *are* avoiding me."

He stopped. "I'm merely tired and wish to rest," he said without turning to look at her.

"Fine, enjoy your rest. I'm going out."

His eyes opened wider, and he spun around. "Miss Darling, don't dare leave this castle alone."

Concern. Yet another curse this woman brought upon him.

"Am I a prisoner?" Her eyes weren't shining, they were blazing.

"No. Didn't you hear what I just told you? I caught two more thieves today. It might be different in your future, but here, you're a temptation few men will ignore."

She didn't say anything for a moment, but her cheeks grew crimson. She patted them and stared at him. "You're different?" she finally asked.

He nodded. "Yes, I am." He resisted temptation every time he didn't run his sword through certain individuals when he saw them. "Ask one of my guardsmen to accompany you."

"Absolutely not," she let him know. "I want to be alone."

He laughed in disbelief and looked behind her at his bedroom door. "Weren't you looking for me?"

"I was," she offered him a cheeky smile, "before I found you and remembered what a dislikable person you are."

"Did you forget so easily?" He mocked her with a lifted brow. "I'll have to try harder to make sure you don't forget again. Should I begin with returning you to the care of Harry Gable? He was about to throw you out in the snow because you refused to mock my dancing, hmm? Thank you for that by the way."

He didn't lose himself to the sweet confusion on her face, the sudden rush of warmth in her eyes.

What was he saying? He shook his head, then covered it with his arm. "Come with me." Before he could stop his own feet from moving, his fingers from taking hold of her wrist, he went with her to fetch her coat and then led her back out of the castle.

"Where are we going?" she asked, letting him lead her to the stables.

"I was hoping you would tell me, since you're the one who wanted to wander out."

She shook her head and shrugged her shoulders. "But I told you I wanted to be alone."

"And I told you not to leave the castle without an escort." He matched her challenging glare and stood his ground.

"Well," she said, looking away. "I can't ride."

He retrieved a small stool close by and set it down on Ghost's left side. He didn't need it. After years of riding the warhorse, he knew how to grasp the horse's mane and mount in a single leap—which was what he did now. Once on Ghost's back, he held his hand down to Miss Darling.

"You might as well take it," he urged with a wide-eyed smile. "Don't tempt me to chase you."

She hesitated another moment, hugging herself and eyeing the stable exit. But instead of taking his second option, she held up her hand. He leaned down and closed his fingers around hers and hefted her up and into his lap.

She landed with a slight thud that rattled Gray's senses. Behind her, he shook his head as if to clear it. "Where to?"

"To the Gable's, then please. I'd like to see Will and let him know I'm alright."

"He doesn't need to know that."

"I *want* him to know. Look, you offered to escort me to where I wanted to go. I want to go to the Gable's house and say goodbye to Mrs. Gable and thank her for caring for my needs when I came here. If you refuse to take me, I'll return to the castle and leave without you at another time."

He said nothing but grasped fistfuls of Ghost's mane and jerked his hips forward, unwittingly grinding them into Miss Darling's bottom. When she turned to send him her deadliest glare, he offered her no response, though his insides were twisting, his blood scaling his veins.

"It's inevitable in our situation," he said evenly.

"What's inevitable? That you're going to touch me intimately again? I suggest you don't. I'm not adverse to sinking my fist into your groin."

He grimaced and shoved her away just enough to make her hold on tighter to his arms. He wondered as he rode her to the Gable's holding as she'd requested, what had come over him. How was his iron resolve deteriorating so quickly? When he realized, after riding through the forest, that she hadn't let go of his arms, he pulled away and then closed his arms around her.

"I won't let you fall," he promised, leaning down near her ear.

When he finally felt her relaxing against his chest, he leaned down again, just a bit closer to her. "Miss Darling, tell me about Mrs. Blagden, the one who gave you the key."

# CHAPTER TEN

Aria closed her eyes and clung to the marquess. Did his red coat smell like pine, or was it the forest all around her? She couldn't think straight with his arms around her while he rode them bareback on his horse. If death had a color, it would be the color of his horse. But the thunderous pounding of her heart convinced her that she was very much alive. Perhaps more alive than she'd been since her accident.

Sitting between his hard thighs was bad enough; thrusting his hips forward to get his mount moving nearly melted her all over him. He hadn't apologized. He'd promised, once again, not to let her fall. Was he so quick and agile that he could stop her from bouncing right out of his lap, or so strong that he could catch her in a grand jeté?

"Miss Darling?"

And the husky tone of his voice when he called her Miss Darling made her belly flip.

"You were about to tell me about the woman who gave you the key."

"Was I?" she challenged. How much should she tell him? His reaction the first time he'd heard of Mrs. B. wasn't a good one.

"After my mother left," he told her, leaning over her to speak close to her ear so she could hear him over the wind and his running horse, "my grandmother took over raising me. Sometimes when I looked deep into her eyes, she seemed infinitely older than a grandmother should be. She left when I was almost ten. Before she left, she gave me the key you now have in your possession."

Aria turned to give him a disappointed stare. Really? "It's the key you want."

"What?"

"Is the key what this is all about?" When he continued to gaze at her, not understanding what she meant, she clarified, "It's one of a kind, solid gold, and it can transport someone through time. Who *wouldn't* want it?"

"Me," he answered dully. "I had it in my possession and I never once tried to use it or even take it from its place to look at it."

"Ha!" she mocked. "So, you're telling me you had the key all this time and you were never curious about the door it belonged to? And that your grandmother is who—? Mrs. B?"

"You can be perceptive when it's spelled out exhaustively for you, lady," he drawled out, moving away from her.

Aria cursed him for taking the warmth from her. "Forget it. I'm not giving it up."

"You're not curious about how we have so much in common?" he asked her. "About why you were sent here—to me?"

"Who says I was sent for you? You weren't even the first person I met. It was Will. Maybe I was sent here for him and not you! Or...or maybe I was sent here for me! You didn't think of that, did you?"

"Miss Darling?" Will Gable called out beyond the early evening mist. "Is that you?"

"Will!" she exclaimed, sounding more excited than she felt. She waited until the horse stopped before she practically leaped from its back and into Will's arms.

"I was beside myself with worry," Will said without letting her go. "I wanted to go to the castle today to check on you, but my mother was afraid of inciting—"

He looked up at the marquess, who was staring at him from

his mount's back, waiting for him to finish.

"—your wrath, my lord."

Aria watched the marquess' smile curl his lips and then spread into a dark grin.

"Your mother knows, then, how easily her son rakes on one's last nerve."

"Will," Aria said nervously. She shouldn't have asked the marquess to bring her here knowing the animosity between them. "I think your mother, and perhaps even you, are wrong about the kind of person the marquess is. He's been nothing but ki—"

"He's not wrong," the marquess interjected. "His family knows well enough that my wrath is not to be trifled with."

"Why?" she challenged, glaring at him with her hands on her hips. "Will you get your horse after him? Wouldn't you have already done that to his brother if it was possible? His coming to the castle to inquire after me would not incite your wrath. You're not that kind of man."

His smile shone in his eyes. It didn't matter if he used his lips or his eyes to show his pleasure. No matter what else she told herself, she liked that she brought out a little bit of him. He angled his head at her as if he wanted to ask her how she knew what kind of man he was.

"You're not wrathful," she told him. "Detached maybe, but not wrathful. You hardly blink an eye when I insult or challenge you. You didn't even get angry when I kicked your sword out of your hand."

His gaze flicked beyond her head, to Will. He shot out a feigned laugh and shook his head. "It's very different, Gable. I don't dislike her." His eyes widened for a second and he coughed softly.

He didn't dislike her. Did that mean he liked her? What if he did? She didn't like him. More importantly, she wasn't staying.

"Okay, enough," she admonished, holding her hands up. "Will, I just wanted you to know that I was alright. He isn't a mad ogre." She smiled, knowing the marquess heard.

"Mayhap just to you, little lion."

She heard him, but she pretended not to. There weren't any men in her past. Her past, like her future, was dedicated to dancing and then to helping her parents. She worked. She had no time for play. Conn needed tuition for an online college or something to help him live. Her mother needed help putting food on the table. How were they eating without her? She felt a sudden rush of panic flood her senses. She had to find a way home and stop thinking of the beautifully expressive dancer trapped behind walls he'd built to keep others out.

"I assume none of the doors in the castle was the one you needed," Will said. Perhaps he hadn't heard the marquess' confession.

"I haven't checked any others yet," she told him.

"Why not?" the marquess asked. "I would have thought that was the first thing you did when you woke up this morning."

"I didn't want to do it alone. If I walked in on someone without you there with me—"

He held up his hand, silencing her from explaining further. But he didn't say another word.

"If you find the door, I will not see you again," Will said in a cracked voice.

Aria didn't know what to say. She hadn't wanted him to get any false hope about them. What should she say to him?

"Ghost is cold."

She and Will both blinked and looked up at the marquess when he spoke. Aria eyed his horse. Ghost. Right. Figures. The beast did look cold though.

"We should go," the marquess said.

"My lord," Will tried, "I can bring her back to the castle after supper. I know my mother would be happy to see and feed her."

"Another time," the marquess said without giving her a chance to reply. "We have many doors to check, and I'd like to get started."

He reached his arm down to Aria and waited for her to take his hand. When she did, he pulled her up.

He didn't ride right off, denying Will another word, but waited for at least five breaths, giving her a chance to bid her friend a possibly permanent farewell. And then he moved around her, encompassing her and tightening his thighs around his horse until the animal bolted away.

"You should use a saddle," she said when the horse slowed to a trot.

"Ghost doesn't like them," he told her, his voice vibrating against her back. She closed her eyes to fight off the dizzying effect he had on her. "She wore one for a long time and would prefer to be free."

Aria wondered if he was speaking of his horse, or himself?

*I'm a puppet.*

His words and the heavy voice in which he spoke them were still fresh in her mind. She had wondered who pulled his strings, but it didn't really matter who. How could he heal from his childhood? That's what mattered. But surely, it couldn't be up to her to heal him. She had a family who needed her! She wanted to shout it—especially so Mrs. B.—wherever or whenever she was—could hear it. Instead, she remained quiet on the way back to Dartmouth—doing her best to ignore the low flying raven above them.

When they arrived at the castle, the marquess dismounted, then instead of helping her down, he leaned in closer to his horse's head and scratched the mare's nose.

Finally, as if what he had to do next was the most unsavory task, he moved closer to Aria and held his arms up to her.

Was she to fall into them? She looked around the stable but didn't see the stool. With her face burning up and her jaw clenched tight, she closed her eyes and let herself tip over.

And would have landed hard on her rump if he hadn't caught her in the cradle of his arms at the last second.

"My apologies," he said, staring down at her. "I wasn't expecting you to collapse as if dead."

He sounded cool and detached. He looked unfazed and unin-terested, but he didn't put her down until she insisted he do so before they reached the castle entrance.

He set her on her feet, letting his sea-colored gaze linger on hers before he glanced up at the raven, then moved away.

"Wash up," he said, taking his first few steps away backward. "I'll see you in the dining hall."

"My lord—" Would she ever get used to calling him that? "I don't know—"

"Sarah will help you."

Was that the hint of a smile she just saw on his lips? What did he find humorous about her not being familiar with how things were run in a castle? He'd almost smiled. That's what was important.

Why? Why did she feel glad that he'd smiled? She wasn't there for him. There had to be a mistake. Didn't she have enough on her plate? She couldn't be responsible for his healing.

Before she could stop him, he went inside and bounded up the stairs.

ARIA FOUND SARAH tidying her rooms. Will's sister seemed sullen while she dusted a table in the small sitting room. She barely looked up when Aria entered.

"Diedre told me you were out with the marquess," she com-plained gently when Aria pressed her to tell her what the matter was.

"Yes, he took me to see Will at your house."

Sarah gave her a hopeful grin. "My brother?" She sighed with relief when Aria nodded. "Will must have been pleased."

Aria smiled but said nothing. What was there to say? She and Will had no future.

"I need to wash up and go to dinner," she told Sarah. "Will you help me? I don't know what I should wear or where I should go."

Sarah seemed to forget the marquess and tended to Aria with great care. Aria guessed Will's sister wouldn't be happy about her and the marquess disappearing after they ate in order to try fitting an odd key into the keyholes of the castle's many doors.

"You know a lot about the marquess," she mentioned to Sarah as the girl tied her hair up with over a dozen pins.

"I admit I've liked him my whole life," Sarah whispered with a giggle. "I felt sorry for him...and for myself because I knew who I was, the daughter of a carpenter. He was nobility, the son of a duke. He would never be allowed to...that's why the other boys hated him, because he was so far above them."

"What happened that day your father died? Do you believe the stories that he can communicate with animals?" She wouldn't tell Sarah about the raven that seemed to follow him all the time. Or about how Ghost didn't like being saddled. "And...just leave the back of my hair down. I don't like all those pins."

"I was young when it happened," Sarah said and plucked two pins from Aria's hair. "Six to be exact, but Harry cried about it every night for almost two months. He and the other boys were shooting arrows to see who had the best aim. Harry's arrow hit Abigail the goose." She pulled more pins and let Aria's long, chestnut tresses spill down her back. "They ran away but Harry returned later to see if she lived or died. Her body was gone. He said he followed a trail of droplets of blood and found the duke's son burying the goose in the forest. Lord Dartmouth knew Harry was the one who struck his friend. How would he know unless Abigail told him? He and Harry fought but then the forest animals began to come out of their hiding places to bite Harry. He said Lord Dartmouth was smiling. A wolf entered the glade and attacked Harry, but our father appeared and shot it. Harry says the boy called out for help and a large raven came and..." She stopped, unable to go on.

Aria took her hand in both of hers. "I'm sorry for bringing it up."

"Oh, Aria, you're shivering. I'm quite alright, really. I

wouldn't say the same for Harry."

"Of course," Aria said. She had the intention of speaking to Harry. According to the marquess, and now his own sister, Harry was a terrible bully toward the duke's motherless son. She wanted to ask the marquess about that day and hear his side of it, not just Harry's.

"Word of the incident traveled throughout all the villages, and soon almost everyone came against the young lord, Grayson Barrington. People wanted to stone him when they heard Harry's sickbed tale. Thankfully, they were too afraid of the duke to lay a finger on his son. None of us were allowed to play with him. He didn't have a single friend, not a soul to cry to—even his grandmother had left. Thank the good Lord for Harper Black. She stepped in and dealt with all the hostility Lord Dartmouth could muster. She finally reached him. She used to take him beyond the wall to the forest against his father's wishes and let him practice his dancing to the music she played on her violin. We knew what she was doing, and we knew the trouble she would get into if the duke found out. He never did. We kept it secret from everyone else."

"We?"

"Will and I," Sarah told her.

"Why would Will care about what happened to the boy who supposedly got his father killed?"

"At the time, Will didn't believe the stories about communicating with animals. He liked Lord Dartmouth, but Harry's rantings finally got to him."

"But not you?" Aria asked her.

Sarah shook her pretty head. "I worked here. I used to sneak off and watch him dance in the woods. I believed that he could speak to animals, and they understood him. Mayhap I should hate him too, but I had seen him with Abigail the goose when it was alive. Every memory I have of him before that day is him with that goose. That's why I believed the stories. I had heard him speaking with Abigail, and many other animals. He would laugh for no reason at all—no reason the rest of us knew. They were his friends. If he was beaten up by my brother, the animals would have gotten involved. It's the only reason so many animals attacked Harry and my father."

"But if he had that kind of power, wouldn't he have used it on your brother when everyone turned against him?"

Sarah shook her head. "After the incident, the village men were permitted to go out and hunt the animals responsible for what happened. They killed everything that moved in the forest. After that, I never saw the marquess smile or talk to an animal again."

Aria wiped her eyes. The punishment was harsh for the animals and for the little boy who loved them.

She had had enough of being pampered and rose up from her seat so fast she nearly knocked Sarah over. She helped the youngest Gable to her feet, then hurried out the door.

When she heard Sarah behind her, she slowed a bit, getting a hold of herself. "I'm so hungry." She laughed when her stomach rumbled to prove it and picked up her steps again. The delicious smells coming from the last set of double doors in the hall weren't the reason her slippered feet hurried to get there faster. She wanted to see the marquess. She shouldn't have asked Sarah so many questions. The more she learned about him, the more she wanted to see him comforted.

For the first time she didn't think about getting home.

Sarah stopped her from pulling open the doors herself and plunging into the dining hall. Instead, she waited while a male servant opened the doors for her.

She entered first, then turned to look over her shoulder for Sarah when the girl fell back.

As if he'd been waiting for her, the marquess appeared at her side and escorted her to his table. There was no one else sitting at it. "Do you sit alone every night?"

"I don't usually dine here," he told her, looking ruthlessly handsome with his naturally raven hair combed back away from his face, his lithe body dressed for dinner in claret velvet and lace. "And when I do, Harper used to sit here."

"She doesn't anymore?" Aria asked him as she sat in the empty chair near his.

"No."

"Why not? I understood her to be very important to you."

He didn't answer but sat down and looked at her, into her eyes as if he were searching for the meaning of life. Her instinct was to look away from such careful examination, but Aria fought it and stared back at him. She felt the risk of it almost immediately when he tore away her layers. What would he do if he discovered the passionate woman buried deep beneath piles of responsibility? She didn't want that part of herself to be exposed.

She almost breathed out loud when he slid his gaze away first. She didn't say anything else while dinner was served. What was she even doing here? Had Mrs. B. really sent her? Why? Lord Grayson Barrington was too dangerous to her. Could he tempt her to forget the doors?

"If we don't find what you're looking for tonight, I'll take you out in the morning to search the forest."

"Thank you," she said with her two-pronged forkful of venison paused at her lips.

She was thankful for sure, but he sounded eager to be rid of her. The thought stung a little.

Then it occurred to her, and she leaned in closer to him. His indefinable, musky scent washed over her and through her, making her dizzy. "You're not thinking of coming with me, are you?"

He blinked at her, then the slightest hint of a smile curled his lips. "It has crossed my mind, but I won't leave Dartmouth in the hands of Cavendish."

She looked across the hall to where his stepbrother sat with a buxom female and a group of other men. Timothy Cavendish was one of the bullies in young Grayson Barrington's life. Now, he stood to inherit everything. Aria scowled at him.

Watching her, the marquess drew her gaze to his widening smile. "You hate those who hate me," he said, sounding almost stunned to Aria's ears.

"Yes," she said without hesitation, then immediately blushed.

"Your reputation might be tarnished if you don't revile me and leave my side. We will meet on the—"

"I'm not going to revile you or leave your side. At least not until I find my door." She offered him her sincerest smile and watched him swallow and look away. "Where did you want to meet? Let's go there now."

"To the next door," he answered hesitantly, then stood and led the way.

He surprised her. She thought, maybe, secretly hoped, that he might try to spend more time with her. He looked and sounded like he wanted to. She wasn't disappointed that he denied himself. It was a commendable trait in a man.

"Do you have the key?"

She reached into a hidden pocket in the folds of her gown and pulled out the golden key. He brought her to the first door on the second landing. It was the door to Lord and Lady Albenum's room while they were visiting. They were in the dining hall, so trying the key in their door wasn't a problem.

By the tenth door Aria noticed her fingers were beginning to shake and her heart rate accelerated with each new door they tried. Would this be the one? Would she just walk through it and enter the future without him? Why wouldn't she? She didn't owe him anything. She wasn't in love with him. She hardly knew him! Why was she having an anxiety attack every time she tried another door?

"My lord," she said after the twenty-third door, "my family can't make it without my help."

"Then you must not tarry, Lady," he said, sounding terribly tender to her ears.

She must not tarry. She followed him to the next door and slipped the key into the keyhole.

"Thank you for helping me," she told him, pausing until she pushed the door open.

He said nothing so she opened the door and looked inside. It wasn't the future. Her heartbeat slowed as she closed the door.

"Why are you helping me, by the way?"

"If you find your door and disappear behind it, I will be free of what they have planned for me."

So, that was the reason he was so eager to see her go, so he could break free.

"You think I was sent purposely for you?" she asked him.

"You were given my key by who I'm certain is...was...my grandmother Tessa Blagden—over two centuries in the future. So, yes, it would seem so." Tessa aka Hester Blagden. Mrs. B. The same person she had blamed when the key sent her here. Was this all Mrs. B.'s plan, as impossible as it was? "It would seem so," she repeated, agreeing. "But why? Mrs. B. knew how much my family needed me. She helped us through so much after the accident. She made my dreams of dancing come true. And now I'm supposed to believe that she's some witch with evil intent."

"I'm told that in a future I may possibly spend with you, we will have sons."

"No, that's impossible," she whispered, horrified. "I can't abandon my family. I'll never abandon them."

Were her eyes deceiving her? Was that a genuine smile forming on his face, in his eyes and on his lips.

"Then let's keep checking."

# CHAPTER ELEVEN

A FTER FIFTY-EIGHT DOORS, they stopped for the night.
"Maybe it's not here."

He turned to her as they walked together through the hall. "There are still more doors. We will check them tomorrow. If your door isn't here, then we'll search the forest. If there was a way here, there must be a way back."

"You're very reassuring." She smiled and his heart went a little soft. There was nothing he could do to stop it. "You must be eager to get rid of me."

"Miss Darling," he said steadily, trying not to think about the fact that she didn't sound playful about it. "I don't think about *ridding myself of you.* If I didn't want to be here with you, I wouldn't be."

"Well," She looked away for a moment to laugh at herself. "I mean, I don't want you to be happy to see me go, but I also don't want you to be hurt when I go."

"I won't be happy to see you go," he let her know, trying not to smile at her like some hapless fool. "I also won't be hurt."

She didn't look any happier, but she smiled. "Good! Well, goodnight then."

Boldly, he reached out and snatched her hand. "Come to my dance hall with me."

"Now?"

What was he doing? He forbade his mouth from opening. His

head betrayed him when he nodded.

She took a step with him and then stopped and smiled at Harper approaching.

Harper smiled back briefly, then turned to Gray. "Can we talk?"

"No," he said through his grounded jaw, and tugged on Miss Darling.

"You should both go talk," she intervened, pulling her hand away. Gray gave her a disbelieving stare. "I'll see you tomorrow, my—"

"Stay right where you are," he ordered.

"It can wait," Harper told him and turned to leave the way she'd come.

Miss Darling stopped her. "We were just going to my lord's dance hall. Why don't you come along? He was just saying earlier that he missed talking with you."

"Miss Darling," he barked. "I said no such thing!"

"Not with your words," she admitted. "But your eyes spoke for you."

He would have laughed at her preposterous statement if Harper hadn't started walking away.

"Harper," he commanded. "Bring your violin." He wanted to sound angrier than he felt. In fact, he wasn't angry at all. Hell, what would betray him next? His heart? His gaze slipped to Miss Darling before he picked up his steps. He'd told her if he didn't want to be here with her, he wouldn't be. So...that meant he wanted to be with her. Hadn't he invited her to the dance hall when she would have left him for the night? Now, she'd invited Harper—and he wasn't angry.

He hadn't taken hold of her hand again and looked down at his shoes while they walked. "I don't think you should go about telling how you hear my eyes speaking for me. These people will think you peculiar."

"Please," she huffed and bunched up her lips, making Gray think about kissing her. He averted his gaze when hers turned to him. "They're the peculiar ones," she continued. "Their heads are as dull as their hearts. They look at art in the flesh and they see something sordid and scandalous. It's their thoughts which are odd and peculiar."

While she went on, he didn't look at her. He wanted to. It took every ounce of strength he possessed not to. He ached to see the indignation play out on her pretty features. She was pretty. He wanted to look at her.

"You should stop growing so angry on my behalf. It's very enchanting—" he looked up from his shoes, finally setting his gaze on hers—"but I have no heart for it."

Her huge eyes opened even wider. "You have no heart for what? Who wants to enchant you? Not me. I'm just passing through."

"As you've said a dozen times now," he muttered.

"And yet you're thinking I want to *enchant* you?" she countered, giving him a look that said he was too ignorant to bother with.

"I don't know if you want to or not," he said, raising his voice, "but you are!"

She dipped her ocean blue gaze, and then he did too. He continued to the dance hall, not realizing she had stopped.

He felt panic rise in him like bile. What was she doing to him? Why couldn't he stop it? He wanted to. Didn't he? He felt a little feverish and flush, so he kept his head down when he entered the hall with her behind him.

He pulled off his velvet coat and tossed it aside, then did the same with his shoes. He thought he might dance for her. He didn't know why he suddenly had such a thought. He wanted to dance for her to show her who he really was. At least a small part, but a vital one, nonetheless.

And that's what frightened him. Why did he want to show her? Why did it suddenly matter?

"What kind of dancing did you perform?" he asked her, wanting to know more about her, despite what his head was shrieking at him.

"Contemporary dance," she told him, then explained. "It's rooted in ballet with more modern movements. The same things are important like clarity of line, and from what I've seen, your lines are beautiful even in the most grotesque way."

He couldn't help but smile but he turned away when he did...and looked straight at Harper who had entered the hall carrying her violin.

"Who is this extraordinary woman that brings a smile to my precious boy's face?" she said in a quiet voice, close to him.

He let his smile linger for another instant on his dearest friend, then turned in the direction of Miss Darling.

"Teach me."

She laughed and shook the foundations of his body. He almost laughed with her. What in blazes—

"Teach you contemporary? No, no, I can't."

"Why can't you? You don't have to dance. Just teach me the steps."

"It's the movement too," she added and turned to Harper when she began playing her violin.

"Yes?" he urged.

"It's...it's interpretation and expression...and...um... freedom."

"Teach me," he asked, lowering his voice and his gaze to hers. "Please."

"Maybe it's better if we don't...I'll return to Will. I'm sure he'll—"

He sighed. He'd heard enough and did three pirouettes away from her. Of course, he'd let her leave if she wanted to go. She wasn't a prisoner. She was correct. They shouldn't spend so much time together. If he wasn't strong enough to suggest it, he was glad she was. Why did she? Was she beginning to feel something for him? His belly flipped. Mayhap he was ill, and these flips and flurries were part of his malady. He looked at Harper. Should he tell her? She would get him feeling well again.

While he twirled on the balls of his feet, he bent forward and then down to his spinning foot and brought his other leg straight up. A classic penché, but he gave it depth and meaning when he brought his shoulders up, and keeping his body parallel to his legs, folded his arms across his chest and then used his graceful hands to indicate him pouring something out of them. Head back, his eyes half closed, he let himself go. He brought his foot down and turned his knees out, contracting his chest, then puffing it out. He raised his hands to his chest again and this time, flicked his wrists, turning his fingers upward on one hand and down on the other. Alternating each position to the shrilling cries of the violin, he turned his face left, then to the right to show her a big part of his childhood. Being beat up by Harry Gable and Timothy Cavendish, and a few others. Leaping into a tour en l'air, or a turn in the air, he thought of how Miss Darling stirred him and how vulnerable it made him feel. He landed on both feet, covering his face with his forearms. Then, his arms fell limp and his head slumped over.

The music stopped.

He didn't open his eyes for a moment while he gathered his control. Sometimes it wasn't easy. This was one of those times. He wanted to keep dancing—but for himself. He needed to release these volatile emotions, or they would erupt.

"That was outstanding," his guest complimented when he walked back to her. "And troublesome."

"Why troublesome?"

Instead of answering right away, she crossed her arms over her chest as if in defense of what she was about to tell him. "I understood what you were saying."

He couldn't remember another time in his life when he felt his bones melt like butter in the sun. He wanted to run from her effect on him. He didn't ever want to trust someone again only for her to leave him...and possibly to the same place the other two women in his life had gone.

He held up his index finger and cast her a playful grin. "Miss Darling, we talked about you saying such things in public."

"We're not in public," she countered. "One like your mother is here."

He looked toward Harper. One like his mother? No. Harper hadn't left him. But she'd kept the truth from him. She knew his future this entire time. She likely knew where his mother was. He pulled his glance away. He'd trusted her.

He felt her coming toward him, moving closer. He breathed deep and closed his eyes.

"Grayson, I still won't leave your side," Harper said tenderly. "You're stuck with me."

He didn't look at her or answer her but remained with his eyes closed.

Undaunted, she continued. "I think your healing has begun."

She offered Aria a quick warm smile, and then turned it on him, seeing his eyes had opened. "I'll see you tomorrow. Good night."

Gray watched her leave.

"She seems to love you very much."

He slid his gaze to Miss Darling. "She kept things from me my whole life."

"Maybe she didn't have a choice."

He dipped his brow at her. "Have you spoken to her about this?"

"No. Why?"

"Did she tell you in some other way…without words?"

She gave him a short laugh. "No. It's just easy to see that she cares for you."

His gaze lingered on hers for a moment before moving to the door, where Harper had exited. Why didn't she have a choice? His grandmother hadn't seemed like the type to strong-arm someone. Had Harper obeyed her out of love? Who was Harper to Tessa Blagden? Now that he was considering speaking to her again, he had many questions for Harper Bla—

"Did your Mrs. Blagden ever mention what her last name meant?"

Aria thought about it, drawing in the corner of her lower lip, making him wonder what it tasted like. "She said it meant blæc dūn, or black hill."

He nodded. Then, Harper *Black* was indeed related to his grandmother. They were both in his life and neither of them ever told him where they came from—where his mother had likely gone. Why lie to him? Was it all to manipulate his life to make certain he had sons to carry on the Ashmore name?

"Did Mrs. Blagden ever mention having a family?" he asked, picking up his shoes to carry them back.

"Yes, but she never told me their names or anything about them. Why?"

"I believe Harper is her relative. Now that I know they have the powerful ability of traveling through time, it's more difficult to trust them."

"Is it more difficult to trust me too?"

"I don't know you," he replied coolly. Almost immediately, he regretted his aloof demeanor with her. "I don't know you and yet I've likely told you more in a few days than I've told anyone else."

He looked into her eyes and was glad to see he'd avoided the storm, though he didn't mind her storms too much.

"So? Will you teach me your contemporary dance?"

She stared at him and then let out a withering sigh. "Sure. Why not? I'd like to see what you can do. But I can't teach you in all these layers and this corset. It's a wonder I haven't passed out with the scant breaths I've had to take since I've been here. Okay, right, I saw that."

"What?" he asked, wide-eyed and trying to look innocent despite the play of a smile across his lips and eyes.

"You smiled."

"So? Is my amusement prohibited?"

"When it's at my expense...well, no, not really," she rescinded. "I suppose not. Better that I amuse you than annoy you. Most of the men I knew back home found me annoying and frustrating.

I wasn't considered amusing."

"My lady, those were boys, not men. They are the ones who are annoying and frustrating. Why else would they look negatively on a sassy spitfire who could disarm them with a kick? You frightened them."

"But I don't frighten you?"

Instead of answering, he popped out his chest, isolating the movement perfectly without a trace of amusement—for a moment, and then the bravado vanished as he broke into a playful smile.

He reigned it in quickly, almost choking on it.

She moved closer to him and leaned in. "Maybe just a little?"

More than a little, but it was a completely different kind of fear. His was a fear of being abandoned again, and his was a fear of her being a willing participant in the Blagden's schemes. Perhaps agreeing to be in their plans for him out of love or loyalty to his grandmother—like Harper. Willing or not, Miss Darling was a puppet too.

They left the dance hall together and walked toward her room.

"Let's start tonight."

She blinked her beguiling eyes. "The midnight bells rang a minute ago."

"Will you turn to mist then?" he asked. "And you don't want me to see?"

"No," she laughed. It was a small, soft sound that permeated his flesh and warmed his blood and emboldened him to move a breath closer.

"Are you too sleepy to dance with me?"

"No," she defended and pressed her knuckles to her temples, her cheeks. "I'm afraid we might not sleep at all."

For the first time, he wanted to nod his agreement. If he had his way, it wouldn't be because they were dancing. "What would be so bad about that?" he asked and gave her backside a short smack.

Before he drew his next breath, she spun around, her arm outstretched, her palm sailing toward his face. Her hand stopped a hair's breadth away from his cheek. With a clenched jaw and fury in her gaze, she held her hand where it stopped.

Staring into her eyes, he was sorry he'd treated her with such careless disregard. For a moment he had thought she was like the others, ready to give in and go with him, even though he never went with any of them. He was wrong.

She wanted to slap his face. He wanted her to slap it too.

Reaching up, he covered her hand with his.

"I won't be like the others and bring you pain," she told him in a soft voice, then yanked her hand free. "But if you ever touch me again without my permission, I won't hold back."

"Forgive me," he repented sincerely. Then, "I'm thoughtless."

"I don't doubt it," she huffed and continued walking.

He leaped in front of her to stop her from leaving. "I'm not really. Not lately."

"Not what?"

"Thoughtless. I think about you often."

When she smiled, he joined her. "So? Do we begin our lessons tonight or do we go to bed to dream about dancing, instead of doing it?"

She kept him waiting while she considered it. "Alright, but let me get my dance clothes."

Her dance clothes? Did she mean the tights and the short veil of a skirt that revealed the strength in her thighs? The oversized pink shirt with the word DARTMOUTH on it, as if she belonged there...with him.

Ridiculous, he thought, continuing to her room. He didn't belong with any woman. What woman would want a man whose heart was covered in barbed wire? No woman had touched his soul, especially not his heart.

But Aria Darling excited him. She soothed him by bringing amusement into his dreary days. He forgot the darkness when he was busy trying not to smile.

He promised to wait when she reached her door and disappeared inside. He wouldn't react to her clothes. He felt his head for a fever, then shook it in disbelief when his hand returned cool. Why else would he continuously do what his head told him not to do? Why else would his heart beat so erratically around her? Why didn't he want to separate from her?

He wondered about these things while he leaned against her door.

He wasn't expecting it to open so quickly and almost tumbled inside. He caught himself before she caught him.

When he straightened, she turned her back to him, half-in and half-out of her room. "Can you untie me?"

"Untie you?" he repeated hollowly as fire shot down between his legs. "I don't know—"

"Just do it. Sarah isn't here. She's probably sleeping, and I'll need this corset loosened before I sleep."

He swallowed looking down at the tie at her lower back. He reached out his hesitant hand and plucked the tail of the bow and pulled. Fire lashed up his back and licked at his fingers as he loosened the ribbon. His flesh felt scalding.

"I won't miss these things," she mused as the stiff fabric fell away and she shut the door in his face.

Was he lusting for her? Since when did he lust after anyone? It was another curse, lust. It gave birth to regret. Damn him! He should go, but he knew he wouldn't. It was as if he no longer possessed any control of himself.

He waited until the door opened again and she stepped out. Yes, he should have left and gone to bed. His belly flipped at the sight of her in hose that were as tight as her own skin, and her heavier top with his name sewn across the front. His heart fluttered, his muscles twitched with an unfamiliar need. In fact, there wasn't a part of him that didn't hurt. His fingers itched to touch her—just one touch. He remembered her warning about doing so without her permission. If she didn't like it, he wouldn't do it. But his fingers still itched.

"You never told me why you wear a shirt that bears my name," he said, trying to ignore her shapely legs—and the rest of her as she walked on a few steps without him.

"It's a college—university in New Hampshire."

"*New* Hampshire?" he asked, catching up.

"In the future America. But I didn't attend Dartmouth. I just like the color."

He took a good look at her again and smiled, obviously liking what he saw. "It suits you."

"Does it?" she asked with a shy smile.

"It reminds me of the delicate flower petals of a musk mallow."

"Oh?" She let out a small, husky laugh, making his legs feel weak. "I remind you of something delicate?"

"Yes," he answered, then looked away when she began to turn to him.

"I'm not."

"To me you are."

"Even though I disarmed you?" she asked, her voice going soft.

"You also didn't put your hand to me when you could have. When you should have."

She wrinkled her brow at him. "And that makes me delicate?"

"Yes. You're like a robin. They are fierce little birds that will fight off a hawk, but they can be felled by the smallest pebble."

She gave him a playful, warning look on the way back to the dance hall. "I'm not sure I like your analogy."

He thought about it for a moment. "Alright then, you're like an ant. They can carry fifty times their weight, but one step can crush them."

He tried not to break into a smile while she stared at him as if he were the most simple-minded dolt to ever live. Finally, she looked away and he released what he'd been holding back.

She slipped her gaze to him and caught him. Without hesitation, she turned to face him fully and took in what he offered her. What he hadn't offered to anyone but Harper since he was a boy. What he'd planned on never offering to anyone again, a full-on, genuine smile and even a short burst of laughter when she swatted his arm and set his feet running the rest of the way.

# CHAPTER TWELVE

"D O WE NEED music? I don't want to disturb Harper. I could wake one of the musicians." Gray entered the hall first and stopped running, turning to her.

"I hadn't thought of music," she said, catching her breath, "but maybe it would be better with a little music."

"Very well, wait here." He hurried back out of the dance room and ran to the main hall. He stopped the first servant he saw and told him to awaken Alexander Pepperton, the castle violinist, and tell him he should go to his lord's dance hall at once—and bring his violin.

When he returned to Miss Darling, he was barely out of breath from running. It took more of his strength to lay his eyes on her stretching with her ankle resting on one of the high bars along the walls.

She saw him and stopped practicing.

"Please continue," he offered and began unbuttoning his waistcoat without taking his eyes off her.

"You should stretch too," she told him tersely, blinking her gaze at him, "since you'll be the one dancing."

He watched her reactions to him, no matter how subtle. It was a lesson his…his…he couldn't remember who taught him to study people, but it was a lesson that had helped him gauge a person's intentions. He tossed his waistcoat and coat away and rolled up his ruffled sleeves, then walked toward her. When he

131

reached her, he lifted his left leg and rested his ankle on the barre in front of her. She smiled. He offered her a slight smile in return and then leaned down and took hold of his ankle, flattening his torso against his outstretched leg.

She followed suit and then turned her hips and curled one arm over her head, holding the barre with the other hand. They stretched together until the violinist appeared in the doorway.

Gray instructed the musician to play Beethoven's *Violin Sonata in A major* and not to speak of what he saw tonight, or it would cost him his head. Of course, Gray had no intentions of taking the musician's head, in fact, he promised to supply food for his family for an entire month for his service tonight.

"Alright," Miss Darling said, slapping her hands together the way his childhood teacher, Philip D'var used to do before he got to teaching before he was accused of being a spy and ran for his life. "I'll teach you the dance I taught at home. You're dancing to the part of Shakespeare's Romeo."

What was this ridiculous rumbling of his bones? He had danced Romeo's part before. Why should it make him happy that she should think him good enough to portray such a passionate character?

"I'll have to tweak the dance a bit since there's no Juliet and you'll be dancing alone."

"There's you," he said in a gruff voice.

"No, there isn't."

He didn't respond, either to agree with her or beg her to dance. He wasn't about to beg. If she loved dancing as much as he did, she wouldn't be able to resist for too long. When she tried to teach him about "hinge" and "hinge variation", he didn't catch on until she demonstrated it for him. He watched in awe of the strength in her belly and buttocks, not to mention her thighs and perhaps mostly in her toes as she pushed up on them, tightening her other muscles all at the same time to lower herself backward to the floor, then back in one fluid movement.

"You're starting with something physically difficult," he pouted.

"You can try holding the barre if you need to," she said with a little smirk. "We'll take it in steps."

He gave her his own succinct half-grin and folded backwards, using his stomach and inner thigh muscles to keep his torso in a straight line while descending. Tightening his abdominals, he lifted his torso in opposition of his descent. As his upper back approached the ground, he pressed his knees forward and stretched his torso and then bounded back up like a snake uncoiling and about to strike.

"Who taught you how to perform a hinge? It wasn't even a dance move until 1930 by Lester Horton."

"You taught me, Miss Darling." He gave her a curious look. "Just now."

"Just...now," she repeated, sounding stunned. "That was the first time you tried a hinge?"

He nodded. "As long as I can see a move, I can perform it. My mother took me to many theater houses when I was a boy. The more I watched a performance, the easier it became for me to dance it."

His pretty instructor gaped at him. "You have photogenic *and* movement memory! I've heard of people like you, but I've never met them. Still, it's one thing knowing *how* to execute the move, it's another to be able to do it."

"Yes," he agreed. "Your 'hinge' requires great muscle strength, which I possess." He lifted his shirt to show her his whipcord belly. Then let the shirt fall again and stepped back. "What's next?"

She blushed and turned away from him. Madly, it made him want to smile at her for blushing over a glimpse of his belly.

"Don't you want to practice the hinge anymore?"

He gave her an earnest look. "Do you think I need to?"

She shook her head slowly. "No, I don't. It was perfect."

He felt his pulse quicken through his veins as if he'd been dancing for a long period of time. "I was just doing what I saw you do."

She set her icy blue gaze on him, but her smile was anything but cold. "Wow, talented *and* modest. A first."

He stared at her for a moment while Beethoven's *Violin Sonata in A major* played across his ears. Then he drew in a deep breath as if he hoped to gather his wits. He did, but only enough to keep from smiling like a fool.

She taught him moves over the next hour, such as "barrel jumping", which was a series of turns, low jumps, and steps. When she demonstrated contorting her body in different ways like "roll downs" and "body waves", he followed along: shoulders back, chest in, stomach and hips out, then reverse, employing muscles all along his back and in his abdomen. Hips and stomach in, chest out, shoulders straight. He loved it and smiled in delight. He took what he learned and let himself move to the beautiful sound in his ears. He couldn't help it. The more he danced, the more at home he began to feel at home with the new style of dancing and incorporating what he already knew in classic and comic ballet into his moves. His burst of movement across the floor and in the air came to an end with him bubbling up with laughter.

"I love contemporary dancing. Teach me more."

"I can tell you love it," she said, a bit breathless as if she had danced with him. "You're very expressive when you dance."

Madly, he felt himself blush. "I haven't felt that way dancing since before I can remember."

"Well then, let's practice more."

He agreed. "Show me the dance for Romeo. Whatever moves I don't know yet that are in the dance, I'll learn when I see it done."

He managed to keep his smile hidden when she quirked her brow at him, on the verge of accusing him of making an excuse to make her dance. "Miss Darling," he continued, "I was made to learn by watching."

She finally nodded and walked to the center of the dance hall, where she turned to face him. She aligned herself and lifted her head, lengthening her neck and her torso, then rolled down until the backs of her hands were flat against the floor.

Gray walked to the single stair where he'd often sat to rest after hours of practice. He sat now to watch her, and he found that he couldn't look away. Her body moved with fluid grace into a hinge. Her arms gently pinwheeled like a cascading waterfall as she arched her back.

For Gray, Aria Darling became the most beautiful being he'd ever seen while she danced. Her body swayed like reeds in a summer breeze. She danced the part of Romeo and Gray imagined every sorrowful emotion she portrayed with her movements. The forbidden love, demonstrated in the skillful push and pull of her dance, the secret intimacy portrayed in her sinuous, seductive movements, and the tragic ending that, if Gray didn't know any better, would believe she had lived through. Her dance was so moving, he forgot to breathe and could barely see out of his misty eyes.

The fact that she hadn't performed a single jump or leap in the dance hadn't escaped him. They were the most difficult, most satisfying moves in a performance. But she was too afraid of breaking again to be truly free.

"You seem to be good at improvising," she said when she returned to him. "I'd like to see what jumps you'll add."

"Miss Darling," he told her, trying his best to keep his heartbeat from making his voice shake, "you bring music to life. Not many can do that."

She studied him for a moment, as if she were trying to read him. Then, she smiled. "You can."

ARIA LAY AWAKE in her bed an hour after leaving the marquess. For the first time in as long as she could remember, her parents' hardships weren't what was keeping her awake.

She'd never fawned over a guy in her life, but the Lord Grayson Barrington Marquess of Dartmouth got her blood flowing. She'd seen enough male dancers come and go to know that not all of them had what it took to be successful, much less to become famous. The handsome marquess was engaging and expressive while his body and the masterful way he moved it stirred heart and soul—hers mainly. From the instant he achieved a hinge without practice and then lifted his shirt to show her his abdomen she'd been doomed. She hadn't had time to look away, which she would have done for her own sanity, before he let go of his shirt and let it drop again. But she'd seen enough. In fact, in that brief instant that felt like an hour, she saw too much. His abdominal muscles were cut into a tight pack of six between his well-defined obliques, which disappeared on either side beneath his breeches and made her a little dizzy. He'd stood, slightly jutting out his hips and creating a sensuous concave curve in his torso. He wasn't overly muscular, but lean and lithe, his body honed for dancing, or... she remembered to breathe and opened her eyes.

She couldn't allow herself to think of him in a sexual way. But honestly, from the instant his feet hit the dance floor he became a different kind of animal. Something dark and dangerous, some that used his body to communicate not only his emotions but his virility, for it flowed from him in waves.

He had a photogenic and movement memory, remembering every move he saw, enabling him to learn whatever dance his heart desired. His first dance tonight had been a masterpiece of longing and pain—a window into his wounded soul. But when he danced contemporary, mastering over a dozen new moves, it was clear that joy filled him.

With his eyes closed and his smile radiant with rapture, he remembered every step she'd demonstrated and made them better. It was the first time she'd seen him happy since she'd arrived in this century. He was truly glorious and breathtaking. When he performed a body wave, moving like a snake and wearing a half smile of scandalous intentions, her legs had nearly given out beneath her. She didn't think she could ever be more attracted to him than in that moment on his dance floor. But when his dance had ended, he turned to her with the residue of his joy sparking his eyes, and with his lips slightly puckered and turned upward, he wrinkled his nose, making one eye close.

She knew if she didn't find her door soon and get out of here, she would fall and fall hard for the Marquess of Dartmouth.

And that's what was keeping her awake. She didn't even know him. It was his dancing that was turning her heart. His deep, passionate love for the same thing she loved. He could be a terrible tyrant—and according to Harry Gable, he had been a demented soul at whose command forest animals attacked Harry and his father, killing the latter. And all while the marquess smiled. She'd seen him dance at his stepmother's ball in his macabre style with no trace of mercy or affection in his gaze. She understood that he was harnessing his emotions because he was afraid of them. He didn't break away from the strings that pulled him along because if he did, his emotions would break free as well, and people might die. He was a puppet and the one pulling the strings was him.

Did she want to be here when all those emotions exploded?

She decided in the dark hours of the night that there was something magical about him. He was, after all, the grandson of a woman who lived in the twenty-first century since leaving him fifteen years ago.

If this was all true, and Aria believed it was because she was living it, then Mrs. B. was a time-traveler, who possessed articles, like a gold key, and handed them out to a woman who had been forever indebted to her.

What had the marquess told her? That she could potentially bear him sons? Why was giving him sons so important? Aria hadn't asked him. Would she stay and do what Mrs. B. wanted for her grandson? No. No loyalty came before that which she felt toward her parents and her brother.

Would she have a choice to stay or go home? Maybe all the doors were closed for good, or at least until she bore the marquess sons! She wouldn't choose to stay here and leave her family. She would never forgive Mrs. B. for this. Even if she succeeded and found her door and went home, she wouldn't forget that Mrs. B. had sent her back to her grandson so his memory could haunt Aria for the rest of her life.

When she finally fell asleep to the sound of birds singing somewhere outside her window, she didn't dream of how her brother would pay for college, or if he would even attend, or how much more her mother would have to work to feed them. She didn't dream of the handsome marquess or how he smiled at her while he danced. She didn't dream at all—and it was wonderful. She slept like a log.

The next time she opened her eyes, sunlight brightened her room enough to make her squint when she opened her eyes. She heard someone scurrying off and disappearing outside her room.

Sarah appeared a few minutes later and with the marquess a step or two behind her.

"Miss Darling, you worried Sarah. Why are you sleeping three hours past noon?"

Aria sat up. Her loose hair tumbled about her shoulders and face. She smoothed it away and tried to think more clearly. It was three o'clock? "Sarah, I'm sorry I made you worry. I didn't fall asleep until the morning," she explained, rubbing her eyes.

"Why did you have trouble sleeping?" Sarah asked.

Aria couldn't tell her that the marquess plagued her thoughts all night or that seeing him now made her dizzy. "I was thinking of my family."

"Oh, Aria," Sarah cooed and went to her. "You will return to them. I just know you will find the way."

Aria nodded. Her gaze involuntarily flicked to the marquess. He was watching her with a warm glint in his eyes.

"Sarah," he said. His voice was gentle but authoritative, "bring your lady some food. I'm certain she hungers."

138

"Yes, m'lord. Right away."

They both watched Sarah hurry off, then Aria flicked her blankets off and hung her legs over the mattress to leave the bed. She'd never had breakfast in bed, and she didn't want to start now. It would be one of those little things that would help spoil her for her real world where her father *had* to be fed intravenously in his bed every day for the rest of whatever was left of his life.

She noticed that the marquess turned his face to look away from her. Was it because she was in her nightgown and her legs were exposed?

She gave the back of his head a slight smile. This was the same man who, while he was dancing, could flash a woman a look that made her snap her fan open and wave it furiously in front of her face. Even women sitting with their fathers who had been threatened by him five minutes earlier. But at the sight of Aria's bare legs, he became shy.

There was too much to like about him. She didn't think he was a tyrant. He might be short and dispassionate with others, but he wasn't cruel to them. Sarah was one of Dartmouth's servants and she was in love with its lord, despite his allegedly having something to do with her father's death. He couldn't be all that bad, unless, like the duke of Hamilton's daughter, Sarah would forgive him anything.

"Are you going to stare at the wall the whole time?"

"Only if you don't return to your bed," he replied just as coolly.

"I have to use the...I have to—" She pointed quickly to the linen partition in the shadowy corner of the room. If she lived here, God forbid, for the rest of her life, she would never get accustomed to urinating in a metal pot.

He caught on and nodded, then without another word, he left the room.

Aria breathed. It didn't help, she still felt faint. How could he look so good in the mor—oh, right. Never mind. She'd never slept in so late in her life. Her thoughts felt scrambled.

139

She was able to clean up without his face or his voice haunting her, but only because her stomach was growling with hunger.

When Sarah returned with a tray of porridge, some berries, fresh bread, butter and honey, she was alone.

"Did the marquess leave?" Aria tried to sound nonchalant and appear unfazed when Sarah informed her that he had, indeed, left. Why else would he stay? "I believe he went to the coffee house."

"Coffee?" Aria didn't even know there was coffee in 1795. She looked at the tray being set down on the bed by Sarah. There was no coffee.

"Yes. It is served at the coffee house. Will sometimes goes but my mother says the drink only serves to make a person quick-tempered and shaky."

"Caffeine," Aria said with a longing sigh.

"Hmm?"

"Sarah," she said as she sat in the bed and picked at her food. "I'd like to go to the coffee house." Oh, how she wanted a cup of coffee.

"Oh, Aria, you cannot go to the coffee house!"

"Why not?" She tasted her porridge. It was bland, but she was hungry and thankful.

"Women are banned from going."

Aria stopped eating. "Hmm? What was that? Women are banned? Why?"

Sarah shook her head. "I do not know."

Aria flung her legs over the side of the bed for the second time that day. "I'll find out!" She looked around the room and, draped over a velvet settee, she saw a pretty, short-sleeved olive-green gown that looked to be silk, volumes of petticoats in white muslin fabric, and a matching green bodice and caraco with full-length, tight sleeves. She went to the gown and ignoring the skirts, pulled the silky fabric over her chemise and pockets. It fell loose on her, a size too big, but after Sarah cinched it below her breasts, it fit better.

"You look romantic and beautiful," Sarah told her, backing up to have a better look at her after she combed Aria's hair and pinned it up, leaving a single curl to dangle over her shoulder. "Will I lose him to you?"

Aria's blood felt as if it were draining from her body. She liked Sarah, and she owed her much. She didn't want to be having this conversation with her. "Is he yours to lose?"

She closed her eyes. Why did she ask that? Who cared? Was she being possessive toward the marquess? "I mean—"

"Perhaps he could be mine one day."

"Yes." Aria's gums itched as she gritted her teeth. "Why are you helping me look 'romantic and beautiful' then?

"If it is you who will make him happy, even...smile that sweet crinkly smile of his again, then that is what I want for him. How could I want anything less without being a selfish wench?"

Aria didn't know what to say. Should she tell her that she'd seen his nose-crinkling smile, and it was glorious? What did one reply to such sacrificial love? "Sarah, I'm not staying. I can't. I have a family to take care of."

Will's younger sister stared at her for a moment, not looking pleased. "So, you will either leave him or take him with you?"

"What?" Aria blinked, trying to gather her wits that seemed to flee whenever the marquess was involved. "I didn't mean—I don't intend—look here, Sarah, I'm not chasing him and leading him on. I'm going to the coffee house for some coffee—"

"Please, Aria, you must not go!"

"I won't sit here longing for coffee when there's a perfectly good coffee house—where did you say it was?"

Sarah bit her lip. "You will need a horse."

"Oh," Aria said with a sigh. She knew nothing about riding horses. Would she risk her life for a cup of coffee? "Maybe I can ask Will to—"

"No," Sarah said. "I do not want to involve him in this scandal. I will ask one of the drivers to take you in his carriage."

"Will this really be a scandal?" Aria asked, fitting on her coat.

"Indeed, it will," Sarah let her know, following her out of the room. "But if anyone likes a good scandal, it is Lord Dartmouth."

# CHAPTER THIRTEEN

G RAY HELD HIS handleless cup to his lips and inhaled deeply. The rich, bold aroma of coffee filled his lungs, and he sighed with delight. The coffee house was crowded on this Sunday and the men seemed more rowdy than usual. Most likely they had been here all day drinking the stimulating beverage.

Without women standing over them, wagging their fingers and scolding them, the men laughed more, smoked more, fought more.

Gray took a sip of his drink. A bottle flew by him. He barely looked up at the two men fighting to his left. If one of them came near him to fight, he would end it quickly. Never again would he crouch and whimper while anyone kicked him senseless.

Usually no one bothered with him. Once they tried to speak to him and received little reply, they gave up and whispered as they walked away about him being the peculiar marquess. He didn't care what they thought. He was here for the coffee, not companionship.

Images filled his thoughts, clearing the smoke, changing the sounds that filled his ears to the music of laughter. Miss Darling. When she stepped right out of bed in her chemise, he almost stopped breathing. She made him smile. She made him want to laugh.

He'd waited an hour after sunrise for her, but she slept. Finally, he had left the castle and headed for the forest on his horse.

Ghost liked the forest. Or was it he who felt at peace there? He hunted thieves but found none. A good thing, despite his disappointment. He'd gone back to the castle, only to find Miss Darling still asleep. They did both retire very late, but as noon approached, he told Sarah Gable to alert him the moment she woke up.

She looked ravishing sitting up in her bed, looking a little disheveled with her messy hair falling around her like a cloak.

He swallowed the hot coffee and felt it seeping into his bones—or was it Miss Darling taking over his senses?

The door to the coffee house swung open and Miss Darling stepped inside in a swirl of cool air.

Every sound stopped. Every man stared at her, stunned by her presence where no women before her had gone.

Gray rubbed his eyes to make sure he was seeing right. He stood up instinctively when two of the patrons stalked around her. What was she doing here? He decided to ask her.

"Miss Darling," he said when he reached her—before the other two patrons did. "What are you doing here? Women aren't permitted here."

"I want a cup of coffee," she told him—told them all. "What's so wrong with that?"

"Women are banned from the coffee house," someone yelled. "Now, get out!"

"I'm not leaving," she let them know, and sat at the nearest table.

"Miss Darling," Gray said, standing over her. When she looked up, he stared into her eyes for a moment, remembering that impossible as it was to believe, she didn't come from this time. "Would you like sugar?"

"No, thank you," she told him with warmth in her gaze.

He held up his hand and told the server to bring the lady black coffee. Men around him were murmuring. Some were moving closer.

Gray sat next to her and crossed his wrists in his lap, the fingers of his right hand touching the hilt of his sword. He waited. "Are you trying to make a statement, My Darli—" he stopped. His eyes opened wide realizing what he said. "*Miss* Darling," he corrected, feeling like he might tip over. She smiled, which made him feel worse…and better at the same time.

Her coffee was served with a bit of force, spilling some of the liquid on the table. Gray stared up at the server, who didn't wait around to get scolded, but hurried away.

Seeing her startle back, Gray leaned in. "Don't be afraid."

She stared into his eyes. "I'm not."

He said nothing, nor did he change his expression when he sipped his coffee and invited her to do the same.

"But if I was," she went on hesitantly. "Why shouldn't I be afraid?"

"I'll keep you safe."

"Why would you?"

He put his cup down. "You have an unfairly low opinion of me, Miss Darling. I would not leave a lady here to her own defenses."

"I don't doubt it, my lord. But don't you enjoy there being no women here? If I've decided to make a statement, why would you stand behind it?"

"For two reasons." He held up his finger. "If you want to drink coffee, you should be able to, no matter where it is. And two," he held up another finger, "By now you should have guessed that I'll stand by any form of rebellion."

"You like trouble," she surmised and sipped her coffee.

He shook his head. "I like fairness and freedom."

She lowered her cup and barely looked up. "Behind you."

He raised his arms and grabbed hold of the man sneaking up behind him and pulled him over his shoulder. The patron landed on his back just inches from the table with a loud thump. Before anyone else moved, Gray dragged his sword free and held it up. "The next one who moves will meet my sword."

"And my foot," Miss Darling added. She angled her head

slightly to see a brutish patron crossing the room to her.

Gray reached for a knife in his boot, but when he lifted his hand to fling the blade, his eye caught Miss Darling lifting her gown over her calf. He watched, spellbound while she kicked out behind her and sent the heel of her foot into the patron's groin. Never in his life had Gray been so distracted. For a moment he couldn't take his eyes off her, and a moment was all it took for someone to hit him in the back of the head and knock him out.

ARIA WATCHED THE marquess go down and was torn between going to him or taking a stand and fighting for her life. She didn't dare move with twelve men circling her. She said a prayer and readied herself against the closest attacker.

Something outside smashed against the window. Everyone stopped and looked toward the sound. When they didn't see anything, they continued moving toward her. But another thud that rattled the yellow glass stopped them again. One of the men took a step closer to the window and then leaped back and fell on his backside when something hit the window and blood spurted against it.

Something hit the east window next, and the men took a collective step away from it. Someone shouted that it was a bird. Aria looked closer. They were all birds! Large birds and small ones flying into the windows with all their might, as if they were deliberately trying to break the glass. If some died to break it, others would get in.

Did birds sacrifice themselves? And for what, or...for who? She looked at the marquess lying unconscious on the floor. She hurried to him. What was happening? Somewhere outside a raven screeched. Around her, the men were fighting with one another about opening the door and running out. Glass shattered and a few of the men cried out. Someone pulled the door open and several of them ran out. After a moment, Aria and the others heard the escapees screaming.

"My lord, my lord, wake up!"

A man behind her shouted a warning and she turned to see a large raven flying through the broken glass window and flapping its great, black wings above her.

She threw herself over the marquess, shielding him. The terrifying bird shrieked close to her ear. She shook with fear.

But then she felt the marquess' arms come around her, and at the same time, the raven retreated and flew out the window.

Aria looked down to find the marquess' sea-green gaze on her. He appeared startled and confused. Someone outside screamed, drawing the marquess up on his elbows with her falling away. He looked toward the open door, then closed his eyes again. Outside the screaming stopped.

Aria watched in stunned disbelief. Was he communicating with the animals? Had the birds been trying to save him? If it was true and he really could communicate with animals, then it was probably true that he was somehow responsible for the death of George Gable.

When the others stopped screaming, the rest of the men ran out of the coffee house.

The marquess tried to stand but clutched the back of his head and only rose to his knees.

"Easy," Aria soothed, moving to help him. "You were hit hard. Is there a physician at the castle?"

"Yes, but…what happened to the birds?"

She looked over her shoulder at the window. It was quiet. "They…they were trying to break the glass. I think they were trying to get inside."

"Inside?"

"Yes, to get to you."

He looked at her, giving nothing away in his stoic expression. "Why would they want to get to me? Do you think they wished to harm me?"

"I used to think they didn't *wish* anything. But no. I think it's clear who they wanted to hurt."

He didn't answer but managed to rise to his feet.

"My lord, you could have a concussion. Let me help you to the carriage."

"I must check on Ghost. I dreamed..." he stopped, unsure if what he said was correct. "I dreamed she was going to kick the front door down. I didn't want her to do it and be feared among the villagers. Men kill what they fear."

Aria listened and couldn't help but remember what Sarah had told her happened fifteen years ago. Men had killed the animals after what happened to Harry Gable and his father.

"We'll have to send someone to come and get Ghost. You can't ride. Don't be stubborn—"

She snapped her mouth shut when he reached for her cheek and ran his fingertips over it. "The last thing I remember is fading out and knowing you were alone. Were you hurt at all?"

His tenderness was difficult to resist. "No, my lord."

"Grayson," he corrected with the slightest smile. "Gray."

He wasn't well. In fact, there was a trickle of blood dripping down his neck. That had to be the reason he was speaking so tenderly to her and telling her to call him by his first name.

"Let's get you to the physician and then we can discuss what to call each other." She took his arm and led him out of the coffee house.

When they stepped outside, she scrunched up her shoulders and looked up at the sky. It was free of birds. The ground, however, was not.

They saw the bird's bodies in the grass under the window. Gray broke free of her aid and reached them first. He gazed down at them, his eyes sparkling with tears that didn't fall.

Aria watched him bend and gently gather the dead birds in his arms. She remembered him shoveling the Gable's front yard and stopping the shovel before it hit the small dead bird in the snow. She scolded him gently while following him just beyond the tree line. Was the forest safe? She looked up at the tangle of bare branches above her. Were those birds?

When he laid the bodies down and began covering them with rocks, she knew he meant to bury the poor birds, and she thought she understood why; they died trying to save him. But she said nothing else and helped him carry the rocks instead.

Perhaps not so remarkably, Ghost pushed him toward the carriage with her long nose and followed behind without a tether when they started moving.

Now, that the marquess' presence filled the small space, the inside of the carriage felt infinitely smaller than it felt on her way to the coffee house.

Sitting across from him, Aria found herself breathing harder at the touch of his knee against her thigh. She was glad he was half hidden in shadow.

"How are you feeling?" she asked, rather than ask if what was settling over her was some kind of paranormal, monumental truth. He could communicate with animals. Really and truly. It made her heart race and skip. And why should it not be true? Was it more monumental than traveling back in time a couple of hundred years? She felt on the verge of an anxiety attack like never before. How had her life gone from the drab, daily grind of teaching to keep her family afloat to some Aria in Regency land spectacle?

"You might want to wear breeches when you leave the castle from now on," the marquess told her, sounding quite well. "It will be easier if you need to use your legs to kick."

"Oh, so you finally accept that I can fight?"

"You felled my guards," he reminded her. "More than that, you unarmed me. I never doubted that you could fight, Miss Darling. I just didn't realize until today how trouble doesn't sway you. If you are going to walk into it, as you did today, you should be properly prepared."

His voice—or maybe it was his words—maybe it was both— seeped into her flesh, her blood, her bones until she was filled with the sound of him, consumed by his slightest touch on her leg.

"Are you feeling ill, Miss Darling?"

"Hmm?" Wasn't she just asking him how he felt? Had he answered? "Why are you changing the subject to me?"

"Because your breathing is labored and you're fanning yourself with your hand."

She felt faint too. He didn't mention that. "It's hot and cramped in here," she replied coolly and shifted her legs farther away from his.

"Are you smiling?" she asked, squinting her eyes at him.

"No."

"Liar. I can hear you."

"Miss Darling, what did I tell you about that kind of talk? You can *hear* me smiling? Come, now."

"But I'm right, aren't I?" she stated rather than asked.

He didn't answer. Then, after a moment of silence between them, "You amuse me."

She was genuinely happy that she brought amusement to his life, but compared to the mountain of obstacles before them, amusement fell panting by the wayside. "You frighten me, my lord."

"Has there been a time when you weren't frightened by me?" His husky voice echoed in the shadows and settled like a blanket around her shoulders.

Should she tell him the truth? She wanted the truth in return, and she wasn't sure she would get it. "Today I felt it when I realized you were communicating with the birds, stopping them from attacking those screaming men. And that raven..." She shivered thinking of how close it had been. "I've seen it flying around you before and I think it might have been about to attack me because I was covering you, but it flew away the second your arms came...around...me. And Ghost..."

"What about Ghost?" the marquess asked quietly without a trace of anger or defense in his tone.

149

"It seems she can understand you."

"Animals communicate differently than we. Ghost can sense my feelings, and she responds to them. Just as you say you can hear what people say without words? So it is with any living thing we care about. Words are not always necessary."

"I understand what you're saying, but you were stopping them with telepathy. You were inside the coffee house. The birds were outside. You weren't sensing anything from them or them from you, unless it was some kind of gift."

"Gift?"

"Yes. You can communicate with animals. That's a gift."

"I can't communicate with animals, lady. I'm not so arrogant to think they understand and obey me. Again, heed my warning not to speak of this with others, or I fear the animals might suffer."

And there was the truth behind it all. The animals would suffer. "I won't speak of it," she promised. "But tell me, do you really deny communicating with those birds and Ghost? And what about that raven?"

He lifted his fingers to his temple. "I can't communicate with them, but..."

"Yes," she urged quietly.

"While I was passed out, I...I dreamed that I could, you know, communicate with animals. There was Ghost wanting to break down the door and the raven wanting me to awaken to stop the birds..." After a short, pitiful sound escaped him and compelled Aria to rest her hand on his knee, he continued. "Perhaps I can communicate with them, but I don't remember ever doing it deliberately. Everyone else seems to believe I can. Even you. Perhaps I can."

"If you really don't know, then maybe you made yourself forget."

He was quiet for the remainder of the trip. When they reached the castle Aria left the carriage first and called the physician.

She wouldn't allow the marquess to get out of the carriage until the physician arrived. When he did, he ordered that the marquess be brought to bed to rest and for observation over the next few days.

"I'll look for the door myself while you recover," Aria told him an hour later when he was urged to remain in his bed by the two nurses of Dartmouth. "Maybe Will can help me."

"He already knows too much," the marquess grumbled, sounding more like a bear than a man. "I'll come with you. I'm perfectly fine—"

"Oh my goodness, are you kidding me right now?" she said as he left the bed again. "How stubborn can one person be?" She ignored his pouty glare. "Get in that bed right now or I'll beg Will to take me back."

She liked that her threat worked. It meant...something, didn't it? Did he hate the Gables so much that he wouldn't allow her to need their help? Or—

"Are you jealous?"

She thought he could handle her directness, but he threw back his head and laughed before he climbed back into bed. Clearly, Aria thought, watching him, her question rattled him though he tried way too hard to pretend it hadn't. What kind of laugh was that anyway? It couldn't be genuine. It was as if he was holding nothing back, His mouth was wide open, and his eyes were half closed as he emanated a nervous, high-pitched sound that was every bit as endearing as his nose scrunching up when he looked at her as his laughter faded.

Adorable, she thought succinctly and folded her arms across her chest like a shield to ward off his extraordinary charm. Not only was he so handsome she didn't think she would ever get used to looking at him, but he was adorable. "Are you going to answer the question?"

"No, it's too ridiculous."

"Is it?"

"Miss Darling," he said with a faint hint of his elusive smile. "I have never been jealous of anyone or anything a day in my life. I simply don't want you around a dangerous man like Harry Gable."

"That's a relief, because I wouldn't ask Will to spend time alone with me checking doors if you were jealous. Well, have a good rest." She breathed a little sigh and turned on her heel to go.

She waited with breath held for him to summon her back, but he didn't. He let her go. Well, then, he said everything he needed to say. She hurried out of the castle before the marquess could call her back. She took her coat, but the weather had changed and left wet, melted snow in its wake.

She knew the way to the Gable's holding. The marquess would be angry with her if he discovered she'd gone out alone, but she was too annoyed to care. Exactly what was so funny about him being jealous of Will?

She was sure he liked her, unless—wait! What if this was all part of his magnetism, the stuff that oozed out of him on the dance floor? He was a playboy, wasn't he? She'd seen his sultry smirk at the women who watched him with hungry eyes.

They wanted him in bed, and his eyes said, "yes, let's go." Was all this tenderness and attention a ploy to get her into his bed? It worried her because she wasn't sure she could hold up her fist and shout in triumph. She'd wondered a few times already what he would be like in bed.

She was a virgin, though she'd come close once or twice with Freddy Harkin when she was sixteen. Freddy was eighteen and putting the pressure on her to go all the way. She didn't let him have his way but stopped speaking with him altogether.

There was no time in Aria's life for a boyfriend or a child. Guys didn't usually get her blood burning like molten lava through her veins. But Lord Grayson Barrington Marquess of Dartmouth in the year 1795 did.

When she climbed the steep hill and crossed above the western wall of the castle, she looked down at the small roof where she'd seen him dance for the first time. She would never forget how beautiful he looked, like an enchanting faerie dancing to music only he could hear.

She heard a sound like a dry twig crack. She turned but saw no one behind her. For an instant she thought her door might appear. Of course, she would run straight to it. Wouldn't she?

Another sound grew into footsteps, and she thought about running. The Gable house wasn't much farther.

A hand grabbed her shoulder and stopped her from moving. She spun around, ready to kick, and saw Will. He smiled, exposing a deep dimple in his cheek. The marquess should be jealous of Will Gable. He was kind, helpful, and handsome.

"What are you doing here alone? Did you and the marquess bicker?"

"No, nothing like that." She told him about going to the coffee house and how the men attacked the marquess and struck him in the head. After Will admonished her for going to an establishment that had banned women, he asked about the marquess' wound and how serious it was. She let him know what the physician said and followed Will into the house at his invitation.

"My mother is eager to see you, and Harry is working at the mill so you will not run into him."

He brought her to the sitting room and offered her a seat near the roaring hearth fire. He smiled at her as if she was his home and he'd been away for a year.

At any other time in her life, she might have been happy to see such a reaction from a kind, handsome man like Will, but after the marquess had torn away all her defenses with his piercing, searching gazes, what made her happy had changed.

"I'll let my mother know you are here."

She nodded and watched Will break away from her and leave the room. She wiped her brow. She had to find the door today. What made her happy had changed. The thought boomed through her mind. Dancing again—dancing with the marquess— staying here with the marquess—no! "I can't stay with him," she admonished herself. "I must go no matter how much of my heart is already lost."

She closed her eyes and brought her mother to the forefront of her mind. Her mother needed her, and she would go.

She didn't see the little mouse watching her from behind the leg of another chair.

# CHAPTER FOURTEEN

G RAY SAT UP with a start. How long had he been asleep? He reached up and rubbed his head as if that would stop its pounding.

"My lord, you didn't sleep very long."

He didn't have to look toward the chair to know it was Sarah Gable who spoke.

"Where's Miss Darling?"

A stifled sigh escaped Sarah's lips. "She will return shortly, my lord. She asked me to watch over you in her stead. Is my company so terrible that you ask for someone else the moment you hear my voice?"

What was this? Was Sarah brooding? She sounded jealous for the first time. Then again, she'd never had anyone to be jealous of. Gray didn't share his affections with anyone. If Sarah were anyone else, he would have pointed out that she didn't answer his question. He still didn't know where Miss Darling was. He would have been brutally honest with her that he couldn't help but ask for his guest because she was the first person on his mind when he woke and the last and only person with him when he laid his head on his pillow at night.

"Forgive me, Sarah. Thank you for seeing to me."

A smile crept over her mouth. "Of course, my lord. Who else would I sit with?"

The youngest of George Gable's children had been a chambermaid and then a maid at Dartmouth Castle since he was a boy. He was seven when he first met her, just before his mother left. She used to come with Mrs. Gable but would end up following Gray around the castle. At three, he thought she was quite adorable and laughed at her antics often. They practically grew up together except that, after the incident, Mrs. Gable left the castle, and Sarah was strictly forbidden to speak to or play with him. The Gables stayed away for four years before returning, offering maid service once again. As she grew older though, Sarah defied her mother and tried to speak to him on several occasions. By then, Gray didn't want any friends, nor did he want to be friendly to anyone.

He ignored her for a long time but just before he left for the army, he found her weeping in one of the turrets. She had admitted that she was weeping because she would miss him. He asked her not to miss him for too long if he never came back. That made her cry more.

He left that day thinking that someone would miss him. Perhaps it was what made him fight back. When he returned, he made sure to speak to her. He promoted her position to a maid and made sure she would be getting 16 guineas a year as her wage.

He was glad she was here. She'd known him the longest with exception to Harper. His sleep had been plagued by dreams and images of foxes, wolves, ravens, and more, all slain and slung over the village men's shoulders and hanging from long sticks. The eyes that had always watched him when they were close, stared lifelessly at nothing. It didn't matter that they had never spoken to him directly. He always heard them when he listened. They were his friends. Kit and Maple, just two of his fox friends, Davith and Ash, his wolf friends, and Matilda and Toric, his raven friends. Dead. *You killed us, Grayson.* He could hear them even in their deaths. *This was your fault.*

His fault. He had to know the truth.

"Sarah."

She leaped from her seat and appeared at the side of the bed. "Yes, my lord?"

He would work at finding her a good husband. "Sarah, you were my friend before anyone else." he said, pushing himself up to sit. He tilted his head to look up at her. It wasn't what he wanted to ask her, but he found himself asking it, nevertheless. "What exactly was it about me that you would miss so much it had made you cry that day when I was leaving for the army? We barely shared five words between us."

She blinked her wide, mortified eyes at him. "You are curious about that now?"

He nodded. "It helped me," he told her and waited.

"I worried that you had nothing to fight for. You were always so moody and morose. You were alone all the time without a person or animal to call friend. I—"

"Animals?" He swung his legs over the side of the bed and motioned for her to pull the chair over and sit. When she did, he leaned in toward her. "Why do you mention them? You've known me even longer than Harper has. Did you believe I communicated with animals?"

"Yes, my lord," she said without hesitation, as if she'd been waiting a lifetime to confess it. "Do you not remember us playing while my mother worked? There were many times when Henrietta, your mother's cat would visit us and meow, and you would laugh and answer things only you could hear. You forbade her and any of her friends from harming the mice in the barns or fields. Even the castle mice used to come and sit around you, me and Henrietta while we played."

His mother's cat? That was before his mother disappeared, when his days were filled with playing and laughter. "I don't remember that."

"I do," she countered. "I know you allowed the animals to kill my father because he killed the wolf."

Gray held up his hand. He didn't want to remember.

"You allowed them to hurt Harry because he killed Abigail. I

157

saw him do it. He laughed while he shot her. He tried to lie about it but I knew the truth. And I know Abigail loved you. I used to watch her follow you after your mother left. I remember seeing her asleep in your lap under the great oak outside. I know she was dear to you.

How was it possible that he had forgotten so much about Abigail when just the thought of her burned his eyes with tears?

"If this is possible then I'm responsible for your father's death and for the deaths of all the animals that were hunted because of what happened."

"You were a passionate child, my lord."

"No. It's impossible to speak to them," he defended. "I only pretended to communicate with them because I was lonely."

"But, my lord, you do not remember any of it?"

He reached for his bed robe and snatched it up. He left the bed and closed his eyes to the sounds of words and voices in his head. Slipping his arms through his robe, he began to pace back and forth. Was she correct? Had he truly spoken with them? Did he allow the animals to kill George Gable? Did he want them to disfigure Harry Gable? Did he…command them to do it? He clutched his head and shook it. None of this could be real. Did he have the power to forget everything?

There was one other person who would know. He stopped pacing and let go of his head. "Bring Harper to me. Find Miss Darling, and bring her as well," he added.

"But she is not here, my lord. Not in the castle."

"Not in the castle?" he repeated, hoping he heard wrong. He glanced at the window. It was dark outside. "Where is she?"

"She is at my house, probably with Will."

It was hard to discern the rushing stream of emotions coursing through him. Most were so unfamiliar and confusing, he almost didn't recognize himself. What did he care that she was with Will Gable? She'd gone out alone to get him. That's what he was angry about. He didn't care if she could fight off five men. One knife, sword, or pistol in the wrong hands and she could be killed. Perhaps she missed Will Gable. The stabbing hook in his chest warned that he was allowing his heart to become involved.

"Send someone to your house to bring her back."

"Yes, my lord."

He watched Sarah leave, thankful that she didn't ask him what to do if Miss Darling refused to return. Wasn't Will Gable the first person his guest thought about when Gray couldn't check the rest of the doors with her. Hadn't Gable taken her in first, and didn't Will have a mother and a sister who were kind-spirited?

He heard the faint squeak of a mouse. It was an unfamiliar sound since every trace of an animal in the castle had been removed or exterminated when Gray was ten to keep them away from him and possibly overthrowing his father.

But vaguely he remembered listening to a mouse named Kitty defend his mother. Kitty. Why was he remembering her only now? He almost smiled at the irony of the head mouse's name.

With a heedless clench of his jaw and his fists, he whispered. "Can you hear me?"

He listened but all he heard was his heart booming in his ears. If he could speak to them, should he? How could he finally face them after running away from them for so long? The thought of it pained him and almost doubled him over. How long could he keep running away? *Find Miss Darling and come tell me where she is and if she's safe.*

Should he laugh at his own madness?

"Grayson," Harper said his name from the bedroom door, then hurried inside. "What are you doing out of bed?"

"Was I able to communicate with animals before?" he asked her. "I've asked you before and you said you knew nothing of what I could and could not do. I'm asking you again. Please speak only the truth to me."

"What happened at the coffee house, Grayson?"

"I was knocked out by a patron and as I'm told, the birds

outside the windows began crashing into them, even dying to break the glass."

Harper nodded, narrowing her eyes on him. "The men who escaped the coffee house were attacked by birds that dove at them as if spit from the charcoal clouds to attack and kill them."

"And then the birds stopped and left them alone," Gray said through clenched teeth. He would never let the animals take the blame for him again. Not ever.

"Were you responsible?"

He nodded. Did she still not know him? "For the latter, yes."

"Then you have already answered your question," she told him with one of her serene smiles.

He remembered coming to in the coffee house. The first thing he'd been aware of was Miss Darling laying on him, shielding his body against...Toric? Hadn't the black raven that killed George Gable been shot down? What was it doing inside the coffee house, circling him and the woman covering him? He had sensed urgency and rage outside and instinctually relayed soothing thoughts to calm and quiet them. He didn't think about doing it. He did it because birds in that condition smash into things and he didn't want any of them to get hurt. When he went outside and found the bodies of the other birds, guilt overwhelmed him again. The least he could do was bury them. She had helped.

"How is it possible?"

"Many things are possible. Especially for you, Grayson."

"Like what, Harper. I can speak to animals. What else?"

"It's unknown. Men of your bloodline are rare. We know of the gifts of time-travel, animal communication, dream communing, which we believe you possess since you were able to speak to your mother in dreams. Seeing the future or the meaning of things, and the ability to see and communicate with spirits are other gifts. And before you get angry at me for not telling you this sooner, there are laws and rules by which the Blagdens must abide. You chose to forget. Forcing you to remember would only cause your mind pain. You had to remember on your own."

He felt numb and then something she said stood out in his mind. "I can travel through time?"

"It's very likely, but—"

"Can I help Miss Darling find her way back?"

"Do you want to?"

He hesitated, then, seeing that she noticed, hurried to answer. "Of course, it's what she wants more than anything."

Harper stared at him for another moment, then shook her head. "You can't time travel without permission, so don't think about it. That is, if you figure out how. You can't time travel until you've been taught how to do it properly. Thoren Ashmore was lost to his twin daughters for over twenty years of their lives and ended up in a noose before he was rescued."

"Who rescued him?" Gray asked.

She waved the question away. "That's another story. Just remember not to fiddle with time. There's punishment for it."

Something in his chest thumped and rose to his throat. "Is that what happened to my mother?"

Harper closed her eyes and gritted her teeth, then with a sigh, "Yes," she admitted. "Yes, Grayson—and before you ask, none of us knows where or when she is."

"Was she running away? From me?"

Tears filled Harper's loving eyes, and she began to shake her head when Gray was distracted by a tiny sound in his head.

*Sir? Are you truly hearing me?*

*What?* Whose was this cautious, curious, squeaky voice in his head? *I think so. Who is this?*

*It's Tabby. We were never introduced. Kitty, my grandmother, was once the head mouse here. She loved you very much.*

*Kitty.* Gray remembered her and felt his belly sink to his feet. His friends were real, and he'd forgotten them. He'd left them.

*I told the others you were back. No one believes me.*

Gray slid his astonished gaze to Harper. "Do you hear this?"

She listened. "Hear what?"

"It's Tabby," he told her. "Her grandmother Kitty was a head mouse here. Harper, I can hear her speaking.

*"The lady you search for is at the Gable home,"* he repeated so Harper could follow along, *"but she waited until the man left the room and then she said, 'I can't stay with him. I must go no matter how much of my heart is already lost.'"*

Harper's eyes opened wider when she cast him a stunned look. Gray wasn't sure what surprised her so: that he was hearing a mouse speaking to him, or that Miss Darling's heart was lost to Will Gable? It didn't surprise him. Why wouldn't she choose the victim over the killer? It sickened him that the one girl he opened to a bit, was thinking of Will Gable when she was with him.

"Grayson, what is it? Has she lost her heart to you already?"

He gave Harper a confused look. "To me?" No. She wasn't speaking about him. Was she? But...she wasn't staying. Whether she meant him or Gable, the point was she had to go. "What do I care who she meant?" he grumbled to Harper, then thanked Tabby for her news.

"Grayson, you're pouting."

"No, I'm not," he said, rolling back into bed. "I want to dance."

"You always want to dance when you're feeling upset." She came near and tucked his blanket under his neck when his teeth chattered. He pushed the blanket off and wiped the sweat off his brow. "The physician said to stay in bed, so no dancing tonight."

How could she sound so calm when he felt as if he were losing his wits, his logic, his strength, someone else in his life?

"Grayson, dearest," she said in a soft voice while she took the seat Sarah had pulled closer to the bed, "are you jealous of Miss Darling and Will Gable?"

He started to deny it, but what good would that do him? He needed to know what to do about it if he was jealous.

"Does thinking of them make you feel angry?" she pressed gently.

"If you must know, then yes, it makes me feel a bit angry. But that's normal possessive behavior. It doesn't mean anything."

"She's not something to be possessed, Grayson."

"We're not living in your twenty-first century," he reminded her stoically.

"She's not something to be possessed in any century."

"Is jealousy more acceptable?"

"It's different," she told him. "It involves your heart."

"I don't know what I'm feeling, Harper," he confessed and sat up again, feeling restless. "I feel like I don't know myself anymore. I learned a new kind of dance, Harper. Did I tell you?"

She shook her head, smiling with him.

"She calls it contemporary," he told her, feeling a little better while he spoke of it. "I danced it, and I never want to stop."

Her smile warmed him. She took his hand. "It seems to have ignited a light in you and for that I'm deeply grateful. I hope you dance until you're an old man."

He smiled, letting his emotion toward her show. She was the motherly one who hadn't left him.

A knock at the door summoned his attention. He waited while Harper rose to open the door. When he saw Miss Darling, he almost left the bed.

"Excuse me, my lord," she said in her dulcet voice. "I just wanted to check on you." She smiled at Harper and then back at him but didn't enter. "I'm glad to see you awake and alert. How are you feeling?"

"Weary and feverish," he answered dryly.

She hurried to his bedside with Harper close behind. When she reached him, she shot out her hand and pressed her palm against his forehead.

He could do nothing but stare at her while she felt him for fever. He felt himself falling as her warm, sweet breath fell over him. Why didn't she wear her hair up in those hideous bundles of curls over her ears like the other women at court? Why was it always falling over her shoulders and down her back like a fragrant veil? Why couldn't he get the images of her shapely legs, her radiant grace while she danced out of his head?

"Miss Darling," he said, moving his head away from her hand, "did you return alone?"

Behind her, Harper shook her head at him.

"Harper, you can go for now."

"Are you sure?" she scoffed at him. "If you feel feverish, you might not be yourself right now?"

He got her meaning. He was going down the wrong path with Miss Darling. Jealousy was never pretty.

He gave Harper a nod. He was sure.

When she left, he returned his attention to Miss Darling.

"Will returned with me," she told him without haste. "I told you I didn't want to check the doors alone in case I'm stopped by—"

"As you can see, I'm alright," he interrupted softly. "You shouldn't keep your door waiting, Miss Darling."

*Or Will Gable*, he wanted to throw at her, but he wasn't one to react or behave rashly. He'd done that once…

"If you find your way home," he said, "I won't see you again. I wanted to tell you that you were right. I can communicate with animals and now I know why I wanted to forget it."

"Why?" she breathed out.

He didn't want to tell her and have his responsibility for the death of all those animals and Mr. Gable be the last thing she remembered about him. "It's not your concern, Miss Darling. Hopefully, you'll find your door and return to your family. Is Will Gable prepared to see you go?"

She blinked and swallowed back something she wanted to say. "I haven't asked him."

"You haven't asked me either."

She cast him a mocking smile. "Why do I need to ask? It's clear you can't wait for me to go."

"Ask me."

She paused, her smile unchanging. "Are you prepared to see me go, my lord?"

"No."

"No?" Her eyes grew so gloriously wide, he wanted to dive into their gray-blue fathoms and never come up for air.

He didn't answer. What could he tell her that wouldn't make him sound like a pathetic fool? Her life wasn't here, and he'd known that since he first saw her. Why did she have to be the one who stirred his heart? How had he let her do it? All the vows he made to himself about never letting anyone touch his heart again, never trusting, never loving again flew off to the four winds and she could be gone at any moment? He'd known she'd be going back. He'd known. He had no right to blame her, and he didn't.

"Miss Darling?"

"Hmm?"

Why was she looking at him with a longing gaze?

"Is your heart lost to Gable?"

No! That wasn't what he meant to ask! But he was curious now because of the way she was staring at him, if she truly meant Gable when she said her heart was already lost to him. He admitted to himself that it shouldn't matter, but he wanted to know.

"No, of course not," she told him to his great relief. "I told you I must go back. Why would I lose my heart to him?"

He believed her. That meant...*I can't stay with him. I must go no matter how much of my heart is already lost*...was the him she spoke of, *him*?

# CHAPTER FIFTEEN

ARIA STEPPED OUT of the marquess' rooms and shut the door behind her. He wasn't prepared to see her go. What was she supposed to do with that? He liked her. Her hands shook. He didn't like many but...he liked her. For an instant she started to smile, but how could she when she was about to go searching for the door home? And why weren't her feet moving? She needed to go. She couldn't let him sway her. Connall needed her. Her parents needed her.

Finally, she stepped away from his door and set off to find Will.

She found Harper instead. "I left the marquess in his bed. He said he wanted to sleep. I think it's alright that he's sleepy. We were up for most of the night. But...well, you know the symptoms of a concussion, right?" Before Harper could answer, she went on. "Watch out for headache, dizziness, light sensitivity, lack of energy, nausea or vomiting. If he's more irritable than usual, that could mean a concussion, any kind of confusion, loss of memory, lack of coordination—"

"Miss Darling," Harper offered her a warm smile. "I know about concussions. I've already informed Sarah and the rest of the maids to be mindful of the symptoms if they're called to see to him for the next few days. But...you sound as if you're going somewhere."

"Home. Well. Maybe, if the door for my key is in the castle.

The marquess and I have already checked fifty-eight doors. Will agreed to help me check the rest."

"I see," Harper said, sounding as if she saw more than what she meant.

Aria narrowed her eyes on her. "How did you get here from the future?"

"You shouldn't have told William Gable and his sister. It's a matter that could get us killed."

"Yes," Aria said with a repentant nod. "I haven't mentioned it to anyone else. When I was flung into the past without any explanation, I asked Will and Sarah what year it was and told them when I was from. I wasn't thinking of being burned at the stake."

"I understand," Harper said. "I can't travel on my own. I was sent here by someone—"

"Mrs. Hester, I mean Tessa Blagden?" Aria asked.

Harper looked around the empty hall, then pulled her into a nearby room. It was one of the rooms built high above the roaring waves. It was furnished with two carved chairs in front of the crackling hearth-fire built into the wall. There was a green velvet settee and a cushioned bench, along with a few tables.

"Tessa Blagden," Harper said, motioning for her to sit in one of the chairs. "She's my great, great..." She looked up as if the answer was there, then shrugged. ... "something grandmother."

Aria stared at her, her eyes wide with shock. "How..."

"She's a time-traveler. She can travel at will."

"Mrs. B. is a time-traveler," Aria echoed, trying to take it all in. "Mrs. B. was also the marquess' grandmother. You're related to him?"

Harper nodded. "I'm his aunt. His mother's sister."

Why was she telling Aria this? Hadn't she refused to speak to Aria about it because of Will Gable? Now, here they were before a roaring fire like two besties and Will waiting for her. "Does the marquess know you're his aunt?"

"Not yet, but I'll make sure he knows everything."

"What else is there?" Why was she sitting here finding out the family secrets of some magical family? She had nothing to do with it. She had her reality, which was responsibility and dependability. "Do you want the short version? I know Mr. Gable is waiting for you."

Her family was waiting for her. "Yes, the short version is fine."

Harper wiggled in her seat, getting settled in. "When Grayson's last son is born, he'll break the curse placed on the Ashmore sons. Josiah Ashmore's six brothers were all killed in one night, but my grandmother and her sister figured out how to reset time and the brothers all lived again. But the curse remained, and they all died violent deaths. Grayson is the last male. He shares the same fate if he doesn't have those sons. When the last male dies, no more will be born and the Ashmore/Blagden name will cease. But the last son—Grayson—if he lives—will have a son who will break the curse.

"Why were they cursed and who did it?" Aria asked, immersed in the story.

"They were cursed by a higher force than we understand. It was placed on them when their mother took the lives of seven others.

"Because the Ashmores share Blagden blood, my family—Grayson's family, will see that the Ashmore name lives on. Grayson needs to have sons. Elizabeth Black, my great aunt, give or take six greats, is a seer and when she looked for Grayson's sons, she found three possible mothers. You're one of them. You could give him seven sons. Lady Rose Planc de'Vere—"

"What?" Aria gaped at her. "Seven? *Seven* sons. Are you insane? You are! You must be if you think I'd have seven kids in 1795. Sure." She laughed, but she felt like throwing up.

"Then there's Sarah Gable—"

"Hmm? Sarah Gable?" For a moment, Aria was happy for Sarah. For a moment. In the next, she glared at the door separating her from the hall, and his room, somewhere out there.

That rat! She'd been right about him. He was a pretty boy playboy! Sarah? Seven sons with Sarah? Aria's blood boiled. It was going to happen. Sarah would be up for it for sure. She was in love with him. If Aria left, it was going to happen.

"That's...that's not my concern," Aria managed. She had to go home. She had to go home. "I'm sure Sarah will be very happy."

"Yes," Harper agreed, "but what about Grayson? He won't be happy."

"That's not my—"

"My grandmother gave you the key. That means it *is* your concern, Miss Darling. He's happy with you. He hasn't left your side since you came to the castle. I know you both spent some time together before that. You must understand, Grayson has never—since before I ever got here—spent more than an hour with anyone. He's untrusting, unfriendly, and uncooperative. But he seems different when he's with you. I've seen him smile."

Yes, he smiled, crinkling nose smiles, genuine amusement that even made him laugh. No. It was better not to think of it.

"I came here to help raise him and over the years I've come to love him as my own child. I'm not still here because of his future sons. I'm here because I can't leave until he's happy."

Aria had to be strong. Yes, she liked the marquess. She thought he was the most talented dancer she'd seen in years...but to abandon her family to stay and have seven sons with a man she barely knew. She stood from her seat. "I'm sorry. I can't stay, so it's better if I go now. Do you know where my door is?"

Harper looked up at her with a somber gaze. "I really have no idea. I was told nothing about you."

Aria nodded and started to leave but then turned back to Harper. "You'll look after him, won't you?"

"Of course." Harper offered her a kind smile. "That's what I'm trying to do."

She didn't try to stop Aria when she left. Aria was glad. She hurried to the main sitting room, where she found Will and apologized for taking so long.

"Is everything well?" he asked, concern marring his brow.

"Yes, of course," she assured him, but she felt anything but okay. She might find the door that leads back to her family, her future—and never see Grayson Barrington again. She would never see him dance again. It stunned her to imagine that she was regretful of never being able to dance with him. She remembered his promise, his voice while he spoke it. *I'll catch you.* After a broken tibia and a couple of bones she broke again by landing from a grand jeté, she wasn't about to go leaping and let just anyone catch her. Would Grayson Barrington catch her? She would never know.

"Which door should we begin with?"

Aria blinked and turned to Will. She'd forgotten he was there. "I'm not sure," she told him. "I don't know all the doors here."

"Are you feeling poorly?" Will asked her. "You seem distracted, and you are a bit pale."

She brought her palm to her forehead and patted it. She felt clammy to her own hand and scowled. Maybe she shouldn't have gone to Will's in the cold. She did have a headache that was threatening to become something to write home about. If she could write home. All at once, she felt the need to cry. She'd lost everything. Well, she didn't have much. She lost her family.

So how could she feel so melancholy over never seeing the marquess again? She shook her head. This had to stop. Yes, she was attracted to him. If she could have dreamed up her perfect partner, her perfect man, he would be the marquess. What did he mean when he said he could communicate with animals *and now I know why I wanted to forget it.* Was it because he remembered asking them to kill Will's father? A chill ran up her spine. Okay, so he wasn't perfect. Who was?

"Miss Darling?" Will broke through her thoughts again, and images of the marquess' beautiful, stoic face shattered.

"I feel fine," she assured her friend, shaking her head free of foolish notions. "We already checked all the upper floors, including the second landing. We should start at the bott—" Her words fled at the sight of the marquess coming down the wide staircase.

He was dressed casually in breeches and boots, a long bed coat, open down the center and a silk shirt barely concealing his lithe muscles beneath. His hair was free of any coloring and as black as Harry Gable proclaimed his heart to be. He looked especially dangerous when, for just an instant or two, his eye caught hers from under his disheveled raven locks and a smile curled his lips. He reminded Aria of a wolf, feral, hungry, and satisfied that he found her. He swept his fingers through his hair, clearing his vision, and in an instant just as deadly to her logic, his entire expression changed into one more pleasant, if not bored.

"What are you doing out of bed?" And why did he look so vital and healthy for one with a possible concussion?

"Why haven't you started your search?" he asked, not answering her question.

She didn't want to tell him that Harper wanted to open up to her about things. He would want to know what things. Things that weren't her place to tell him. "Do you realize how dangerous it can be for you if your head is...broken and you don't rest? You could die."

He smoothed back his hair to see her better and set his powerful gaze on hers. She shifted in place and turned to Will just to break contact.

"Miss Darling," he said like a siren, calling for her attention again.

Why did he say her name as if he were using it as an intimate endearment?

"Your concern should be in getting home, not if I live or die."

She would have told him he was right and headed to the cellar with Will if something completely different wasn't already spilling out of her mouth. "How can I just leave when I don't know if you're too stubborn to stay in bed? Of course, I'm concerned for you. What do you take me for? I'm not heartless."

PAULA QUINN

The slightest trace of his smile didn't escape Aria's notice.

"I can't rest knowing you're looking for a way out," he confessed.

"Out? You mean home."

He cocked one corner of his mouth and shrugged.

"My lord," Will tried to intervene. That was as far as he got when the marquess turned his glare on him. He didn't try to say another word but backed down.

Aria bristled and she turned on the marquess. "You're as bad as Harry Gable."

The marquess wore the expression of a man who had been unfairly struck.

"You're over there pushing your weight around. You know Will won't retort for fear of losing his property."

"What?" Gray balked—partially pouting his lips that already looked luscious and needed no prompting. He turned his gleaming gaze on poor Will. "Tell her now how many times I have threatened to take your property."

"None, my lord."

Aria stepped in front of Will and tilted her neck to stare at the marquess. "How many times has he disobeyed you and given you a reason to do it?"

"Very often!" the marquess said, raising his voice an octave. "Even more since you arrived!"

"Are you raising your voice to me?" She let her tone do the threatening.

He tightened his lips but kept them shut and blew out a little extra breath through his nostrils. When she folded her arms across her chest, he wrinkled his nose slightly, but he wasn't smiling. It looked more like he was...snarling.

She swallowed and looked away first. Just how dangerous was he really?

*I can communicate with animals.*

Or, as that first dance she'd seen him perform atop his castle rooftop had suggested, was he truly mad?

"I'll come with you to check the doors."

She stopped breathing and looked at him again. "That isn't wise. Go to bed. I won't go anywhere tonight."

He looked so surprised, she almost smiled. "You won't go tonight?

"No."

"For me?"

He was so much more transparent than the men of 2024. She thought honesty and naivety were very attractive.

She nodded. "Now we're even. You shoveled the front of Will's property for me. I'm not checking the doors tonight for you."

He smiled, then turned stoic again when he looked at Will. But Aria had seen it. It was genuine. Not just something given to shock or beguile.

"I'm sorry that you came all the way here with me, Will," she said, genuinely sorry for dragging him out of his warm home only to send him out again.

"It was nothing," Will assured, keeping one eye on the marquess. Will had seen him smile too and risked much. "I hope to see you again tomorrow."

The marquess parted his lips, then shut them when he caught Aria watching him. He let her bid Will a peaceful night without saying anything mean or worthy of another Harry remark. She knew that would prick him and she felt a little guilty for using his enemy's worst trait against him.

"Where are you going?" She hurried to cut him off when he turned for his dance hall instead of his bedroom.

"I need to move."

"Move to your bed, you stubborn—" she stopped when he looked at her. "You aren't dancing. I won't let you."

She realized what she said and who she sounded like the second after she said it. "I don't want you to get very sick. It's just for a couple of days. I know it's hard," she said standing in front of him, blocking his path, "but please, stay safe and rest."

He stared into her eyes and then finally nodded. She was about to smile... "Stay with me until I can dance. If you go while I can't, I'll go madder than I already am."

"Blackmail?"

"Only if it works."

She hated herself for it, but she smiled. He smiled back.

The more time she spent with him, the more she began to realize that he didn't always mean what he said, and when she thought he was being serious, he wasn't. It wasn't always easy to tell because his expression remained unchanged.

She insisted on walking him back to his room. On the way, they met Timothy Cavendish.

"Ah, the boy who could talk to animals," the marquess' stepbrother said with a sneer. "Word is spreading fast about how the birds did your bidding today. Tell me, do you always use birds to fight for you? Did you do so in the army as well?"

"Excuse me," Aria said with a polite smile. "I don't know how to address you. You're not the lord of anywhere, are you?"

"Not yet." His sneer darkened when it left her and turned on the marquess, who was smirking at what she said.

"Well, Mr. Cavendish," she continued, still smiling politely. "The marquess had been knocked out cold. I was there. Whichever of your friends is spreading that rumor, they are dishonest, and to trust them would be foolish."

"Are you calling me a fool?" His sneer faded into something more serious.

"Only if you believe them," she replied.

The instant Mr. Cavendish drew his next breath—or perhaps before then, the marquess stepped in front of her.

"I'm warning you now," he said, sounding more like a snarling animal than a man, "speak to her again and I'll show you why I don't need birds to do my bidding. For addressing her without my permission, I may have a thousand armies of fleas make your life an unbearable living hell." He stared level into his stepbrother's eyes and then smiled—chuckled even.

Aria didn't say a word when he took hold of her hand and led her away from a sputtering Mr. Cavendish.

"Why did you defend me when I told you that I *can* communicate with animals?" he asked Aria, growing serious—or at least appearing serious—as they neared the door to his rooms.

"If you wanted him to know the truth, you would have told him. Seeing how you made yourself forget, I'm *sure* it's something you don't want him to find out."

He looked at her with a surprised smile and something else in his eyes. She wasn't sure what it was, but if a man in the future had ever looked at her the same way, she would be married by now.

He turned to the door, and then returned his attention to her, the residue of his smile evident in his eyes. "Come have a cup of wine with me in my private solar."

Drinking alone with him was the *last* thing she should do. She shouldn't. But instead of refusing, she nodded her head and followed him as one hypnotized. She realized miserably that deep down, she didn't want their time together to be over so quickly. And even though it was best over now, she clung to something that may have been possible in another time and place.

His private solar ended up being below stairs. She knew where to find it since it was one of the first of over fifty doors he'd allowed her to open—in the cellars, close to where dozens of casks of wine were stored.

"I thought solars were usually situated on the upper floors," she remarked as they reached the door.

"I prefer the unusual," he remarked. He lifted his arm over her head and pushed the door open. Aria looked up at him, so close she could make out flecks of gold in his cerulean eyes.

When he dipped his gaze to hers after a moment without her moving, she cleared her throat and stepped inside. The interior was bathed in the light of a slow burning tallow candle and a low hearth fire instead of sunshine from a world two-hundred and twenty-nine years in the future. He moved past her and entered the room.

Unlike the large sitting room above the cliffs where she had sat with Harper, the marquess' solar was a small, cozy sanctuary for one. One oversized, cushioned chair with a woolen blanket thrown over the top was set before the carved-out hearth. A full bookcase lined another wall, and a small, polished walnut writing desk was set against another wall with a window.

"You come here alone," she ventured.

"Yes." He poured her a drink from a decanter on a small table near the chair, then poured a cup for himself as well. Aria watched him, wondering how far she should go with her questions. She wasn't one to hold back. "My lord—"

"Gray. Call me Gray," he offered along with the chair.

Would speaking his name make it that much harder to forget him?

"I—" he sealed his lips and then began again. "Harry killed Abigail. He told me that he planned to eat her and warned me to dig her up from where I buried her. We fought. I asked for help. I—I asked the animals to avenge me and Abigail. They did. Not because they obey. They came because I was their friend. Abigail was their friend. George Gable died because he shot Davith, a black wolf, whose fur lines my hood. He died because of my call. By the next morning, most of my friends were dead. The villagers hunted the rest and on the second day, nearly every one of them was dead."

He lowered his head for a moment as if looking at her was too difficult. A moment later he lifted his macabre grin and wide eyes and pointed to his head.

That time must have been unbearable for a boy of ten. He'd gotten all his friends killed. He couldn't live with it. Aria could tell by his red, glassy eyes. He wouldn't let any tears fall though.

Aria didn't know why he was confessing all this to her. Was she the first to hear it?

"You were just a child," she said softly. "That experience shaped your life. I'm sorry it was so difficult for you, Gray."

"Not all my friends perished though," he said, more to himself than to her. It was as if he was remembering everything as the moments passed.

"The raven that follows you," she guessed.

He nodded. "Toric."

Aria wiped her eyes. "I'm sorry about the coffee house," she said quietly, remembering birds smashing into the window. "My determination not to be unfairly excluded cost a lot of birds their lives."

A trace of his warmest smile shone on his face. "You did the right thing. Those men chose violence against me. That's what caused everything. It was nothing you did."

The birds protected him, some giving their lives to do so.

Who was he that he had such a powerful gift to be able to communicate with animals? And why had Mrs. B. sent her, of all people, back to him? Was it because they both loved dancing? Or was she sent back to have his sons? Would the key work on any of the doors, or would Mrs. B. close the way to ensure the marquess' sons were born? Knowing now the powers the marquess possessed, she understood why his heirs would be so important. She didn't believe she was the one to give him his sons. She had a mountain of responsibility to her family. She wouldn't let them down. But could she let Gray die an early death if he didn't have sons with Sarah Gable?

The thought of Sarah Gable having his children made her blood boil.

"Tell me what it's like—your home."

She nodded, happy to change the subject.

They didn't hear Timothy Cavendish creeping around outside the solar door.

# CHAPTER SIXTEEN

"**Y**ES, THEY FLY and yes, kind of like a bird, but more like a dragonfly," Miss Darling told him while they sat together on the woolen blanket strewn beneath them before the hearth in his solar. "They have long, metal wings on either side and—"

Airplanes. They sounded fascinating to Gray's ears, but Miss Darling's soft, sweet voice began to sound more like music to him and he became less attentive to her words and more to the music of her. *Aria*. The more he basked in the pleasing shape of her face, illuminated in the firelight, framed by her glossy chestnut locks, the alluring curve of her jaw, the beguiling shape of her lips, the ocean blue of her fathomless eyes—

"Gray? Did you hear a word I said?"

He blinked and tried not to look too guilty.

She smiled.

His heart began to race.

"Am I boring you? You asked about my home."

"No, of course you're not boring me," he defended. "I was just…" He remembered that she was bold and honest enough to call his bluff if he tried to veer her from the truth. … "I was just admiring you and how you look in my poor eyes."

Her face turned pink, and she lowered her gaze shyly. He marveled at the difference in her from when he or someone else fired up her temper.

He ached to touch her, to run his hand over her hair, his

fingers against her creamy cheek. It made him feel as if he'd just finished dancing and needed to catch his breath. He stared at her, not knowing what to say, not caring if he ever spoke again. Feelings didn't need to be spoken, did they? They were passed one to another by thoughts, gazes, and actions. But his staring made people feel uncomfortable. Now he understood it was because words were usually useless with animals. But Aria Darling wasn't an animal.

"Miss Darling?" He softened his tone to one he thought sounded most soothing. "May I touch you?"

She lifted her firelit gaze to his. "Touch me?"

He nodded, never taking his eyes from hers. He lifted his fingers to a strand of her hair falling down her cheek.

Watching her for a sign of her displeasure, he moved his outstretched fingers closer. When she still didn't protest, he touched the tendril. Instead of clearing it away, he ran a fingertip down it, touching her cheek, her jaw, her bottom lip.

He didn't breathe. He couldn't think clearly enough to tell himself to stop. Don't touch her. But even as alarms were blaring in his head, he leaned in closer, slowly, dipping his gaze slightly to take in the ravishing sight of her waiting mouth. He wanted to kiss her. He hadn't wanted anything so badly in years. To draw her close and close his arms around her. "May I kiss you?" he whispered, slowly moving closer.

She closed her eyes. He could hear her breathing echoing in his ears, seeping into his bones, his heart. His breath mixed with hers, warming him for an instant. Her eyes shot open. She moved away on the blanket. "Don't kiss me," she pleaded, holding her fingers to her mouth. "I'm afraid I could fall for you, my lord— Gray. I could fall so hard that when I return home, I won't heal."

His heart thumped hard in his ears, replacing the sound of her sweet breath. Was she saying that she might fall in love with him? He didn't want her to go home broken again because of him. No, never that.

He didn't want her to go, to disappear without a trace. He

feared he might break this time. But he couldn't ask her to stay and abandon her family.

When she stood from the blanket and gave her skirts a pat, he leaped to his feet. She was correct to get herself away from him. He wouldn't stop her from leaving.

"Let me walk you back to your room."

"You don't have to," she said, holding up her palm.

"I know," he told her. "But let me. Please. I won't try to kiss you or anything like that. I agree that it would be more harmful for both of us when you return home."

She paused to stare at him, biting a corner of her bottom lip. He glanced there and felt the mad urge to groan out loud. He fought the urge the way he fought not to beat Cavendish and Harry Gable and the rest of their friends to bloody pulps every time they opened their mouths.

"You do understand why I have to return, don't you?" she asked, pausing before she turned for the door.

"Of course," he assured her. "I find your loyalty to your family commendable. I'm even a little jealous of them." He didn't realize he was smiling until she grew somber.

"I'll look for your mother. If she's in my future, I'll find her."

His smile remained but grew darker. "What will you tell her?"

"I'll tell her the boy she left has grown into a remarkable dancer with more passion in the tips of his toes than a hundred men on their wedding night—"

His brows lifted in surprise and humor.

—"and that he lives in the obscurity of abandonment. And I'll ask Mrs. B., if I see her, why her seer sister didn't see what would happen to you with the Gables and the animals. Why didn't she stop it from happening?"

They left the solar together with Gray feeling glad that she would defend him to—he stopped walking and looked at her.

"How do you know my grandmother's sister is a seer? I didn't tell you. I didn't even know."

For a moment, she gave him a confused look, and then a guilty one. "Harper told me."

He felt the blood drain from his face. "What else? What else did she tell you?"

"She told me this seer supposedly saw the possible mothers of your sons. Seven sons. I was one of them."

"That must be why she gave you the key."

She nodded her agreement and felt the pocket in her skirts. Her eyes opened wider, and she patted her thigh more urgently and then rummaged through the folds in her skirts and beneath. "Gray! The key is gone!"

"Gone?" he repeated quietly. She had to be mistaken. "Are you certain you had it with you?"

"Yes! I had it. It was in my room when I returned from the Gable's house. I planned on checking the doors, so I went to my room to get it."

"Alright, you had it up to that point. When do you remember having it last?"

She thought about it. "I had it when I checked in on you in your bed. After that, I went to the sitting room on the second floor above the cliffs, then I found Will, then you."

He hurried back into his solar with her close on his heels. He lifted the blanket from the floor and seeing no key, hurried around the room moving everything out of its place. Not finding it in the solar, they backtracked, checking the stairs, and almost every inch of Gray's room, and finally made it to the sitting room. Aria checked frantically in the chair she had been sitting in earlier. The key was not there.

"I'll wake everyone," Gray said. "Someone must have found it."

Aria held up her hand. "No, please don't wake everyone. If someone found it, I'm sure they'll return it tomorrow."

Gray felt an odd spark of hope where there had been only darkness before. "You don't sound worried."

She choked out a short laugh. "I'm terrified, don't get me

wrong. I miss my family so much, but..."

"Hmm?" he urged gently when she didn't continue.

"But it's been nice getting to know you."

He couldn't help the slow smile bubbling up from that newly illuminated place inside him. He hadn't heard words like the ones she had just uttered since he was seven and his mother left him. This alluring woman, whom he'd known for a mere ten days, spoke them so easily, so honestly. She made him feel like a different person. A man who didn't know he needed to hear someone tell him they enjoyed being with him. A man who wasn't hated or mistrusted by all. A man. Even now, watching her rein in the terrible panic shining in her eyes, he wanted to step forward and take her in his arms. He wanted to protect her, comfort her and promise to get her home, despite something deeper telling him to beg her to stay.

"I feel the same way," he admitted and stepped away from her. The sun would be up in a few hours, and it was safer to walk her to her room and bid her good night.

"Is that so?"

Gray heard the teasing lilt in her voice as she hurried to keep up with him.

"Then why are you running away?"

"I'm not running away," he corrected coolly, then spread his gaze on her. "But if I was, it would be because I feared I might pull you into my arms to see what that was like next."

"Huh?"

He glanced at her and shook his head. "Miss Darling, aren't you sleepy yet?"

She stopped and put her fists on her hips and a playful smile on her lips. "Oh, so all of a sudden you want me to be sleepy. You just said it was nice getting to know me too, and now you're being rude and aloof. What happened?"

"Nothing happened," he said and kept walking. The last thing he wanted was to get into a discussion about why he was still running away from women at the age of twenty-five—or, more importantly why he was running from her specifically. Not just for her sake, but for his.

"Oh, right, Harper told me you were untrusting, unfriendly, and uncooperative."

He stopped and turned to her. "You both had a long talk, hmm?"

She nodded.

"What else? Out with it!"

Her eyes widened. "Out with it?"

"Yes. If it was about me, I want to know what was spoken about."

"You think everything is about you? There's no way Harper and I just talked and got to know each other better?"

"I know as a fact that every time Harper has something to say, it involves me," he told her and then scowled when she rolled her eyes and giggled. "Mock me if you like but test me tomorrow. Strike up a conversation with Harper about anything other than me. See what happens." He picked up his steps again, but not before tossing her a playfully benevolent smile. "Rest assured, I'll forgive you for doubting me."

He heard her blustering behind him and something down deep inside some long-forgotten chamber of his heart compelled him to throw back his head and leap toward heaven.

*It will help you heal.*

He almost staggered. It wasn't an animal he heard in his head, but a memory. A memory of his grandmother's voice. What would help him heal?

With his heart thrashing, he turned once more to look at her. Aria, like the music he loved, was helping him heal. And all at once the weight of choices he would have to make hit him squarely in the chest.

What would happen to his healing when she left? Was he going to make a choice between feeling something other than...nothing? Of walking in the light of her smiles and his own, or in the gloom of loneliness and controlled rage? Would he send her home to her family, whom she loved or selfishly keep her to himself? "She would hate me," he whispered so low he didn't realize he'd spoken out loud until she reacted.

"Who would hate you?" she asked. "And why? What have you done?"

"I'll get you home, Miss Darling," he promised as they reached her bedroom door. "With or without the key."

"Wait, what do you mean?" she pressed. "You know a way without the key? Why didn't you tell me? Tell me the way."

"Harper said that besides the ability to communicate with animals, I may possibly have other gifts. One of them is time-travel. But she warned me against trying."

"Why?"

"Apparently the last Ashmore who could do it, did it wrong and was separated from his daughters for twenty years. I don't know how to do it and I'm not sure Harper knows either. But I would find out. I would learn how to do it right, and I would send you home."

She stared into his eyes, and he watched in wonder as something dawned on her, widening her eyes and parting her lips.

"It's me. It's me who you worry will hate you."

He leaned over her and opened the door to her room. "I'm not worried, Miss Darling. I won't keep you from your family because of some trickery of my grandmother's. We'll find your key tomorrow. Pleasant dreams." He spared her a smile and hurried away before she could call him back.

He longed for the days when his heart was lost to dance, and dance alone. Now, thoughts of pirouettes, penché arabesques, and tours en l'air were replaced with images of Miss Aria Darling's shining eyes when she blinked at him, memories of her graceful body moving across his dance hall, when she laughed and when she was busy reviling him. He thought of her and nothing else all his recent days as well as nights. Awake or asleep she plagued him.

When he reached his room and entered it, he wished someone was in the hall to lock him inside. He already missed her company. He didn't want to be tempted to go to her.

He went to his bed, tearing off his bed coat and shirt underneath. He checked the room one more time for the key, then kicked off his boots and hose and went to stand by the glass window. He could see the moon outside, round and illuminated as a sunlit pearl.

"Grandmother, if you can somehow hear me, stop being a coward and come back. Of course," he mumbled when he heard nothing back. "You never cared how I was. Not even on the days when I crumbled and wanted to give up was there even the slightest sign of you near me. You obviously came back to get the key to give to Miss Darling. Even then you didn't come to see about me. So, don't return. In the end, you were just another puppet master."

From his window, he could see the castle turrets. Perched on the highest one, was a large black raven.

*Toric.*

Immediately the bird swooped down from the turret wall and flew closer, landing on another narrow perch.

Toric. Memories came flooding back of Toric, Gray's clever protector always flying above him. When Gray found him as an abandoned fledgling, he took him home and cared for him until Toric could fly. He flew alright. Everywhere Gray went, Toric flew close by. For a long time, Toric thought Gray was his father, but even after the raven understood their friendship, he still called Gray "Father".

Where had he been all these years while Gray chose to pretend he and the others didn't exist?

Gray opened the window, then rushed to the other side of the bed to get his shirt against the cold.

Someone knocked on the door. He stopped on his way to the window. It could only be Harper knocking at this hour, or perhaps it was…he hurried to the door and pulled it open. He'd been correct. It was Miss Darling. He couldn't help but smile at the sight of her. "I was hoping it was you."

She looked nervous and shy for someone with a feisty spirit. Her gleaming blue eyes dipped to his bare chest and belly of his open shirt. She was already pale but at the sight before her, she grew pale gray, like a ghost.

She brought her arms around herself and tore her gaze off him to look at the window. "It's chilly. Why is your—"

He heard the flap of Toric's wings and sensed the raven's presence before he turned around to look where Miss Darling was looking. She stepped back almost into the hall, her eyes wide.

Gray reached out and took her by the hand. "Why are you here so late? Are you unwell?"

She shook her head, reassuring him, but her gaze returned at once to Toric.

"Come inside. Toric won't hurt you. He's a friend of mine."

At his words, Toric flew into the room and landed on Gray's shoulder. Was that Miss Darling's heart he could hear pounding? And harder still when Toric bent his glossy, black-feathered head and rubbed it against Gray's cheek.

Gray closed his eyes and let out a sigh and a smile riddled with relief and joy to be reunited with *his friend*.

*I'm sorry I stayed away so long, Toric. Forgive me.*

*There is no need for forgiveness, Father,* Toric spoke in his thoughts. *You have returned. We are all overjoyed.*

Gray opened his eyes and found his smile resting on Miss Darling's face.

"You're talking to him right now, aren't you."

"Yes," he told her.

"I'll go then," she said to Gray, keeping her eyes on Toric. "We can talk in the morning. It'll be coming pretty soon anyway."

"Aria."

She stopped trying to free her wrist and waited for him to continue.

"Yes, like music," he answered Toric out loud after he did so silently so she wouldn't feel excluded.

She gave the raven an awkward smile. "Tell him I said it's nice to meet him."

Forgetting himself, Toric gurgled, piercing Gray's close ear. Gray brought his fingers to it and closed his eyes.

Toric made a whispering sound and pressed his beak to Gray's cheek.

"You really can communicate with them," Aria said, sounding as if she had just discovered the truth.

"Yes," he told her with the hint of a smile on his lips. "Didn't you believe me?"

"Yes and no. I mean how many people do you know who can speak to animals? And it hasn't been proven."

That wasn't a problem. "When you were at the Gable's home, the mice heard you say that you had to leave, no matter how much of your heart was lost."

Her eyes opened wide, and she gasped. He had the notion that he should have remained silent.

"They told you that?"

He nodded, not sure of what to say next, or if he should say anything at all.

"Did you ask them to listen in on me?"

Yes, she was angry and growing angrier by the moment. Her brows knit together, creating shadows in her eyes and she scowled hard enough to make Toric's feathers ruffle.

*Never ever cause her harm, Toric.*

*Yes, Father.*

"I asked them to find you and make certain you were safe," Gray explained to her. "It was the first time I've spoken to them in fifteen years."

She nodded and he was glad he avoided her anger. He turned to go to the window to close it while Toric was here, but he felt a little lightheaded. What was this? He felt like laughing. He didn't but the thought occurred to him. He remembered his friends and it seemed as if they forgave him for getting so many of them killed and then abandoning them—he had abandoned them. He stopped and turned to look at Toric still perched on his shoulder.

*You are human, Father,* the raven said before he spoke. *You were very young—*

Gray shook his head and said out loud as well as in his head. "That's no excuse. Toric, I denied our friendship. I denied all of you."

*For our safety, Father. If you denied us, it was for our good, so that more of us didn't die. As I said, you are human. It is what humans do. They sacrifice themselves for their children and their friends.*

Gray looked to where Miss Darling still stood by the door. She knew he was communicating with Toric. He wanted her to stay the night. But she wasn't his wife, and her name would be dragged through the filthy streets. If she didn't find her door, she would have to live with whispers and pointing fingers. If she didn't find her door, would he keep her close? Would he ask her to be his wife? He smiled and then chuckled softly at the preposterous thought. Him! Married! Never! At least, that's what he told himself since he had become an adult. And now, to fall for a woman who was more welcome than the sun after a harrowing night on the battlefield, a woman who could disappear through a door, never to return.

No. He wouldn't laugh or smile. Life didn't deserve to see him happy.

"Gray," she said his name softly across the room. "It was a heavy load for a boy to carry alone. Now your friends are back to help you."

Damn it, he didn't mean to smile yet again. How did she know the thing to say to give him hope and help him feel better? "Come," he said, ready to do anything to help her find her way home, even if it meant breaking his barely held together heart. "You need to sleep so you can get an early start finding your key and your door tomorrow."

He wasn't prepared to see her leave, but it didn't matter as long as she was happy.

It's what humans did.

# CHAPTER SEVENTEEN

A RIA DESCENDED THE stairs the next morning with the marquess on her mind. It hadn't been any better during the night in bed trying to sleep. She may have fallen asleep for a minute or two but dreams of him opened her eyes and made her breath quicken. The scariest part was that she was disappointed when she woke up and he wasn't there, in her bed, staring at her with his lagoon-colored eyes as if she was his and he loved her beyond reason. She could close her eyes now and feel his fingers tracing her jaw, her chin, her lips.

It wasn't real. It would never be real. Once they found the key and the closer she came to opening the last door in the castle, the closer she came to finding a way home. If the door wasn't here, she'd search every inch of the forest. She thought of her dear brother. Conn had had such a zeal for life. Now, he was an empty shell. Her heart broke as it had all night every time she thought of the key. They had to find it.

And what if she did get home? Who would believe that she'd traveled back to the past and met a man who could communicate with animals? He could. She had no doubts anymore. He'd clearly been communicating with the giant raven last night when the bird flew into his room. She still had trouble coming to terms with it. He did have some responsibility in the Gable's father's death. When he was ten. No wonder he had not only stopped communicating with the animals, but he had also convinced himself none of his memories of them were real and let himself forget them. Would she forget Gray? She had no picture of him. If she spoke of him, they would admit her into a mental hospital. It would be as if he never existed.

Should she turn around and go search for the key again? Should she rush to the marquess? She'd run into Elspeth Gable when she left her room and was advised that Sarah was in the dining hall with the marquess.

Uncomfortable with Sarah and the marquess together, Aria hurried forward toward the hall. Even as she went though, she realized they would spend more time together after she left. Sarah would likely have his seven sons. Ugh! She wanted to slap her palm into her head. She had no right to be jealous—

She looked up from the wall she'd walked into and found Timothy Cavendish smiling down at her. She truly didn't like him. He didn't seem as if he'd changed much in fifteen years. He was still a sniveling bully-wanna-be.

"Ah, Miss Darling," he greeted with a sneer. That was another one of the things she didn't like about him. He didn't smile. He sneered. "No doubt, you are looking for my brother."

She refrained from reminding him that Gray wasn't his brother. She was thankful for it, too. "I'm on my way to the dining hall. If you'll excuse me, Mr. Cavendish."

"It is truly a shame, Miss Darling," he said when she stepped around him and continued on her way.

She knew she shouldn't have, but she stopped. "What is?"

"You are standing on the wrong side. I could give you everything and more."

Her jaw almost dropped as she turned to him. Was he really—? No, yuck. She couldn't finish the thought. All at once she saw him without his ugly personality to get in the way. His long dark hair was curled around his ears and the rest in the back was twisted into a thin braid. His eyes were dark gray and too small on either side of his long, pointy nose. His permanently mocking lips were thin like two worms.

"I assure you, you have nothing I want."

"That was the wrong thing to say, Miss."

She took a step closer to him and glared at him through narrow eyes. "Are you threatening me?"

He loosened the knot of his cravat. "You sound quite confident in your boldness. What makes you so? Hmm? Do you think the marquess will protect you from the worst that can happen?"

She curled her hands into fists even as her heart thumped hard in her ears. "And what's the worst that can happen, Mr. Cavendish?"

"Remember, Miss," he said with a taunting curl to his lips, "you chose the wrong side."

She watched him go, glad he was getting out of her sight. What a loser, she thought as she set course for the great hall once again. Should she tell Gray that he threatened her? No, she didn't want to leave them pitted against each other even more than they already were.

She finally reached the dining hall doors and pulled them open. She hated entering alone with all eyes on her. She wished the marquess had waited for her.

With a slight shrug, she stepped inside. Her gaze sailed immediately to the small crowd in the northwest corner. A dozen women pushed in around a man standing by one of the windows. The marquess.

The ladies all giggled, sounding like turkeys waiting to be fed.

Aria huffed a little and ventured closer. If he was saying something funny, shouldn't she hear it since he barely cracked a smile most of the time?

"Oh, Lord Dartmouth, the good Lord was certainly smiling on the day you were born."

Aria scowled at the red-head and her perfect curls like grape vines hanging over her ears.

"With the way Lord Dartmouth dances, I do not think the Almighty had anything to do with him."

Against her will, Aria recalled him dancing, grinding his hips in the air and smiling at the crowd as if he were grinding them into something else.

"Clare!" Two of the ladies admonished. "Do not say such blasphemous things."

"Will you dance for us now, my lord?" one wench called out.

"Yes, please do!" cried another.

Aria fumed. Was he the most careless man she had ever met? Didn't she warn him last night that he needed rest? Was he really going to dance for these hens? What about her key? What about Mr. Cavendish's threats? So what if she wasn't going to mention them to the marquess. It still bothered her. And now she was supposed to watch him dance—

"Sadly, ladies, I've been warned not to dance for a few days."

Aria's heart warmed—just a little. At least he was taking her advice.

"Warned by who?" one of the hens clucked.

"A frightening woman who can fell any man in this hall," the marquess quipped and took a step forward, parting the crowd of women. He saw Aria and smiled. Every lady surrounding them, including Sarah, stared agape. Was the marquess truly, genuinely smiling at someone? A woman?

Suddenly their stunned expressions turned sour.

One of them whispered as he passed them on his way to Aria. He stopped and looked over his shoulder, his smile still intact but with a touch of ice. "Lady Millicent, see yourself out, and don't return.

"Pardon me, my lord?" Lady Millicent balked.

She said a few other things, but Gray didn't pay attention to her. He kept his eyes on Aria as he started back toward her, and all she could do was feel thankful that he didn't treat her with such disregard. Then again, she hadn't called another woman a derogatory name, and simply because the marquess smiled at her.

"Good morn to you, Lady Aria," he greeted in front of the others and let his smile linger on her.

There was something about him saying her name. Even with

the courteous title of Lady, her name sounded personal when he spoke it. If she liked the way he called her Miss *Darling*, her first name felt like an intimate caress. How could she be so angry with him a minute ago, and now she was fawning all over him for saying her name? Ridiculous! The heart certainly was a traitorous thing.

"You're certainly at home with an audience," she remarked, looking him over from head to foot.

His smile remained and he even added a quiet chuckle to it. From the corner of her eye, Aria saw Sarah Gable wiping her eyes and smiling.

"I was questioning them about the whereabouts of my key."

His explanation pulled Aria's full attention to him. At times, like now, he was incredibly impossible to read. "Thank you," she said, speaking what was immediately on her heart.

His smile warmed and then he shifted his gaze to the gaping women watching him. "Have a pleasant day, ladies," he said dismissively.

They all scattered, and watching, he shook his head, then looked up from under his black hair. "None claim to have seen it. I'm waiting for Harper to arrive. She may have found it in the sitting room after you left her and then couldn't find you when I took you to my solar."

But they hadn't gone straight to the solar, had they? Harper could have found them with a quick search. But Aria didn't speak her thoughts. He was already defending the woman who had raised him on her sister's behalf.

"I worry that because it's made of gold, it won't be returned," she told him and sat when he offered her the seat.

"I thought of that," he agreed, sitting next to her. "No one here will keep what belongs to me. I've spread the news through those women. I lost the key my beloved grandmother gave me. I will reward them handsomely if they find it and return it to me or punish them if they find it and think to keep it. Everyone will hear of it within the hour." He grinned at her when he was done.

Aria shook her head in disbelief and a touch of admiration and smiled back. "You're clever."

"It means you will have to wait a bit longer to go home."

"Another day shouldn't hurt," she said, shocking both herself and him. "We should find the key by tomorrow. How come you haven't demanded it back from me? It *is* yours and it *is* solid gold."

He thought about it for a moment. His tea was served, and he sipped it. Aria shifted in her seat. Was he going to answer? She wouldn't be surprised if he didn't.

"My grandmother told me it would heal me, and she told me something else, but I can't remember what it was. She had said whatever it was and gave me the key the day she left me. I always thought of her when I looked at the key. I began to hate to look at it. I only just remembered her telling me the key would heal me. She must have known about my future. What else would I need to be healed from? She knew and she still left."

Aria put out her hand and rested it on his leg—more toward his thigh than his knee. She hadn't meant to touch him. She pulled away, her eyes wide and repentant.

He leaned in. "Miss Darling," he said in a quiet tone that sent ripples through her blood, "I give you permission to touch me."

If she could have turned pale enough to become transparent, she would have. She didn't know where to look. She didn't want to stop at touching him. It made her want to cry how much she wanted to dance with him, be touched by him, kissed by him, undressed—

Something warm covered her other hand, breaking through her thoughts like a hammer. She looked to see the hand that had taken hers wasn't Gray's.

Will. He must have slipped into the chair on the other side of her. She pulled her hand free and put it in her lap with its twin. Gray was staring at Will as if he were thinking of ways to tear Will apart, beginning with his head.

"My lord," she whispered, hoping to calm him.

His gaze dipped to hers. "My lord? What happened to you calling me by my Christian name? Gray. Remember?"

She wanted to pinch his arm. He'd given her permission to touch him, hadn't he?

She could feel Will's eyes on her. She slid her gaze to his for a quick look. When their eyes met, he reached for her again.

Gray's arm shot out like a snake and snatched her fingers away before Will touched them. His eyes blazed with warning.

Aria sighed and pulled away from both of them. "What's going on here?" she demanded.

"Will, have I given you permission to touch me whenever you wish?" She motioned to the marquess. "He learned the hard way. Do you want to be next?"

"Then why do his fingers still rest atop yours?" Will asked.

Aria looked down at Gray's fingers, and then at him. The instant her eyes met his, he smiled. It felt as if a warm breeze swept over her, through her. Grayson Barrington was so much more than the duke's mad son. She wanted to find out how much more. "Because I have given him permission."

Will sputtered for a moment. Aria felt awful. He'd been nothing but kind to her. But she'd made herself unavailable to him, hadn't she? Could she have done more?

"Will, I—"

"Gable, have a drink." Before Will could accept or refuse, the marquess called to one of the servants to bring another cup.

"You should not have stayed here with him," Will said, ignoring Gray's offer and sounding as if his heart was in his throat.

Aria peeked at the marquess. He didn't appear to be angry, but she was learning not to trust his expressions.

"I would not have let Harry throw you out," Will continued.

"Will," Sarah reached the table and took her brother by the arm, "come away now. You have troubled our lord enough."

"Did you know about them?" Will demanded, pushing his sister's hand away.

Aria caught the slightest wrinkle of the marquess' nose. It

lifted his upper lip and made it look like he was showing his teeth. At Will.

"Brother," Sarah said, quickly recognizing the danger to her brother, "let's not interfere with them, hmm? We will lose. He will not give her up."

Sarah said the last thing in a hushed voice, but Aria heard her. She was wrong about the marquess not giving Aria up. What could he do? What *would* he do? They hadn't agreed on anything between them. They both knew what was coming.

Still, Aria considered, looking away, would he stop her from leaving by taking the key?

She didn't want to think such a thing about him. He wasn't mad—and he wasn't a bad guy, despite what he believed he was responsible for as a child. No. He wouldn't have stolen the key, trying to stop her from being reunited with her family. She turned her attention back to him. He gave her a bit of a concerned look, as if he feared Sarah's statement had upset her.

She winked at him to reassure him. He turned into something like a soft teddy bear before her eyes, his gaze warm and his smile wide.

None of them noticed Harper approaching, her gaze fastened on the marquess, her soft smile growing into a look of astonishment—until it settled on Will. "Mr. Gable, please pay heed to your sister's wise words. I've never seen the marquess so happy. He will only let her go for one thing, and it isn't you."

The thankful look Gray flicked to Harper didn't escape Aria's notice. He was trying to behave as civilized as he could…for Aria. She could tell he remained calm for her sake by the way he chewed the inside of his cheek and glanced at her numerous times.

"Will," Aria said. He was having a difficult time because of her. She wanted to handle it herself and not have Harper or Gray do it for her. "When I search the rest of the doors, I'll make certain you're here."

He breathed out a great, silent sigh and nodded. "When will that be?"

"Well, I lost the key, so as soon as—"

"You lost the key?" Will gaped at her. "Did you lose it or was it stolen?"

Aria could sense the marquess' patience nearing an end. "It would have had to be stolen while on me. It wasn't. It must have fallen out of my pocket somewhere. We're searching," she added quickly when he opened his mouth. "We will find it."

He nodded, but Aria could see the doubtful tug of his brow. "Very well. I must finish building three tables today so I will leave you if I must."

The growling bear that was the marquess roused and rose to his feet. "Gable—"

"You better go then, Will," Aria smiled and stepped between him and the marquess.

When he left them, Sarah turned to the marquess. "My brother is a good man."

The marquess slid his gaze to Sarah and took his seat again. "That's why despite him insulting me in my own house, I let him leave with his head atop his neck."

Aria wished he wouldn't say such things, especially about Will, but Will's sister smiled and curtsied. "You are very kind, my lord."

Kind? Well, Aria pondered, maybe he was very kind. What would other lords of their castles do?

"You wouldn't hurt Will, would you?" Aria asked him. She thanked the young man who served them—and Harper when she took a seat opposite the marquess—fresh eggs, baked bread and warm porridge.

"Do you like him?" Aria asked him hopefully.

"No. I like his sister."

"Hmm? What?" Aria asked, lowering her spoon to her bowl.

"Sarah," he said, as if he had to clarify. He didn't.

"Right. You like her?"

He nodded and set about eating. "She's like a little sister to me."

"A little sister?" she echoed.

He forgot his food and stared at her. "Are you jealous?"

She nodded, not bothering to conceal the truth, not even caring that Harper sat with them and was listening—and probably judging her. "Yes. Yes, I am."

The marquess grinned at her.

Harper's spoon paused for the briefest of moments.

"Harper tells me that jealousy involves the heart."

Harper continued to eat and didn't lift her gaze to the marquess when he spoke.

Aria knew she was listening. She turned her attention to the pretty older woman. "Were you speaking of the marquess' heart?"

The marquess gave out a short burst of mocking laughter, and then without a word in his defense, grew sober.

Aria smiled inwardly. In fact, like some high schooler, her heart fluttered and flipped at the thought of him being jealous.

"Harper," the marquess said, "you heard Miss Darling's key is lost. Please use everything at your disposal to find it."

Harper asked a few questions, like when Aria saw it last and agreed to have the sitting room searched from top to bottom.

"There you are!" They turned to the entryway to see Eloise Barrington gliding toward them, chin up, hands held aloft as if she might get contaminated if anything nearby touched her. "Grayson, your father has insisted on a marriage ball to find you a wife. I did my best to postpone it, but he wants to secure an heir through you."

"I'm sure you fought him tooth and nail."

"Of course, I fought him," she answered him candidly. "An heir makes my Timothy one step further away from the duke."

Aria opened her mouth to tell this horrible woman that she wouldn't stand for any threats against the marquess or his future children. From the corner of her eye, she spotted Gray watching her with quiet fascination lighting his turquoise eyes. Whatever she wanted to say to his stepmother faded like dark smoke on a cloudless, breezy day. She was going to miss the way he unabashedly stared at her.

"Hmm," his stepmother followed his gaze. "Perhaps there is no need for a ball now that Miss Darling from York has graced our home."

"What makes you say that?" Gray asked her in a tone like cool steel. He turned his steady gaze on the older woman and waited while she sputtered a bit—much like her son.

"The way you were looking at her..."

He lifted his brows, urging her to continue.

"...it just seemed as if you...had an...interest in her direction." At her last words, her temper flared, and she spoke with a bit tauter boldness. She produced a handheld fan from somewhere on herself, snapped it open, and waved it in front of her face.

"You can tell my father that the only thing I'll be doing at his marriage ball is mocking him for being such a poor example of a husband."

The duke's wife expelled a short laugh. "What are you talking about? Your father is fine—"

"I'm not talking about you, Eloise." It wasn't just his words that sounded like acid spilling merrily from his lips, but the snarl he aimed at her revealed that he was almost at the end of his patience. "He made his first wife hate being a wife and mother and drove her away. But I'll tell everyone all about it at the ball. I'm sure they would all like to know how the duke used to berate his wife and then go sneak off to you. I wonder what the king will think about adultery and your marriage. He will likely have it annulled. If that happens, the only thing *your Timothy* will inherit will be a tin can to collect the coins for which he begs."

"Grayson!" she gasped as if he'd kicked her in the guts.

Aria quickly realized that there were those for whom Gray had no mercy. His father's wife was one of them.

He chuckled softly at her shock and dismay and then turned away from her as she hurried off. Aria thought she saw a trace of regret flash across his eyes. But then it was gone again. She glanced at Harper, whose empathetic gaze was fastened on Gray. The woman who raised him knew him best. She knew the aloof "madman" was really just a wounded little boy who'd lost everyone he loved, including his furry friends. Wasn't it cruel of her to pursue any kind of relationship with him and then leave him the same way the others had? Another thought sounded out like an alarm. It was a thought that plagued and haunted her almost every waking moment. What if she could never leave? Now that her key was gone, never seeing home again was even more of a possibility. No key. No door.

"What is it?" the marquess' soft, low voice resonated through her blood. "Are you thinking of your home?"

She nodded. "How did you know?"

"You suddenly look very melancholy."

What other man would bother to notice a shift in her mood? Why did her heart have to be imprisoned by responsibility? If he wanted her to, she'd stay with him if her family didn't need her. But they did.

"We'll find the key, Aria," he promised softly, watching a tear escape her eye and slip down her cheek.

She wondered as she wiped the tear away whether she wanted to cry for a week because she prayed he was right, or because she didn't want him to be.

# CHAPTER EIGHTEEN

ARIA SPENT THE third day in a row talking out loud to Mrs. B. She hoped her old friend heard her. There was nothing left to do but entreat her benefactor to help her yet again. "If this was all your doing to get me to marry your grandson and have his sons, I'm sorry to disappoint you but you should have chosen a young woman who didn't care what happened to the people she loved and left behind. Do you think I'm like Gray's mother? Do you think I can just leave my parents in such dire straits? My brother? You chose the wrong girl. Yes, I could love Gray in different circumstances. I know I could. But you knew me, Mrs. B. I mean, I thought you did. You took me from them on my brother's birthday." She stopped to blow her nose and wipe her eyes. "But I forgive you. Just knowing there was a man who once lived—even if I am the only one who believes it—a man whom I could have given my heart to, is enough to help me forgive you. Just please, please bring me back before I'm completely lost to him, and I betray my family."

It was the third day without finding the key. Maybe Mrs. B. couldn't hear her. Maybe she was ignoring Aria's call for help.

Aria left her room and went in search of the marquess. His presence drew her, compelling her to question others about his whereabouts. She checked the dining hall, the sitting room, and his private solar, but she couldn't find him and no one she asked had seen him. Sarah suggested Aria go look outside, in the woods between the castle and the eastern village.

"You know a lot about him," Aria complimented with a smile.

Sarah nodded and turned two shades darker red. "He was my first friend, that's all. After his mother left, he went off on his own path. But I was always here cleaning his chamber. I watched him go so deep inside himself, no one could reach him. I couldn't reach him—and I tried. Many of the girls, whether ladies or chambermaids, tried, but no one touched him. It seems though, as if you have. He's been smiling again."

"I'm selfish, Sarah," Aria confessed. "I don't want him to let anyone else touch him, but I can't stay here. I must return home. He will be—"

"He will be broken, mayhap beyond repair," Sarah finished for her. "Can you not see that he loves you, Aria? He makes it obvious enough by the way his face lights with joy when you walk into a room. I can scarcely believe my eyes when I see the way he smiles when he looks at you, whether you are looking at him or not. He ignores the other girls—and when it comes to the marquees, they are sometimes difficult to ignore. But he only has interest in you."

They were words Aria would have loved hearing in any other situation but this one. Now, they felt like knives being flung at her body. "How is Will?" she asked to change the topic. She knew she made a mistake when Sarah frowned at her.

"He is a fool," his sister sighed. "But he is resilient."

"I didn't mean—"

"I know." Sarah smiled at her and sent her on her way to find Gray.

She took a coat that one of the seamstresses called Aggie made for her. Aria marveled at how quickly the seamstresses worked, crafting gowns, coats, petticoats, and more in days. This coat, dyed a rich royal blue, was fashioned of lightweight wool for the warming weather. It had claret embroidery around the cuffs and hem, and claret piping around the thin hood. She wished she could take it with her when she went home.

She left the castle and followed Sarah's directions. She entered the tree line around the castle grounds and looked around. Every inch looked the same. Every tree, almost identical to the one next to it. She called Gray's name and listened for a reply but even the birds went silent. She walked deeper into the forest, calling out. She looked around again. She couldn't see the castle or the village. Just trees. She was lost. For a minute, she panicked. Having grown up in New York City, she had no experience with forests. But also growing up in New York City helped her to swallow back her panic and get ahold of herself.

She looked up at the arboreal canopy trying to see the birds. Were there any up there? "Hello," she called up. "I'm looking for Gray. The marquess. I know you know him. Can you lead me to him please?"

She waited, feeling a bit foolish for talking to the birds as if they understood her. But after another few minutes, she heard a familiar sound from above.

The croak of a raven.

The bird soared toward her just beneath the canopy. Its wings were blacker than a moonless night. Its beak and eyes, legs and feet were all just as dark. It folded its great, glossy wings just as it landed on the forest floor in front of her.

There, it simply stared at her.

"Toric. I remember your name," she said to the animal. "I'm lost. Please lead me to Gray."

At once, the bird unfurled its wings and took off. She was about to call out for it to wait, but she realized it was flying toward her and then away again, helping her keep pace.

She wanted to stop her brisk pace and take a minute to marvel at the fact that animals understood her. Could they all understand what she said? And not just what she said, but what every human said? She thought about the little parakeet her mother had found last summer and how her mother stopped to talk to it every time she walked past its cage. Did the parakeet understand her?

While she pondered the wonder of it all, she heard the faint hum of the wind, the soft singing of birds, the snap of dry twigs when a roe deer walked on it. Together it all took on a musical quality.

Following a bird while the forest sang around her made Aria feel a kind of freedom she hadn't felt in years. Her shoulders didn't feel weighed down with worries and responsibilities. She had the mad urge to skip and dance her way along the path Toric led.

And then she came upon him in a small clearing. The music of nature rang out louder. Not everyone heard the song, but it lifted the spirit of those who did. Grayson Barrington heard it. He moved to it. Alone, he danced for the sheer love of dancing and expressing himself through movement.

Breathless, Aria watched him spread his arms and toss back his head. His ebony locks swung back and then fell over his eyes when he bent forward and bowed his head. He folded his arms as gracefully as Toric had when it landed.

He saw her through eyes eclipsed by his raven hair. She knew it was coming and her heart beat frantically, thumping in her ears, adding to the music of the woods. He didn't make her wait but smiled when he saw her—as he did every time he set eyes on her.

Did he care for her as Sarah had said?

He didn't stop dancing but spun and twirled in perfect pirouettes and pas de basques. He leaped in graceful jetes. She marveled and felt moved to tears when he incorporated contemporary movements in his dance. His extension was impressive, creating beautiful lines. He used his breath as the force that fueled his movement. She was too busy mesmerized by his breathtaking contractions and releases, his soft falls and recoveries to notice the squirrels, foxes, pine marten, and deer all still with their eyes on him.

He was a master at isolating his moves, popping—or what he called 'twitching', with an almost natural ease and power.

He came closer, his dance coming to an end. Placing his palm over his chest, he rolled and popped his chest out three times as if his heart compelled his movements.

She smiled when he reached her. "You're beautiful." The instant she spoke, she blinked as if waking from a spell. "Your dance is beautiful. That's what I meant to say."

He gave her a doubtful smirk that turned soft the instant a blush rushed across her face. "I dream of touching you." He feigned surprise and covered his traitorous mouth. "I dream of dancing with you. That's what I meant to say."

Aria didn't know which was more intimate and giggled at the poor comparison.

"How did you find me?" he asked.

"Toric led the way. I was lost."

He gave the bird perched on a bare branch a few feet away a curious look. "Toric doesn't usually offer his aid to strangers. Thank you, old friend."

The bird croaked and flew off.

"Gray, can all animals understand humans?"

He took her hand. His was warm, as was his gaze when he pulled her toward the center of the clearing. "I'll tell you the answer if you dance with me."

She followed, and without telling him what she was doing, stepped into him, close to his chest. His arm came up instantly to hold her, but she stopped him, taking one arm and closing it around her waist. He smiled. She took his other hand and held it up and away.

"This is a more intimate way to dance in the future," she let him know with her body a hair's breadth away from his. She could feel his heat radiating off him. It felt nice in the cold. Her steps were loosely taken from the waltz, but she went where they took her.

He caught on quickly and swirled her around the circle until she threw back her head to laugh. When her gaze settled on him again, she saw that he'd been staring at her. At her neck. She blushed a little and then leaned her head on his chest.

His heart beat against her cheek just before he pulled her one step closer. Holding her hand, he pressed it to his chest and held it as if it were a treasure.

She'd never been held so. Was it because she'd never had time? Or could she have had all the time in the world and still never found a man like him?

Sighing against him, she closed her eyes and let him naturally lead. He held her, safe against the weather.

Around them, the animals dispersed. All were happy their "Grayson" had returned. They squeaked and buzzed and made a variety of other noises. Was it as they had done when he was a boy with no human friends? They had all been there for him, with him when his mother left, and when Gable and Cavendish and their friends beat him to a pulp. They were there when his grandmother left—until Harry killed Abigail the goose. Because he loved his friends, he'd pushed them away.

"All animals have the ability to understand human language, if they hear it enough," he told her as promised. "They pick up emotions first. It's more instinctual than learned. Most humans don't communicate with them, so they never learn to interact."

"But you don't communicate by speaking to them," she pointed out.

"I can communicate through telepathy," he told her. "Thanks, I'm told by Harper, to my distant grandfather."

They spoke briefly about the Ashmores. Aria didn't tell him Harper was his mother's sister. That truth was for Harper to tell.

Finally, they headed back to the castle where a steaming hot meal of partridge and turnip stew with fresh bread awaited them.

Harper appeared beside his chair and slipped into the one next to it. "You weren't dancing in the forest, were you?"

He didn't answer but spread his gaze over everyone in the dining hall with the slightest of smiles curling his lips.

"You know what the doctor told you, Grayson. Are you dense?" Harper leaned forward to set her angry gaze on Aria on the other side of him.

Gray's smile vanished and was replaced by a pout that made him look like a repentant puppy. "Why are you snapping at her? I left the castle three hours ago, long before she found me."

"Did you stop him?" she asked Aria.

"You know I do as I please," he interrupted, leaning forward to block her view.

Aria understood why Harper was angry. Aria had been careless with him. She was wrong, and the very least she could do was not hide behind him but admit it. "No, I didn't try to stop him."

He turned to her and reached for her hand.

Harper covered his hand with his and stopped him. "Do you want to let your enemies know what your weakness is?"

His hand retreated slowly. His eyes told her he was sorry.

"Grayson," Harper said in a low voice, but loud enough for Aria to hear. "You shouldn't touch her, and especially not so intimately. Don't let Cavendish or Harry Gable know how you feel about her. It puts her at risk. Remember they hate you. Hurting her is just as good as hurting you."

What? A wave of confusion went through Aria. Hurt her?

"And don't think you can touch her in private and remember to catch yourself from doing it in public," Harper continued. "Your enemies would jump at the chance to do something that will make you lose your title. What would you do if she's found dead, Grayson?"

His gaze turned deadly in an instant as it slipped to Mr. Cavendish across the room.

Aria's stomach flipped—and not in a good way. She felt sick. Would Mr. Cavendish really try to kill her to hurt Gray? She turned her diamond-hard gaze on him. Let him try.

"Grayson," Harper pressed, "Keep your cool. Stay calm."

He took a breath through his nose and blew it out like a dragon getting ready to burn a kingdom—or his most hated enemy.

Almost instinctively, Aria spoke his name softly. "Gray."

He turned away from Cavendish and returned his attention to Aria. "I'll be more vigilant."

"You too, Miss Darling," Harper warned. "Whatever you feel for him must wait."

How long? Aria didn't ask. She didn't want to know. She didn't have the luxury of time. She nodded, and brought her spoon to her lips, though she felt as if she were going to be sick.

She understood. No touching. It was different when the choice was her own. Now, she had felt his heart beating against her cheek. When she'd been held within the circle of his arms and danced around a forest clearing. No touching. They couldn't even pretend. Harper was correct. They would forget in public. One small mistake and she could be in danger.

It was a good thing, really. They couldn't touch. That included kissing, or just reaching for a feather in his hair. It was for the best. Soon as she found that key—

"Also," Harper went on, "take care of yourself. You're not an infant, Grayson. If the doctor says no dancing, then no dancing."

At that moment the castle physician walked by the table and paused upon seeing Gray. "You can dance, young man. Enough time has passed for me to observe that you're well."

Gray brightened considerably. "Thank you."

When they were finished, he asked Aria and Harper to meet him in his dance hall above stairs. "And Harper, please bring your violin."

Aria smiled behind her fingers when Harper grumbled under her breath and set about her task.

Aria walked with her to her chambers, where she retrieved her beautiful violin. Aria wished she knew how to play an instrument. She'd like to play for Gray while he danced.

"I really am sorry I let him dance earlier," Aria said as they went to Gray's dance hall. "Even though it was okay, I didn't know that, and I should have stopped him."

Harper glanced at her and nodded with an exhaustive sigh.

"He's hard to tame, that one."

"Hasn't he been tamed enough?" Aria asked her quietly.

Harper stopped walking. Aria stopped with her and looked at her shoes. "Yes. I guess he has."

"Maybe instead of trying to get even more control over him," Aria went on gently. "Help him cut the strings."

Harper leaned in closer. "That's not what you're here for."

Aria shrugged and smiled. "I'm not so easy to tame either."

"What will you be able to do if you're sent back, no longer useful. Back to the future while he's here making Sarah fat with his children?"

Did she have to go so far? Aria sped up her steps. Now she couldn't get the image out of her head.

"You confuse me, Miss Darling."

Aria turned to her. "Why?"

"Are you in love with him or not?"

Aria's mouth went dry. How should she answer that? Harper might as well be his mother asking a question like that. "It's a bit early to—I mean I like him, sure, but—it's difficult not to fall in love with him."

Harper smiled and kept going. Thankfully, not pressing Aria about it further.

When they reached the hall, Gray was already there warming up.

Aria envied him that he was able to do what he loved most. She also liked looking at him while he stretched his long, shapely legs on the bar.

When he saw her, he smiled. There were people in the future who smiled when they saw her, but not every single time. Gray made it clear that she pleased him no matter what was going on in his life.

Without speaking a word, Harper took her place on the stool and readied her violin to play it.

Aria thought she was going to sit and watch him dance, but when he lifted his leg off the barre and went to the corner nearest her to retrieve something from the shadows, her blood swooshed loudly in her ears.

He went to her carrying something that hung from his fingers like a cloth.

"I had this made for you," he said thickly. "I used your tiny skirt as a model for something a bit less scandalous in the ballroom." He opened his fingers and let the peach silk fall over them. "The women tried to match the color of your Dartmouth top. This was the closest they could get to it. Are you disappointed?"

Aria stared at his offering. If she wasn't mistaken, that was silk chiffon. She reached out to touch it. As expected, it felt like a sheer veil in her fingers. "Silk chiffon is very costly. I couldn't wear it."

Immediately, he gave her a pout that made her want to give in to his every request. "Why can't you wear it because it's costly?"

She took it from his hand and held it up to her waist. It was made of three sheer layers that fell at midcalf. She looked down at herself and then closed her eyes. No. She wasn't meant to wear ballet skirts anymore. What if she fell here in this century and broke something? She'd never recover.

"Gray, it's beautiful, but it's for me to dance in, right? I can't. I can't da—"

He closed his fingers around her waist and lifted her straight up into the air. Then set her down as softly as a feather. "I won't let you fall, Aria."

When she still hesitated, he asked her to just try the clothes on. The ladies would be disappointed if she didn't at least try them on.

She agreed and disappeared behind a screen closing off another shadowy corner with a clean bucket inside. She hurried. The skirt fit perfectly around her waist with plenty of room for spreading her legs if she danced. There was a small top with it, the same color peach that made her smile warmly at the thought of whoever dyed the fabric trying to match her pink Dartmouth sweatshirt.

She dressed in the set they made her, keeping on the hose she already wore. There was no mirror to see herself, but Aria filled with tears—an ocean of them waiting to spill forth from her. She felt like a dancer wearing these clothes. She hadn't felt like a dancer or hoped to be one in so long, it was incredible how deeply she missed it. Before she stepped back into the light, she heard Harper's voice.

"So, you're both on a first name basis."

"Yes," Gray replied.

"And you had a costly skirt made for her, thoughtfully trying to match it to a color she likes."

"Harper," he drawled, "do you have any other obvious observations to make?"

His aunt said nothing more and began to play her violin.

When Aria stepped into view, the music stopped. "I haven't seen twenty-first century fashion on anyone in a long time," Harper said with a smile aimed at Aria. "You look like a dancer."

Gray said nothing but just stared at her. His eyes dropped to her legs donned in hose visible behind the flowy chiffon. Then he smiled. "It's perfect."

She blushed and took a seat near Harper rather than go to him and be tempted to dance with him.

He surprised her when he sat beside her instead of dancing. When Aria asked him what he was doing and why he wasn't dancing now that he had the go-ahead from the physician, he shrugged his shoulders.

"I don't feel like dancing alone."

"You've never danced any other way," Harper, pausing in her song.

He looked at her and laughed softly as if continuing their previous conversation. "That's correct, but now it all seems a bit dull."

"Dull?" Aria asked him, her eyes going wide.

"Yes. Now that I might finally have someone to dance with, I find the prospect of dancing alone dull."

"So, you're not going to dance?" she asked incredulously.

"I might never dance again."

She couldn't tell by his stoic expression if he was joking or not. She waited another minute but when he made no move to get up, she slapped her palms on her thighs. "Fine! I mean, I'm dressed for it."

He tried to hide his satisfied smile when she stood up, but she caught the corners of his lips rise. She chose to ignore her defeat—and the cold floor and walked to the center of the hall on her bare feet.

"Harper, please play something slow—maybe a little haunting," she requested.

"I know just the thing," she said and lifted her bow to the strings.

Aria recognized the melody right away. She paused, but only long enough to draw back her tears. It was an old folk song she had danced to in a college play that she was in about King Arthur. The song was a poignant ballad about longing to go home. The score meant something different to her at the time. Now, she let the haunting melody direct her movements. She swayed and swirled into triple pirouettes, losing herself to the music as if it were casting its heavy spell on her. In fact, she didn't know tears were spilling from her eyes until she spun, and the crystal droplets flew upon the marquess' shirt.

Her next movement found her falling into his arms. She looked up into his eyes, not understanding for a second how she'd arrived there. Had she jumped? Had he caught her?

Then her hearing adjusted, and she heard Harper's lovely voice singing the lyrics.

"I will go home, across the sea
Don't look, my love, don't look for me."

There was more, but no more was needed. The eyes she stared into understood. Or he *thought* he understood.

"Aria, you make me want to give you the thing you want most. Even if it's the thing I think will finally destroy me."

# CHAPTER NINETEEN

GRAY WAS SELFISH. He couldn't remember doing an unselfish thing. Perhaps before his mother left, he was kinder and more thoughtful. He doubted Sarah would have latched onto him if he had treated her poorly. But he couldn't remember, and he never cared. Until now.

He felt the desperate need to offer Aria anything she wanted if she would stay with him. But he knew what she wanted most, and he'd just made the most unselfish offer he'd ever uttered. No matter what losing her would do to him—and he finally admitted that he would be heavily affected—he would send her away. He would make sure of it, even if it destroyed him.

He gazed into her eyes, holding her in the cradle of his arm while Harper ended her song that tore his heart from his chest and made his eyes grow red with unshed tears.

"I'll get you home," he promised her in a whisper. He didn't want Harper to hear him. She obeyed his grandmother, and his grandmother wanted his sons to be born to Aria Darling. If Sarah Gable were an option, Aria never would have needed to come. Harper wanted what his grandmother wanted. She'd do what was needed to keep Aria here.

Something occurred to him suddenly. He pulled Aria up and let her go, remembering what Harper said about him touching Aria and putting her in danger. He looked at the woman he loved as his mother, then turned away.

*Tabby, are you close?*

*Yes, Grayson.*

*I need you to search Harper's chambers. Bring as many of your friends as you need.*

*What are we searching for?*

*A gold master key.*

*Master key?*

*It's a fancy looking, long key,* he explained. *It's fashioned of pure gold. If you find it, bring it to my chambers, please.*

When he was finished communicating with the head mouse, he turned his attention back to Aria.

"Teach me more contemporary dance," he asked, wanting to watch her, dance with her, and keep Harper here while the mice searched her room.

His beautiful dancer laughed softly, having no idea that Harper might be the one who took the key. He wouldn't mention it, especially since he didn't know yet if she was guilty.

"You already know so many moves," Aria complimented. "Hmm, let me see now."

While she thought about what to teach him next, he glanced again at Harper. How would he feel if she had taken the key? Grateful that she was able to help Aria stay longer? Or angry that she hadn't told them the truth even after knowing how the lost key had affected Aria. If she had the key, he would know how loyal she was to his grandmother.

"Harper," Aria called to her. "The rendition of the Romeo and Juliet we were practicing was performed to modern ballads. If you would play whatever you think is pretty—"

"One that has nothing to do with the previous topic," Gray interjected to the violinist, then sat on a step close by to watch.

Aria began in tendu, then into plié and then sprang into a succession of slow, lyrical movements that blended into each other. Her hinge variations showed the power in her movements, while her long stretches into allongé, then arabesque were performed with deliberate delicacy. He took special note of the

215

control of her breath, giving life to her isolations and contractions. She combined it all into an expressive work of art that brought love and passion to life.

Gray found himself on his feet. The longing to go to her and lift her off her feet and into his arms was like nothing he'd ever felt before. His skin tingled and tightened over his muscles with the need to touch her. His blood burned like molten lava through his veins with the desire to bend his body close to hers in a dance that would last forever, ignited by a touch for all time.

Harper stopped playing and stared at him. "There's something else I haven't told you. I can sense your grandmother. She's back here—in this time."

For a moment his head didn't register what he heard; the instant it hit him, his heart thrashed so violently in his chest, he grew lightheaded and reached for the wall.

Aria and Harper were there seconds apart.

"Are you alright?" Aria asked, coiling his arm around her shoulder as if she could hold him up. He smiled as if something had just fluttered across his heart.

He remembered what Harper said. His grandmother was back. Emotions roiled through him. Anger vied for preeminence over all the hurt and unforgiveness for leaving him alone. There was only one reason for her to be here. It had to have something to do with Aria.

He stood straighter, taking his weight off Aria's slight shoulders. "Harper, you're telepathic."

"Only with her," Harper let him know. "And give or take a spirit here and there."

Gray closed his eyes and shook his head. "Tell her to stay away from me. And she better stay away from Aria too."

"Gray," Aria said softly. "I want to speak with her. I want to know if she has seen my family."

He closed his eyes. Yes, he had to give in to her request. He nodded. "Harper, if she brings Aria home, I want to bid Aria farewell."

Harper nodded.

*Grayson* came Tabby's squeaky voice in his head. *We searched Miss Black's chambers but did not find any key.*

For that, at least, he was grateful. He thanked Tabby and returned his attention to the two women with him.

"Grayson, how can I tell grandmother you won't see her when she came to see you?"

But he'd only heard one thing. "Grandmother? You call her grandmother. Harper," his voice was low with growing detachment triumphing over trembling emotions, "are you my aunt? Are you my mother's sister?"

He noted Aria's small intake of breath first. She knew about Harper. He wanted to turn to her, but Harper began to speak.

"Yes, I'm your aunt but I consider you my own son, Grayson," she told him. "I'm your mother, Emma's sister."

"Harper," he said. His expression matched his cool tone, "how much more are you keeping from me?"

"Grayson, I—"

But he'd stopped listening. He'd heard enough—from Harper, at least. He set his gaze on Aria and prayed silently that she wasn't a part of whatever schemes Harper planned out for his grandmother.

"Who are you, truly?" he asked her. He had to know if she was a part of this all along. How much did she know?

Had she cast some spell on him to make him look at her differently? To see her as what she was. A woman. Had her fiery temper and sweet smiles softened his heart and breathed a fog over his mind, blinding him to her feigned interest in him?

*I can't stay with him. I must go no matter how much of my heart is already lost.*

He remembered her words, spoken to no one but heard by a tiny mouse. What she felt for him was real. She was too spirited and honest to pretend.

"I'm just me, Gray," she said in her dulcet voice. "I'm a dance teacher, a sister, and a daughter. I was ripped from my life and brought here—into the snow. I know less about all this than you."

He nodded, relief showing clearly on his face. He wanted to take her hand and leave Harper's presence. They were trying to make Aria a part of the Ashmore/Blagden destiny by taking her from her family. He wouldn't let them. But he kept his hand at his side. Touching her, even the slightest touch of her hand, would make him think about touching her all the time—and it might cause him to be less careful with her under the watchful eye of his enemy.

"When is she coming?" He asked Harper about his grandmother. He veered off topic when something occurred to him. "Grandmother is your mother."

"She's not my mother," she told him with a slight shake of her head. "She's older than that. And I don't know when she'll be at Dartmouth. But it won't be long."

He didn't answer her but turned inward to Tabby the head mouse instead. *I have a favor to ask of you.*

*Ask anything,* came the quick reply.

*I would like to know everything Harper says for the next forty-eight hours. Can you do that?*

*Of course, Grayson! I will have a thousand ears on it.*

He was tempted to smile at the gift of having ears everywhere. But Harper was watching. She would realize that he was communicating with something and would be more cautious about things she said out loud.

"Grayson," Harper began. She looked miserably repentant yet again. "It was more important to try to help you heal. You would have mistrusted me immediately if you knew I was your aunt—another family member who could leave you anytime. That's what you would have thought. You would have been obsessed with finding your mother if you knew I had anything to do with her."

Perhaps she was correct, but he would never know. There was no point telling her how betrayed he felt by her. She told herself she had done the right thing. It was an argument he didn't want to have.

"Grayson, I know you don't trust me anymore, but..."

Gray waited, giving her a chance to defend herself if that was what she wanted to do.

"But everything I did, every decision I made was made with love in my heart for you. I was thirteen years old when I pulled you from your mother's body and held you in my arms before she did. I've loved you from that moment on. But this is all bigger than you, Grayson. One or all your sons will break a curse that has plagued families for centuries—and will save your life."

"I have no destiny," he whispered in a low voice.

"You do have a destiny," she corrected. "We don't know which of the three women you will choose, if any—or what that choice will mean. Your destiny is to father sons in love."

His eyes turned involuntarily to Aria. He could father sons in love with her. He could feel his blood rising to his face and then to his head until he felt feverish. Was it a spell?

He fought to regain control of himself by concentrating on Harper's voice and words.

"...to keep the Ashmore line alive."

He shook his head. "No. I'll decide what my destiny is. But I can tell you that if she goes home—" He paused to look at Aria— "no child born to me after that, if I have any, will be conceived in love."

Harper set her gaze on Aria. She understood what he meant, if not Aria, then no one.

"Harper," he said, dragging her gaze to him. "Aria's wish is to return home, and I'm going to help her do that. Don't get involved."

"What are you trying to say, Grayson? You won't have any sons? In that case, I must warn you Tessa will see it done herself."

"What do you mean?"

"She'll manipulate time. She'll bring you a few years back, a few forward, over and over until you do it her way."

"That's not destiny."

Gray's and Harper's gaze flicked to Aria when he spoke.

"That's not free will, Harper," Aria continued. "Does Mrs. B. believe herself to be God?"

"No. She—"

"She should stay out of it. Everyone is entitled to discover their own destiny."

"I wish she would," Harper said with a groan.

Gray didn't realize tears had fallen to his cheeks until Aria slipped her hand in his. He thought it mad that such a small, intimate gesture could make his heart feel lighter in seconds. His gaze found hers as he turned to her.

She reached her free hand up and wiped his tears with her fingers. "Don't worry. Everything will be okay."

She had no way of knowing that for sure, but she said it to comfort him. And it did. He began to smile at her, but Harper put her hand between theirs and severed their connection.

"You must both keep from touching—" she began to admonish, but Aria stopped her.

"I don't care about any would-be threats," she told Harper. "I'm not going to let anyone dictate my behavior. If I want to touch him, I'm going to touch him." She took his hand again and this time entwined her fingers through his.

Caring for her wellbeing, he tried to pull away.

She held on tighter. "Gray, if I haven't made it clear enough already, let me say it in plain English. I won't stand for being told what to do. In my time, or yours."

His or hers. Separate. Different. If he hadn't grown used to pain, he would have doubled over at the ache in his belly at her words and the meaning of them. There was nothing in her that considered staying with him.

He'd go with her then. What did he care for anyone here? Let Cavendish have it all. That's what his father wanted anyway. He'd go to Aria's future with her and live and dance there. He'd wed her and have seven—no six sons and one daughter, destiny be damned—who would rule them all. The thought of it made him smile slightly. She saw it and rubbed the pad of her thumb over his skin.

"Are you staying then, Aria?" Harper asked her.

Aria stared at her but didn't answer.

Harper turned her attention to him. "Grayson, she's going to leave."

"Right," he said, purposely meaning neither this nor that. "Harper, it's late. You should retire to your chambers. Aria and I will remain for a bit longer."

"I shouldn't leave you alone."

He set his cool gaze on her. "Harper, I'm not a child. Goodnight."

He was glad when she didn't argue but marched out of the small dance hall in silence.

"Let's dance," he swept around Aria and said in her ear. He wanted to forget what Harper said and had done, and just dance with Aria. He wanted it more than anything he'd wanted in his life—to touch her in the intimate throes of dance, in a timeless embrace.

"Gray, I can't help but worry about falling."

Her confession reached his heart. He backed away, but his eyes beckoned her forward. She didn't go to him, but he would keep calling. If tomorrow came and they found her key and she found her door, he would regret not dancing with her more.

Without Harper's violin, he relied on the crackling of the hearth fire and his heartbeat in his ears to make music. He moved to it, isolating different parts of his body with each beat.

Turning his knees outward, he bent in plié. He twisted his arms to the left, then to the right, bending his wrists, curling his fingers. He smiled, feeling her eyes on him. He didn't look at her yet, but scooped his hand over his raven tresses and closed his fingers around the back of his neck. He looked up then and smiled at her and almost laughed softly when she brought her hand to her throat—as if she could read his thoughts. He drew in a corner of his bottom lip between his teeth and scrunched up his nose at her. He danced around the hall, combining contemporary moves he'd recently learned, and ballet moves he'd known since he was a boy. He reached her in a vortex of spins and beautiful lines, intimate smiles and playful winks. When he stopped before her, he held his hand out to her and prayed she accepted.

She did and stepped into him. His heart thrashed and thundered within. For a moment, he completely forgot how to dance and just stood there with her, letting the beats of their hearts produce a whole new sound.

He wasn't exactly sure how to dance with her facing him save for traditional pas de deux or ballet dances for two, some ballroom dances, and what she taught him in the forest.

She arched her back and, draped over his arm, bent far back enough for her fingertips to touch the floor. Gray leaned over her, dipping his nose closer to her neck. They moved together in perfect synchronicity. When she moved in a variation of what he knew, he followed and kept up with her.

Finally, he pulled her closer with gentle force and smiled then tossed back his head and closed his eyes.

"Gray, you're a very passionate dancer," she whispered close, beguiling his senses. "You know perfectly well how to seduce."

"Am I seducing you, Miss Darling?"

She nodded, looking up at him, pressed to him. "Don't you feel my heart beating?"

"I thought it was mine," he said, close. He dipped his head and pressed his lips to hers. Harper's warnings about touching her grew fainter and then were gone altogether.

He lifted her chin and deepened their kiss. She curled her arms around his neck, standing on the tips of her toes to receive him. She tasted of warmth and desire.

He felt himself going a little harder when she darted her tongue into his mouth. He cupped one of her buttocks in his hand and drew her in closer until he could feel all her soft curves.

They heard someone moving about outside the front door.

They separated and stood apart staring at each other until whoever was out there passed.

"Come," he said, taking her by the hand. "It's getting late. I'll walk you to your chambers."

"Let me change back into my petticoat and shirts—and all the rest of it."

Gray waited while she disappeared behind the partition. She didn't like all the clothes women had to wear. He didn't like them either.

When they left the hall, he wouldn't let her hold his hand on the way to her rooms. She proved she wasn't from his time by not taking the threat of danger to her life seriously enough. He would speak to her about it tomorrow. For now, they didn't touch or speak on the way toward her door.

The silence was not awkward or uncomfortable, especially since sometimes—Gray believed—more could be said without words. A lingering glance, an intimate smile, a warm gaze—or a heated one resounded off the walls of the heart and sank deeper than any words.

That was why, for so long, his expression remained impassive and unreadable. He'd been careful not to communicate anything to the people around him. But that didn't mean he was passion-less. He took delight that it seemed Aria from another lifetime understood and remained silent, save for a soft round of giggles here or there, like bells of celebration to his usually somber ears.

He liked the sound of her, not just her laughter, but her voice and the cadence of it that often made him want to tip his head, smile, and move his feet.

"Tomorrow let's spar."

He turned to her and nodded. "Alright. Do you want me to teach you how to wield a sword? It's not likely something you learned in the twenty-first century."

"I want to fight you," she clarified with a hint of playfulness gleaming in her eyes.

He smiled. The more time he spent with her, the more she

tempted him to toss aside every concern, every speck of hatred within him, and dance without the weight of any of it. "You don't have to wait until tomorrow to do that, my darling."

"Gray?" she said, wide-eyed.

"Hmm?"

"You called me your darling."

He never wanted to stop looking at her. "Yes, I know." Reaching her door, he dipped his head to hers to kiss her.

He was stopped by two of Dartmouth's guards.

# CHAPTER TWENTY

"FORGIVE US, LORD Dartmouth," one of the guardsmen said, sparing a nervous glance at Aria. "Your father sent us to take Miss Darling away."

Away? Gray thought he was hearing wrong. But when one of them put his hand on her arm, Gray yanked the hand away. "How dare you touch her!"

"My lord, your father—!"

"Touch her again and I'll cut off your arm," Gray warned, stepping between the soldier and Aria and resting his hand on the hilt of his sword.

"Grayson!"

Gray turned, surprised to hear his father's voice on the stairs.

"What are you doing protecting her?" the duke asked him. "Are the whispers true? Do you share affection for this woman? Step away from her."

"What's the meaning of this?" Gray demanded, not moving a hair away from her.

"She is accused of stealing my best wine from the cellars last night," his father let him know.

"Ridiculous," Gray told him. "She was with me last night."

"Then it is true," his father accused, "you were with her when she stole my wine. Did you drink it with her too?"

Ah, so this was about him, then. Now Gray understood. Cavendish was her accuser. He must have heard Gray and Aria in

Gray's solar and hatched his plan.

Had Gray made it so obvious that Cavendish went after her? He knew that if anyone was familiar with him at all, they'd know by his uncharacteristic behavior toward her that he cared for Aria Darling.

"Where was Cavendish last night, Father? I'm quite certain I heard him in the cellar while Miss Darling and I were in my solar."

After all that had happened, and all the time the Duke of Devon hadn't been there when his only son had needed him, Gray thought he would have learned that this man he called Father was nothing befitting his title. But the duke surprised him yet again.

"Grayson, step away from her or I'll have you stand before the council with her."

Gray didn't move. Finally, Aria gave him a shove with the side of her body and pushed him away. *Use your head, not your heart,* her look seemed to say. He nodded slightly and moved aside. "But I'm going with her," he told his father. "You'll have to kill me to stop me."

Resigned to not letting *that* happen at least, the duke nodded to the guards and turned to descend the stairs.

Gray looked for Cavendish while they were led to his father's sitting room, but his accuser was nowhere to be seen. That is, until they stepped into the chambers, and he saw him rise from Gray's chair.

Gray wanted to warn him not to step foot out of the castle, but if disaster struck, the animals would be blamed. He ground his jaw instead. "Did you tell the duke that Miss Darling stole his wine?"

"I saw her take it with my very own eyes, Brother."

"Then you admit to being in the cellar," Gray said with a deadly smirk. "I know why Miss Darling was there, but why were you there, *Brother*?"

"My mother needed something for her headache and dispatched me to see to it."

Gray chuckled without a sound of amusement leaving him. "Why would she use you as her dog to fetch her things, when she has a perfectly good husband she has trained even better than you?"

Cavendish smirked, then snorted. "Are you calling your father a dog?"

Gray stared at him. "I think I was perfectly clear."

His father bristled but didn't say anything.

"Are you going to answer my question? Why would your mother send you and not one of her many servants?"

"Are you accusing me of deceit?" Cavendish asked, feigning disbelief.

"Yes," Gray told him without hesitation. "But we will save that for when I throw you and your mother out on your arses." Without waiting for a response, Gray turned on his father again. "Are you truly going to listen to this worm? I suggest you have his chambers searched for your wine."

*Tabby*—

*I sent fifty of my best mice to search Mr. Cavendish's chamber, Grayson,* the head mouse answered before he finished asking.

*Thank you, Tabby.*

He would have smiled at the thought of having such good friends, but his father was glaring at Aria.

Gray moved to stand in front of her, blocking his father's view. When his father glared at him instead of Aria, Gray shook his head in disgust at him. "Why would you be so careless about making an enemy of me?" From the corner of his eye he saw Harper in the doorway. He thought for certain the sound he was hearing was Aria's heartbeat. He had danced to it. He remembered its rhythm. She was afraid. He wanted to turn to her and tell her not to be afraid of him.

But right now, he wanted to make the others around him tremble. "You already abandoned me as my father. Do you provoke me now as my enemy's father?"

"Grayson," the duke began, but then he stopped.

Gray scoffed at him. What was there this man before him could say? Son, forgive me. Gray scoffed at himself.

"Grayson," the duke began again, "who is this woman you seek to protect?"

Gray couldn't help the snarl that wrinkled his nose and scrunched up his lips. "What right do you have to know?"

The duke didn't answer. His stepson did.

"Your Grace," he said, addressing the duke, "allow me to drag this ungrateful sot to the prison tower for speaking to you with such disrespect."

Gray smiled and turned to aim it at Aria. She was deeply intuitive and seemed as if she could understand him without him speaking any words, like the animals did. If she could, in that moment he wanted her to know that nothing was about to happen. No one wanted to die.

In the next instant, he drew his sword and slashed the air with the sharp edge, coming to a stop over a hair rising off the pulse at his stepbrother's throat. He turned the smile he wore like a mask on Cavendish.

"You were saying?" he asked.

No one breathed. No one dared. It was one of those times when being believed to be mad proved helpful. He knew he could kill Cavendish, but he wouldn't do it in Dartmouth. No reason to stain the floors with a rat's blood.

Gray could have demanded that Cavendish take back his accusation. He knew with a sword at his throat, Cavendish would have complied. But then he would have used the excuse that he only withdrew his accusation because he feared for his life.

"Cavendish, if her name ever leaves your mouth, I will hear of it, and I'll come and kill you."

"Fa—" the worm tried to call out to his father for help.

Gray's blade drew a thin line of blood from Cavendish's neck. The guards surrounding Aria left her and drew their swords, aiming them at Gray.

"Am I not your lord?" he asked them with a mixture of curiosity and anger staining his words.

Lucky for them, they nodded and withdrew. "Step away from the lady," he warned them, keeping his blade completely still while a droplet of blood fell from the gleaming steel. They obeyed.

"Grayson," his father shouted, "drop your sword! Have you gone completely mad?"

"Long ago," Gray answered him. For a moment, even he believed it. Madness had eaten away his brain, so why not kill the boy who had broken his ribs three times and was responsible for almost as many bloody noses and sliced lips Harry Gable had inflicted on him?

"Grayson."

His thoughts faltered at the sound of his grandmother's voice. He had never forgotten it.

"Put down your sword this instant," she warned calmly. "Or I'll send her back right before your eyes."

He blinked. What did she just say? He turned to look at her standing near Aria.

He dropped his sword as she commanded, but his eyes burned with blue fire when he set them on her. She hadn't changed, save for the first time he saw tears in her eyes. He didn't care how she looked. Trembling anger coursed through him. The first thing she did when she returned after fifteen years was to threaten him.

"If you disturb a hair on her head without her consent again, I'll never forgive you," he promised just as calmly. "I'll figure out how to use my gifts and I'll find her—if it takes me a lifetime, I'll search—disturbing every moment of time I get my hands on—until I find her, and then I'll send us back to this moment when I cut my strings from you once and for all."

She looked horrified, with tears misting her eyes. Aria too, looked heartbroken with tears streaming down her cheeks. The sight enraged him more. Why would she ever want to stay in this miserable place?

"Why did you return, Grandmother?"

"It was time. Come, you've already said too much. Let's go speak in private."

"I'm not going anywhere without Aria."

"Have you been in contact with my family?" Aria pleaded the instant his grandmother's eyes met hers.

"They are well, dear girl," Aria's Mrs. B. assured her. "They think you went on a trip to Germany for the school."

"They know I wouldn't leave without saying goodbye," Aria muttered to her as his grandmother passed her on her way to him. Gray heard her.

"You took her from her family," he accused, tight-lipped.

"I can't discuss it here," Tessa told him.

He ground his jaw, wanting to hear what she had to say.

Taking Aria by the hand, he pulled her toward the exit.

"Father," he heard Cavendish boldly say, "are you going to sit by and let them all walk out of here?"

*Grayson,* he heard Tabby's voice in his head, *we found the wine in Mr. Cavendish's chambers. My family found three casks behind a curtain in his bedroom.*

Gray smiled slightly and turned to one of the guardsmen. "Go check Cavendish's chambers for the wine casks. His bedroom to be precise."

"Yes, my lord," the guard said, then hurried off, taking three other men with him.

Gray made a promise to himself that he would send fleas to visit Cavendish's prison bed before the sun rose. For now, though, he thanked Tabby and followed his grandmother to the castle doors, where their wool coats were strewn over a chair.

Gray eyed Harper, who stayed with them, then slid his gaze to Aria. He moved closer to her and gazed into her cloudless blue eyes. "Are you well?"

She nodded but didn't speak. They both felt the same weighted concern. Now that Tessa Blagden had returned, she could send Aria home. Gray believed her when she used Aria with which to threaten him. She didn't need a key.

They stepped out of the castle and into the cool night. Gray turned his ear toward the night sound of the forest. His grandmother led them closer to it.

"Why are you leading us into the forest?" he asked the old woman. What if she was bringing them there to send Aria back without anyone witnessing it?

"No one will follow us there," she answered him.

Of that, she was correct. No one would follow Gray into the woods without a quiver full of arrows, or even a pistol. He looked around. If anyone tried to harm the animals—

Finally, they came to a small clearing. His grandmother turned to him. Gray wanted to look away. She had hurt him so deeply he didn't think he could look into her eyes without weeping the way he should have when he was ten.

"I know you both want answers," she began, addressing Aria, as well. "I had no choice but to put you together when I did. Grayson, I'd hoped you would have used the key to leave here, but you chose to die on some useless battlefield instead."

"How was I supposed to know what that key was for?" he accused.

"I told you it would lead you to your heart's desire," she argued while his thoughts drifted to Aria. "You don't remember?"

"No, not really, but your surprise that I didn't abandon Dartmouth the way you and my mother abandoned me, disgusts me. And why had you hoped that I would use the key to leave, Grandmother? Did you know what my life would be like? Did you know and you still left?"

"Your mother did not abandon you, Gray." She shook her head sorrowfully. "Harper doesn't even know this." She cast the younger Blagden a guilty glance. "It was thought best that she wasn't told, saving you and her unhelpful heartache. Emma was fleeing punishment for using time as her vengeful arena. But she didn't need to be present to receive her punishment. When she brought her fourth victim to the harrowing future, she was sent back here and stripped of her time travel ability. The council of Devon was told of her whereabouts. She was captured and burned as a witch."

Gray took a step back, shaken to the marrow. His mother was dead. Burned as a witch! He heard a sound and thought it came from his own heart, but it came from Harper's. Her older sister was dead, and no one had told her.

"Perhaps if I had known my mother didn't walk away from me..." Now, he set his murderous gaze on his grandmother without the threat of tears. "You pull all the strings, don't you, Grandmother. If the end you desire is seen to fruition you don't care about any of us."

"That's not true—"

"It is," Aria interrupted her. "You took me from my family without my consent. That's kidnapping, and on my brother's birthday, no less. You took away a big chunk of my mother's help, both financially and mentally."

Gray snorted at his grandmother. "But you don't understand loyalty, do you? Or compassion. Did you think for one moment what this would do to Aria? Worrying night and day about her family? To Harper, who now must live with the knowledge that her sister was burned to death, and she wasn't told?"

"Emma chose the way she wished to live," his grandmother told them. "And she chose the way she wished to die."

Harper turned away, her face a mask of grief.

But Gray had no place for such sentiment. Not yet. First, he would tell his grandmother that he never wanted to look upon her face again. Even though...even though he still loved her. "So, my mother died because she broke some law of time travel, yet you would have me do it. You provided a way for Aria to do it."

"I would have hidden you from the pain you suffered here," his grandmother told him. "But I couldn't take you. It's strictly forbidden, even if... I could only give you the key, my dearest grandson. You had to do the rest. The key would have brought you to the future. I had to leave you to prepare that future for you, but you had forgotten about the key. You forgot everything. So, I sent her here to you to heal you. But this isn't where she belongs."

He closed his eyes. What if Aria chose to stay? Would she be punished, as his mother had been? "Then...why would you send me where I don't belong?"

"My grandson," she began tenderly, "you belong to either here or there. You see, you were conceived in Dartmouth Castle in 1767 and born in 1999 in an apartment in Astoria, New York."

He laughed, it was a mocking sound, not a merry one. "You're mad—"

"In an effort to escape your father, your foolish mother traveled there with you in her belly. She knew better than to give birth to you here. She knew the rules. She couldn't stay. So she brought you back with her and returned to your father, until she grew miserable again."

"Maybe," Aria said scornfully, "she had him in the future because of things called hospitals and painkillers."

Gray looked at her and found himself wondering what hospitals and painkillers would be like in the future. He was allowed to go. He was being told to go.

His gaze warmed on Aria. He didn't have to lose her. Did it mean that much to him that he didn't? How could his heart feel light when he'd just learned the truth about his mother? But his mother had been gone for eighteen years. He didn't want to miss Aria for that long, or even for a day.

*This key will lead you to your heart's desire.*

He reached out his fingertips and touched Aria's temple. She was his heart's desire.

*It will help you heal.*

The key had brought her to him, and she was healing his weary soul. He thought about what Harper had told him. He wouldn't mind giving Aria seven children. He smiled slightly thinking about it.

She blushed as if reading his thoughts. He knew she didn't possess that gift, but she could read his different, very subtle facial expressions.

"My dear, Aria," his grandmother said, breaking through his thoughts of a future with Aria. "First, I know your dedication to your family. Dear girl, I know it better than anyone else. I saw the sacrifice you made every day for them. I wouldn't leave them with nothing. I gave your mother your "pay" while you were away. Plus, a hefty bonus, which you deserve. She no longer has to worry about paying the rent or buying food. I didn't take care of all of it while you were there because not having help strengthened you and made you an even better person."

While she spoke, Gray noticed that Aria was holding back her tears. The tip of her pert nose turned red, and so did the whites of her eyes. Her cool blue irises grew more vivid and sparkling. But she remained silent, letting her friend explain herself.

"Perhaps I should have told you that you would be leaving them. But you never would have agreed to come here."

Gray caught Aria's eye when she glanced at him. Was she thinking that she wouldn't have met him? How did she feel about that possibility?

"I'll send you home, child."

Gray turned away at her words. If he went with her, he'd be giving Dartmouth to Cavendish. Why did he care about people who thought he was a mad monster, or worse—a witch like his mother? Let Cavendish rule over them. Let them all be stuck in this drab life, void of creativity and originality. Aria showed him a little bit of her future in the way she danced and in the way she passed no judgment on him when she saw how he dressed and how he danced. He wanted to go with her when she went home.

"I'm sure the key will turn up," his grandmother said, sounding convinced.

"Where is it?" Gray asked her. She didn't answer him but continued speaking to Aria.

"The door is any door in this castle. When the time comes,

just focus on something from home and turn the key."

"All this time," Aria said softly, "the door was any door?"

His grandmother nodded. "I am sorry, child, but…was coming here really so terrible?"

Gray faced her slowly, awaiting her answer.

"Does meeting him cancel out what you did to me?" Aria asked. "I was close to being frostbitten, alone and clueless in the *past*. My logical mind had to stop working. I had to trust a stranger and sleep in his sister's bed. Every day, every second of being away from my family was difficult, but no, it wasn't terrible after seeing Gray dance. After seeing him dance, I became selfish."

His grandmother smiled. "You haven't a selfish bone in your body. Aria," she said a moment later, growing serious again. She glanced at him. "I love this boy desperately and I hated being away for so long, but…" her gaze rested on Aria again. … "I wouldn't let anyone who wasn't worthy of him get so close to him. Sarah Gable and Rose Planc de'Vere are lovely women, but they couldn't make him happy. And after being alone for so long, he deserves a woman who will stay by his side all her days."

Aria slipped her gaze to him. Did she look worried? When her teeth chattered, he stepped closer to her and took her hands in his. "Let's return to the castle."

"Gray," his grandmother said, stopping him. "Don't go tonight. There are affairs to be seen to here so that they will be uncontested in the future. I need you here for at least a day."

He nodded and turned back for the castle with Aria's hand in his.

>>>«««

TESSA BLAGDEN HAD lived through many centuries. She'd seen many wonders. But this—this—

"He's holding her hand," she leaned in and said to Harper.

"I told you he cares for her."

"Did you note the way he stared at her, how he smiled at her?" Tessa asked exuberantly. "From your past reports I was beginning to lose hope for his happiness. I wanted it for him so much." Shaking her head with regret, she brought a napkin to her eyes and patted them dry. "Some things must be done."

"What are you talking about?" Harper demanded. "Tell me the plan. I won't be kept in the dark this time. Not when it comes to him."

Tessa gave her a steady look full of love and compassion. Harper had done all and had given up all to do what was asked of her. In that, she was very much like Aria Darling. She deserved the truth about her sister, and now she deserved to know the rest.

# CHAPTER TWENTY-ONE

A RIA'S HEAD SPUN in all directions while she let Gray lead her back to the castle. She'd almost been thrown into some prison on false charges. Harper's warning was happening. Gray's enemy was going after her. But Gray showed her tonight that he wouldn't let anything happen to her. His warnings were frightening. She heard his icy voice in her mind when he posed his question to his father. *Why would you be so careless about making an enemy of me?*

Indeed, why would anyone?

Mrs. B. had also arrived and if that weren't enough to make Aria's head spin, she then dropped a bomb that Gray had been born in the twentieth century. He was urged to return to set time right.

They'd had no idea that time-traveling was against some sort of time rule. Aria doubted Gray would have let that stop him. Would he leave with her? So many possibilities flowed through her mind about what she wanted to show him: lights, cars, planes, trains, movies, restaurants and more.

They entered the castle, and Gray helped her out of her coat. His fingers brushed her shoulder and then upper arm. His touch sent warm charges through her. Like the charge of lightning that made one's hair rise up. His breath, falling on the back of her head made her want to turn in his arms and kiss him.

"I'll walk you to your chamber." His fathomless voice reso-

nated through her.

"Gray?" she said as they walked together toward the stairs.

"Yes?" he answered, sounding like a satisfied cat while he took her hand again and held it to his chest.

"I'm sorry about your mother. I'm sorry you didn't know."

He was quiet for a moment in thoughtful contemplation—or he wasn't thinking at all. His expression didn't offer her a clue. Just when she thought he didn't want to talk about it, he turned slightly to look at her.

"I haven't had a mother since I was seven. I hate that things were kept from me, but I understand why they were—when I was a child, at least. As I grew older, I wish I would have been told the truth."

Aria nodded. Her heart broke for him to have such a sneaky, thoughtless grandmother. Mrs. B. had been sneaky and thoughtless with her too. Aria wasn't so sure she wanted to forgive her.

"Perhaps things were meant to be this way."

She gave him an askew look. "Will Dartmouth's rebellious lord suddenly accept that things are meant to be a certain way, and follow along?"

He stopped and turned his body to face her fully. With his free hand he reached up to gently swipe a tendril of her hair off her cheek. He smiled, looking into her eyes, and then grew serious in the next breath. "Not only follow along but go joyfully if it involves you."

She stared into his eyes, where Grayson Barrington lived, still survived after being alone for so torturously long. Oh, she thanked the good Lord that Gray hadn't given up what made him wonderfully, expressively human. Dancing.

She had given up. She felt her eyes burn and tried to blink her tears away, but they filled her eyes, nonetheless.

"What makes you cry?" he asked in a quiet tone. "Tell me and I'll see that it never causes you to shed a tear again."

She gazed at his lips while he spoke and while two full, fat tears fell from her cheeks. "I want to dance."

He let her words sink in for a second, and then his smile returned, and he pulled her by the hand the other way—toward his dance hall.

"I didn't mean now," she protested, stopping him with laughter escaping her. "It's the middle of the night! I mean in general. I want to dance with you again."

"Oh, with me," he said with a playful grin. "We don't need a dance hall to do that." He made a sharp turn and veered off the path, leading her to the doors of his chambers.

This time she didn't protest. She followed him when he stepped inside and looked around while he bolted the door. She'd been inside his chambers before, though the first time he'd been attacked at the coffee house, and he lay in his bed recovering. She'd entered quickly and left the same way.

His chambers were like a huge New York City apartment with separate rooms. The first room was a fancy living room of sorts, with heavy wood tables and four chairs upholstered in olive silk damask. There was a settee of brown velvet and an ornate walnut armoire against the east wall. A large hearth with a stone mantel was built into the west wall. Above it was a painting of a dancer. Aria thought it to be Gray from the graceful lines.

She followed him through a doorway into another room bare of furniture with moonlight streaming through the eight tall windows along two walls. Aria knew glass was scarce and expensive nowadays. She also knew that Gray liked being outside and these tall windows were probably the closest he could get to it sometimes.

"Another dance hall," she remarked looking around while he lit candles throughout.

"This one is significantly smaller," he told her, coming closer. "For when I just want to dance without leaving my rooms."

Immediately following his words, he bunched up his nose. His eyes closed and his lips puckered. "Do I sound horribly spoiled?"

She shook her head, smiling dreamily at him. "Goodness, my

lord Dartmouth, but you're charming."

Proving her words to her own heart, he laughed, freeing all traces of guile, opening his mouth wide and releasing a ridiculously adorable sound. This part of him was a stark contrast from the raw, sensual charm he emitted when he danced to the stoic, detached warlord who was harder to read than a book of braille if you weren't blind.

She could read him though, most of the time. He possessed emotions—and they were strong.

"You're not spoiled, Gray," she assured, taking a step closer to him. "You're wonderfully fresh. Like a cool breeze in the dead of summer. You're a welcome breath of life using your body to be known."

He looked down at her and smiled. "I like how you see me."

He dipped his head to kiss her. She was sure he could feel her heart pounding against him. She thought she might faint. It wasn't that she'd never been kissed. She had been, but never the way Gray had kissed her.

She almost groaned out loud when the luxuriousness of his full lips pressed against hers. His mouth was curious and cautious, opening to her and closing again around her tongue, her lips.

He didn't keep kissing though, but rather hauled her against him, and cupping her right hand, he twirled her on her feet, around and around in place, and around the empty hall. They danced to music only they could hear.

He brought it to a whole new level when he ground his hips against her and began dancing contemporary. He kept her pressed against him, one arm curled around her waist, the other hanging at his side while he moved his hips, his chest, his hard belly. She matched his movements, keeping her left leg and hip between his legs. She thought she could seduce him, but she was the one whose knees almost buckled three times. But it wasn't until he ground himself against her and smiled like a beast with nakedly male intentions that she had to close her eyes to fight against the sight of him and what it was doing to her.

When he bent his face to her neck and inhaled her deeply, she shuddered against him. He lifted his face and looked at her, then smiled and lowered his mouth to hers. His hand at her back closed around her fully, holding her closer.

Briefly, she thought about passing out. Could she stop it from happening? Was this what it was like to kiss the man you loved? To barely breathe waiting for the touch of his lips?

She coiled both of her arms around his neck. She wouldn't let him go if he backed away from kissing her.

He didn't. In fact, he matched her eagerness, and, taking her jaw in his palm, he kissed her and made her heart dance. His warm tongue became light, flickering around the darkest shadows—warm, golden light streaked with crimson. His breath, seasoned with desire, became fire, igniting her nerve-endings, setting flames to her blood. As the fire in his gaze had promised, he wreaked havoc on her with his mouth, his tongue, his teeth, the latter of which he used to nibble on her lower lip and chin. He was like some*thing* that wanted to eat her alive. She was willing to be consumed.

She tightened in his arms, like wound coils ready to spring. At once, she felt him harden. Instinctively, she rubbed herself against him. She almost melted in his arms when he withdrew from their kiss, drew back his lips and ground his teeth. He jutted out his groin as if he meant to impale her but was stopped by the confines of their clothes.

Aria was a virgin. It wasn't too unheard of for a twenty-three-year-old in 2024. She didn't have time for a relationship, and she wasn't about to give her body to just anyone.

Gray wasn't just anyone.

She pulled at his shirt, then stopped to run her fingers down the taut nooks and crannies of his abdomen. He yanked the rest of his shirt over his head, then pulled the laces of her corset and threw the contraption over his shoulder. She worked the laces of his breeches, stripping him down to his hose, while he freed her of her skirts.

PAULA QUINN

She thought they might do it right there on the hard floor, but he scooped her up in the cradle of his arms and carried her through another doorway that opened to his bedroom.

The urge to giggle like a schoolgirl was tempered by the desire to weep like a woman who had lost everything. No. She wouldn't lose him. He was everything.

She wondered, fleetingly while he carried her to his bed, when she had stopped worrying about her family. Was it after Mrs. B. swore that she'd helped them out, or before that—when she began falling in love with an eighteenth-century dancer?

He set her down on the soft mattress and stared down at her. He swiped his finger over a tear dripping down her cheek. "What is it? Do you want to wait?" he asked patiently.

"No," she told him, "Because no matter what, I won't regret it."

His expression melted into a smile and then he shed his hose like a second skin. She looked at him in the light of the hearth fire and swallowed. She might be a virgin, but she wasn't ignorant of where he was supposed to put that thing springing up between his sinewy thighs. But as frightening as it appeared, as a part of the rest of his sculpted body, it was beautiful and enticing.

He climbed into bed with her and pulled two blankets over them, up to their chins. She shivered with him in the cold and then laughed with him. She was thankful that he didn't jump on top of her and begin humping her like she had once overheard one of her students complaining that was how her fiancé did things.

Aria doubted very much she'd be complaining about Gray in the future.

A thread of panic coursed through her, and she pulled him closer. "Gray, promise you won't leave me. No, no." She fought to gain control over herself. "I have no right to ask that of you. I'm sorry. Maybe we shouldn't do this. If we do, I'm afraid I might fall too deeply in love with you. We don't know what's going to happen—if we're separated, I won't be able to—"

"Aria, my darling, why are you worrying over things that will never happen? I won't be separated from you. Take me as your husband and let's let this whole place know it tomorrow."

"No," she shook her head. "I won't marry you to spite anyone. Ask me again at another time."

His smile deepened, watching her while she spoke. "Aria?"

"Yes?" She glanced at him as she wiggled out of her petticoats and hose under the blankets.

"I love you."

She stopped and looked at his face close to hers. He was so handsome he stole the breath from her body.

"I'm more stunned than you are," he confessed in a soft voice. "I thought no one could ever touch my heart again. I wasn't even willing to let it happen. But you, you came roaring like a fearless little lion and tore away my defenses as if they were made of parchment."

She tried kicking her legs out of her hose but to no avail. He laughed, and she was sure he crinkled his nose in the soft glow of the firelight. He helped her out of her binds, and she swore silently to help him with the same.

Free, she vaulted over him and smiled down at him. "Gray?" she whispered. "I love you too. I love you enough to throw the key into the estuary when we find it."

"Aria," he said, settling her atop his thighs. "I would never let you abandon your family."

She didn't doubt his words, and she loved him even more for them. She didn't want to think about being apart from him now. But who would he be abandoning here? His father and his father's horrible wife and her son? The villagers who'd raged to stone him?

She lowered herself and kissed his waiting, smiling mouth. She felt him beneath her trying to guide himself into her. She smiled like a cat and rubbed herself over him, encasing him in her fiery hot niche, almost taking him whole as he shot his hot lubricant into her.

She didn't let him retreat when he was spent but held him down and pumped harder. To her surprise and delight, his stamina didn't fail, nor did his appetite for her. What had been her victory quickly became his when he turned her on her back and spread her thighs with his knees.

She wasn't sure how she'd taken him the first time. She wasn't sure she could do it again, but he drove himself into her and made her drip around him and take him deeper.

They slept for a little while but soon he woke her again by drinking from her tight nipples. She could do nothing but smile as molten fire coursed through her and made her legs spread.

Turning her over, he mounted her from behind. He leaned over her and spoke close to her ear, telling her what she meant to him and how much he needed her in his life.

Pushing her down he slipped his finger under her and rolled her hard nub in his fingers until she cried out. His thrusts grew more urgent as she found her release in his hand, and he found his inside her warm body.

Aria wasn't sure how many times they'd woken up tangled in each other's arms. How many times they made love before he finally fell asleep for over two hours.

Aria was sore but ecstatically happy as she made her way to her chambers just before the sun came up.

She didn't want Sarah to find her bed empty this morning, and she also wanted to let Gray sleep, so she slipped out of his bed without disturbing him.

She managed to get to her rooms without anyone seeing her. She smiled, opening her door and stepping inside. Hands came around her mouth right away and a hard body pressed up against hers.

"Scream and I kill him before I kill you."

Mr. Cavendish's voice against her ear made her want to scream and claw his eyes out. She wouldn't scream but she would kick him in the—

Another set of hands appeared out of the shadows. One hand

lashed out and punched her in the jaw, knocking her out.

GRAY DREAMED HE was a child wandering about in the forest. All around him animals foraged and prepared for the new day. None of them stopped to speak with him. When he tried to communicate with them, nothing happened. Panic and loneliness engulfed him. Suddenly, they began running for their lives away from him and out of the forest.

*Wait! Why are you running? Can you not hear me?*

They didn't respond or even stop running. Then he saw Abigail the goose flying toward him. She quacked but he shook his head, not understanding.

"But I can understand," he told himself. "I can understand." He closed his eyes and listened. For a moment he heard nothing but quacking, and then he was no longer in the forest. His dream changed. He was still a young boy, but now he was inside the castle, in his chambers, asleep with his head on a woman's lap.

"Grayson, I came back for you, but I was captured."

"Mother, I have been so afraid without you."

"Forgive me, my darling," she cooed, stroking his head. "I couldn't live the way they wanted me to live in that time. I was so miserable by all their ridiculous rules and regulations against women that I prayed many nights for death. I didn't know that I could travel through time until I was twelve. My younger sister Joan was just eight when she was thrown from her horse and broke her neck. She died later that night. My parents were inconsolable. I was...I was crying. Joan was a beautiful, sweet little girl. I didn't want to lose her in my life. I wept, brokenhearted. All I could do was wish we could go back in time and stop Joan from riding that horse. And then, it happened." She paused to wipe her eyes and then smiled. "I don't regret it. Joan was with us again. I didn't travel again for ten years. Grandmother Tessa had warned me so many times not to try it that I never did. But I was desperate to be away from this time. At first, I flitted around searching for a time that would suit us. My goal had always been to find a place for you and me, Gray. But then, traveling became fun and I began to forget my life here."

"Me," he whispered.

She didn't answer but stopped stroking him and looked up at the door.

"Wake up," she said, returning her attention to him. "Wake up, Son."

Then he heard another voice, *Grayson, it is Tabby. Open your eyes! Wake up! They have taken your lady!*

Gray's eyes shot open. He sucked in a great gulp of air and sat upright in his bed. An instant passed while his dream and what he just heard settled into him. He looked at the side of his bed where he'd left Aria before falling asleep. She wasn't there. Without further hesitation, he leaped out of the bed, pulled on his breeches and boots and ran from the chambers.

He went directly to Aria's chambers. She wasn't there.

*Tabby! Where is she?*

*Mr. Cavendish and Mr. Gable have taken her out of the house and are heading for the Gable holding.*

Gray felt his blood boiling in his veins. Cavendish and Harry Gable, he thought with murderous intent flashing across his eyes as he fled the castle. He would kill them.

He called for Ghost and the horse barreled out of the stable, bareback.

*He took her on Chester*, Ghost communicated to him, *after Esper kicked out at him every time he attempted to saddle her.*

Gray smiled. Esper was fast. Chester was old. *Remind me to give Esper extra carrots later.*

*I bit Mr. Gable's finger when he tried to saddle me.*

*That's my girl. You'll get carrots every day for the rest of your life. But now, help me find her.*

The horse took off at top speed. Then Gray heard Ghost in his mind, *May I say, lord, that it is good to have you back.*

246

*It's good to be back,* Gray replied and leaned forward to pat Ghost's neck. *Forgive me for staying away for so long.*

They came upon Chester and one of the horses that had followed him home the day he caught the two thieves. There was no one with them. There were droplets of blood on the snowy ground. Gray's blood drained from his face. Was this Aria's blood? If it was…if she was hurt in any way…

*I sense two people alive within a kilometer of here,* he alone heard Ghost say.

Immediately, his head snapped up. He sniffed the air as he'd seen his friends do for ten years of his life. But he smelled nothing beside the scents of the forest.

But Ghost could smell better than he could. *This way,* the horse told him and turned north.

"Aria!" he shouted out.

*This way!* something answered.

*Over here!*

*This way!*

He followed the path to where the birds and foxes and other forest animals led him. He passed the Gable's holding and didn't veer in its direction. He trusted the voices he heard more than his eyes.

They led him in the right direction. He came upon Cavendish hovering over her, pointing his arrow, nocked and ready to fly into her beautiful face.

Gray didn't think. He acted on pure instinct, ready to kill for her.

He charged like a horrifying beast set loose to wreck its worst havoc. He smashed into Cavendish, grasping the arrow at the same time. He heard ribs cracking.

Landing on the balls of his feet and palms almost hitting the ground, he turned, snarled, and leaped at the man writhing on the ground. A knee crashing into Cavendish's thigh would ensure the bastard didn't stand to his feet again. But that wasn't enough. Cavendish had kicked Gray and broken his bones more than once. He'd teased and ridiculed Gray about his dancing and after the incident, Cavendish made his life a living hell. Gray wanted to pay him back for it all.

When blood from Cavendish's face splattered up onto his cheek, he became aware of someone grasping his wrist and almost falling over him when she tried to stop his fist from striking again.

Aria! "Aria!" He grabbed her face and grew furious again when he saw her bruised jaw. But he didn't hit Cavendish again. Aria needed to be seen to.

"Are you hurt very badly?" he managed to ask her, not breathing until she answered. "Where's Harry Gable?"

"I'm not hurt," she assured him with her smile that worked to calm him. "And Harry Gable is off somewhere nursing his hand after Ghost bit off his finger."

*You'll get apples too, Ghost.*

"You should be promising her apples for the next month."

"That's what I'm doing! How did you know?"

She shrugged. "I can tell by your tender expression that you're speaking to her. And I just know what I would say to her."

She made him laugh. He laughed! Then he kissed her jaw as gently as he could and pulled her into his embrace.

"How did you find me?"

He looked at his horse. "Ghost has a good nose."

*Why, thank you Grayson.*

His smile deepened and Aria laughed. "My boyfriend is Dr. Doolittle."

"Who?" he asked.

She let him help her to her feet and then, standing above Cavendish, she let him kiss her.

# CHAPTER TWENTY-TWO

THE DUKE'S MARRIAGE ball for his son was in its second hour and Gray still hadn't shown his face. That was because Aria didn't want to stop kissing him. They had stolen away to his private dance hall so he could practice his dance. With his grandmother returned, Aria had convinced him that they had so much to be thankful to Mrs. B. for. His grandmother knew that out of the three women suitable to take him as a husband, only Aria would appreciate his love of dancing and his dedication to it. She understood how it made him feel.

Earlier, when he mentioned practicing, despite all the musicians being in the main ballroom, she leaped at the chance to watch him. She had watched him often. Tonight though, tonight his dancing made her desire him with a force that wouldn't be tamed or stopped. One look at the flames in his eyes, the decadence of his smile, and she melted from the inside out.

Boldly, she had gone to him on the dance floor and moved like a cat in heat against him, around him until he pushed her up against the window, yanked up her skirts, and pulled at other garments to take her. Their love was passionate and swift, leaving them both pulling their breath and resting against each other.

Looking up at him, Aria knew she loved him enough to stay with him for the rest of her life. But as much as she loved looking at him, she loved touching him, holding him even more. She pulled him close. She was about to tell him how much she loved him, when he said her name.

"Take me as your husband. I promise my life to you. I want to stay by your side forever and share our journeys together. If you cry, I want to be there to hold you and comfort you. And if it was me who brought tears to your eyes, I'll spend forever making it up to you. "Let's...ehm..." He smiled at her from under his long, dark lashes ... "have seven children together."

"Yes," she told him softly, "I'll be your wife and have your children, however many there are."

They kissed until someone banged on the locked door. Gray adjusted his periwinkle velvet breeches.

Aria considered him the sexiest man alive, who could fire up her insides just by tucking his shirt into his breeches.

Blushing uncontrollably, she adjusted her clothes—and there were so damn many layers.

The intruder happened to be Harper, looking for them. "Cavendish is bedridden—and very drunk I'm told. Now is the chance to speak to your father without his interruptions."

Gray scowled at her. "How can you not know me by now?"

"Oh, please," Harper chided. "Do you think I don't know you would rather have your nose cut off than consider an opportunity to defend yourself to your father?"

"And why exactly should I defend myself to him?" Gray bit out and began buttoning his periwinkle coat with magenta embroidery along the edges and cuffs.

"Because he's your family, Grayson. Remind him of that. You must not lose everything to Cavendish. While your father lives, he can still change his will. You must make certain that nothing changes. You must inherit everything. Grandmother will make herself your beneficiary should you disappear. It will all be in a bank, waiting for you in the future."

Gray looked at Aria. She nodded and left the dance hall with him and Harper.

She was with him when he stepped through the ballroom double doors and strolled inside, smiling as if he hadn't made them all wait for two hours before they could begin their gossiping. He smiled at no one in particular and Aria couldn't help but notice that when his eyes reached her, his smile grew noticeably warmer.

The music stopped and every eye turned to him. Walking at his side, Aria tilted her chin and held her head up, proud to be walking beside him.

His grandmother was there, sitting at his table with Harper, waiting for them. When Gray saw her, he acknowledged her with a nod and a wink.

Mrs. B.'s gushing reaction to him didn't escape Aria's notice. Aria smiled, happy that they were reunited.

After he walked her to his table, Gray turned to the musicians, mainly the pianist, with whom he had pre-arranged a musical piece. They exchanged a nod and Gray walked to the center of the dance floor, cleared when the guests saw him enter.

"I'm here to dedicate this dance to my grandmother, who has returned to me."

Aria had a hard time seeing Mrs. B. wiping her eyes because her own were blurry with tears.

The music began. He stood slightly bent forward and then threw his arms back with a snap of his head. He extended his arms to the left. His body followed and then he swung to the right. He flowed to the music as if he could feel every note and chord in his blood. Aria believed he could.

Around her she could hear the sighs of the women in the ballroom.

"He is like living art."

"…a feast for my poor eyes."

"I like this way of dancing more than ballet. What is it called?"

The questions and comments buzzed around Aria's ears. She smiled, not worried in the least about any one of the women there. Somehow, she had won the bitter heart of the marquess and then watched him shed his chains and step into the radiant light. He danced, free of the strings that had moved him this way and that. She would cry her happy tears later. It wouldn't do to have her, Harper, and his grandmother all crying like fools at the table.

He sprang from one foot, spreading his legs and arms wide while in the air. He landed on the other foot in a perfect grand jeté. Aria felt goosebumps rise on her arms.

His body was long and lean in all the right places, creating beautiful lines whether in the air or on the ground. He was light on his toes, his feet moving as if in the air. Though he'd just begun practicing lyrical dance, every move was completely natural. His pushes and pulls were forceful, yet graceful. From his raised head to his pointed toes, he was glorious to behold.

But it was the way he closed his eyes and delighted in flying that made him most breathtaking.

Aria remembered to breathe and looked across the table at Mrs. B. Gray's grandmother wore a smile that Aria was sure would never completely leave her face. She knew what his dancing meant to him and, as Aria told Gray, his grandmother sent Aria to him because she knew Aria would appreciate his marvelous talent. Maybe she also knew that Aria would never allow anyone to stop him from dancing again.

When Gray was finished his grandmother and Aria began the applause, but everyone joined in until the sound of clapping hands filled the ballroom.

Gray waited until the applause died down before he turned his attention to his father, who stared at him as if he'd never seen his son before.

Aria held her breath. Gray hadn't told her what he was going to say to his father. With him, it could go either way. She had no idea what to expect.

"The other reason I'm here tonight, dancing at your ball is to announce to you and everyone here that I've found the woman I love with every ounce of my heart." He looked to where Aria was sitting with her face aglow in the firelight. "Miss Aria Darling will be at my side as my wife for all time."

With nothing but his warm smile, he eased her nerves.

But too soon, he returned his dark attention to his father. "Whether you approve or not."

When the duke opened his mouth to speak, Gray held up his finger to stop him. "I am your only son. I am sound of mind, and I have fought for the king. I won't let Miss Darling or Dartmouth be taken from me."

He paused for a moment to let his words sink in. Aria wondered if the duke was thinking about his stepson, Mr. Cavendish, lying in his sickbed at the moment with a broken nose and three missing teeth and two broken ribs.

"Since I was a boy," he continued, "you have never done a single thing for me. Now I ask you to do one thing. Declare that Timothy Cavendish is no longer your son, even by marriage because he tried to take Miss Darling's life. No such man should ever rule."

"He was doing what I ordered him to do," his father said, shocking Gray and Aria alike. "She's a thief! I should have had her thrown into prison instead of listening to that old woman, Tessa Blagden! Where is she?"

Aria stared at Mrs. B.'s empty chair. She was looking at her old friend while the duke ranted on. And then, before Aria finished blinking her eyes, Mrs. B. was gone.

Aria took a moment before the guards grabbed her to wonder why Mrs. B. was allowed to jump around in time, but Gray's mother had been punished for it.

She looked at him in time to see him turn his stoic expression on the men around her. And then, in an instant, fire lit his eyes. He drew his sword and hurried toward them. Most ran, some waited until he was almost upon them before they ran too. When Gray reached her, unhindered, he grabbed her hand and closed his eyes.

Aria had no idea what he was doing. His father shouted behind her. Harper joined her and Gray.

"Aria, tell me something about your mother. Quickly!" Gray held his blade out while he waited for her to answer.

"Um…ah…she's a hard worker. She…it's hard to think when all this was going on!

Gray opened his eyes briefly and gave her a caustic look.

Aria narrowed her eyes on him but focused her thoughts. "She has blonde hair and her eyes are blue like mine. Um, she's five feet, six inches tall. She has a burn scar from two years ago on the back of her left arm, from her shoulder to her elbow. She…"

Aria's words caught in her throat at the sight before her.

The air blurred, as if she were looking over the heat of flames. The western wall of the ballroom tore away. On the other side was…was her mother's living room.

With his hand covering hers, Gray ran for the tear.

Home! It was home! Aria's heart was ready to explode.

A pair of hands stopped her dead in her tracks, ripping her hand from Gray's, then dragged her in the opposite direction.

She turned to look up, horrified at Harry Gable. "Let me go!" She tried to fight her way free.

"Aria!" Gray screamed her name. He was close to the blurry tear. "I can't keep it open if I run back. Come to me!"

Aria tried to pull herself together and concentrate, then she snapped out her leg, but her captor merely shook his head and held on. Aria panicked, but a pair of hands grabbed Harry from behind, one arm coiled around his neck.

Aria saw that it was Will and kicked out. Finally, she broke free. She looked toward the rent in time. Gray was there, waiting for her.

A shot rang out. Sarah screamed. It was Will! Will had been shot! There was no time to even look back. Barely an instant for a shadow to rush by Aria as she took a flying, fearless leap into Gray's arms. And the rent closed.

GRAY HELD OUT his arms when she leaped and caught her. He smiled as if it was the single most important thing he succeeded at in his life. It was.

Then he looked around. They were in a square room with odd candle stands giving off soft, golden light. There was a settee-type, thick-cushioned place for sitting, along with a chair, upholstered in the same cream-colored fabric.

He wanted to ask Aria if she saw the shadow shoot by them—seemingly going from this world to that one.

"Mom?"

Before he asked her, Aria's voice broke through his thoughts.

Mom. They were in the future. It worked! He traveled through time!

A woman appeared from another room carrying a basket of clothing. "Aria? What are you doing home so early? Did you finish prac—"

The older woman's words were swallowed up in a tight, tearful embrace. "Mom! Oh, Mom! I'm sorry I wasn't here."

"Here for what?" Her mother gently pushed her out of her arms and gave her a careful looking over. "When did your hair get so long? And...what's with the medieval clothes?"

"Regency," Aria absently corrected. "Mom—"

"And who is this handsome young man?"

"How's Dad?" Aria asked, hurrying out of the room and into another. "Where's Dad?" She shouted, rushing back to them, pale of all color. "Did he...?"

Her mother gave her a concerned look. "Your father went off to the batting cages."

"The batting cages?" Aria shouted, looking faint.

"Aria," her mother said with a concerned look, "what's the matter with—"

"What about the accident? Where's Conn?"

Now her mother gave Gray the same worried look. "What is she talking about? What accident? Has there been an accident?" the older woman leaned her hand against the wall. "Aria, what accident? Is it Conn? He was just—"

"There hasn't been an accident," Gray reassured her. "Aria," he said, turning to her next and lowering his voice. "I think I brought us back a few years early."

She stopped moving. He wasn't sure she was breathing. Then, "A few years early?"

He smiled. "Yes."

"You mean the accident—"

"Hasn't happened yet," he supplied.

Tears immediately filled Aria's eyes, and she threw her hands to her mouth. "Thank you, Gray. I don't know how to thank you."

"I'll figure something out."

They exchanged a smile and then Aria turned to her mother. "Mom, I know this is going to sound crazy, but what's the date?"

Her mother scowled at her, and it reminded Gray of Aria when she was angry.

"You're right, it does sound crazy. Do you have a fever?" She hurried closer and pressed her palm to Aria's forehead. "You're acting very strange. It's April 7th."

"And the year?" Aria pressed.

Her mother slapped her palms against her thighs. "2022."

"2022?!" Aria began to cry. When her mother and Gray went to her, she reassured them that they were happy tears. "The happiest of my life." She looked at Gray and smiled. "Thank you."

"Young man, since my daughter hasn't introduced us yet, I'm Rose Darling. You are?"

"Grayson Barrington, my lady." He bowed and smiled at her on the way back up.

"Oh, my," Mrs. Darling said, bringing her hand to her chest.

"He's the Marquess of Dartmouth…in England," Aria announced.

"Oh, my." Her mother repeated and backed up a step to size him up from head to toe. "How do you know my Aria?"

"I'm a dancer."

"Romeo?"

Aria took her mother's hands and nodded. "Better than Romeo."

"Better?" Gray and her mother asked together.

"So much better," she answered them both with a slight blush that tempted Gray to go to her and take her in his arms. He wondered if a lifetime would be long enough to spend with her.

When Mrs. Darling offered him a seat on the couch, he gave it a curious look first. It seemed to be bursting at the seams with cushioning. Was there any wood used to keep it from sinking into the floor? He sat down cautiously and then smiled and snuggled into the deep cushion and closed his eyes. A man could sleep well on this fat couch.

"Don't get too comfortable," Aria said and tugged on his arm. "I have a million things I want to show you."

"Oh, sightseeing?" Mrs. Darling smiled at them. "You'll need energy. Let me make you some lunch."

Aria agreed and Gray knew she wanted to spend more time with her mother, whom she feared she had lost.

He was surprised to find Mrs. Darling so accommodating, without a trace of sourness in her tone when she spoke. He wondered if his mother would have been so pleasant had she lived. In his most recent dream of her, she seemed thoughtful and kind, stroking his tired head in her lap. Would he have learned her modern English and called her mom? Would he have had a couch?

"I made tuna salad for sandwiches with the boys, but—well, now, where is that boy? Connall, you're going to be late!" She turned to tell them, "He's leaving today for the week on his hiking trip with Charlie and Jack Bantor. I told him I'd pack a launch."

"Hiking trip?" Aria echoed in a shaky voice. "He can walk," she said in a quiet whisper and wiped her tears in a heedless attempt to stop her tears.

When no answer came from her son, her mother shrugged

her shoulders softly. "I guess he left already. He was here a minute ago."

Gray's heart skipped in his chest when he looked over his shoulder at where the rift had been.

"But don't worry, you two," Mrs. Darling declared on her way into the kitchen. "I made plenty."

Aria looped her arm through his and locked him in entwining her hands when he began walking. "Gray, you gave my brother back his legs and my father his life."

"I'm glad, my love. Do you think your brother left already for his trip?"

She nodded and smiled. "He was always...is always very active."

Gray smiled with her and looked over her shoulder one last time at where they had entered and swallowed his panic that the shadow might have been...

"You're going to love my mother's tuna salad sandwiches."

And Gray did. He'd had fish before but never crumbled bits of tuna fish and chopped onions with delicious white sauce Aria called mayonnaise—and all of it spread out on *rye toast*.

It was the first of many wonders of the twenty-first century Gray experienced that day. After they changed clothes—her into her own garments, and him, into *jeans* and a button-down shirt that belonged to her brother, Gray discovered that there weren't any candles beneath the cloth covered candle stands—which was a good thing because the cloth would have surely caught fire. Almost everything worked off electricity. He'd heard of it before, but it was a relatively new marvel in his century, and there was nothing like personal electricity to power a home's lighting, among hundreds of other things that needed electricity to run.

It was almost nothing compared to what he saw when he stepped outdoors with Aria to go meet her father at the batting cages.

There were people...everywhere. And modern, metal behemoths rolling to and fro, called, according to Aria, cars. Modern vendors owned *stores*, where they sold everything from food to clothing, cigars, and footwear. Everything moved at a quickened pace.

When music began to play from somewhere around him, he stopped. "What's that?"

Aria stopped with him and smiled. "It's music coming from that electronics store. Pink Floyd. Great soundtrack."

He closed his eyes and began to sway. Aria took his hand and pulled. "Not in the middle of the street. I'll take you to the school later."

Following her, he asked a dozen questions about the musicians from the electronics store, then stopped again in front of a hotdog cart. His eyes opened wide and then closed again to take a deep breath.

"Hot dogs," she told him.

He made a look of disgust. "People eat dogs now?"

She explained, as best she could, what hot dogs were and brought him one from the odd green paper money she found in her pocket. He scarfed it down, then requested another. Twenty-first century food was truly a wonder!

While she paid the vendor, a male voice called out her name. When she heard it tears immediately filled her eyes. She turned to see her father coming toward them.

"My father is walking, Gray," she said with such joy in her voice it almost brought tears to his eyes, as well. "It's been almost two years since I saw him walk to me." She turned to Gray and her gaze on him warmed. "I'll never forget this. He was given a death sentence and now he's alive and well."

"It sounds a bit how life left me until I met you," he told her softly. If her father hadn't almost reached them, Gray would have kissed her.

"Sweetheart, what are you doing home early?" Her father stepped up to her and put his arm around her, then kissed her forehead.

Aria hugged him and never wanted to let go. "Daddy, you

look so young and healthy."

"What? What are all the tears, Aria?" he inquired gently, studying her.

"It's just...I'm happy to see you up and around."

"Hmm?" He gave her a confused look, then slipped it to Gray.

Gray gave him a little bow. "I'm Gray. Grayson Barrington."

"The Marquess of Dartmouth in Devon, England," Aria added as she had for her mother.

Mr. Darling grinned at him and held out his hand. Gray looked at the offering and then offered his hand, as well.

"What brings you to our fair city, my lord?" her father asked, still smiling.

"Your daughter, Sir."

He and Aria explained how they met at an audition and danced together. Gray had returned home but he missed Aria too much to stay away.

"It sounds like you might want to marry my little girl."

"Daddy!" Aria's soft laughter drifted like a siren's song across Gray's ears.

"Yes." Gray said, smiling at her like a fool before he grew serious again. "I intended on asking you for your blessing."

"Let's go home and talk about it with my wife," her father suggested. They agreed and turned back for the *apartment.*

"Daddy?"

"Yes, love."

"I'm so happy to see you well." She looped her arm through his and walked with him.

Her father gave her a soft chuckle and then smiled at Gray. "If you ever have children, pray for a daughter."

Gray nodded, having seen glimpses of a girl child with flaming red curls falling around her cherubic face. "I will, Sir."

"That's good. So, Marquess, you love my daughter?"

Smile intact, in fact, Gray thought he just might not ever stop smiling, he answered, "Yes, I love her."

# CHAPTER TWENTY-THREE

ARIA STOOD BY the counter in the apartment she grew up in. The coffee she waited for began to perk. She looked at the people sitting at the kitchen table laughing together and thought she could die right now and be happy. Her parents were restored and delightfully ordinary. Her marquess sat among them, transformed into a friendly, easy-going, cheerful man. Her brother had his legs back! She wanted to throw her head back and laugh and cry.

Gray's charm worked on everyone in the family, that is, after he refused to get into the building elevator until he'd climbed eight flights of stairs and realized he couldn't make the other nine. Water—hot or cold—from the faucet kept him perplexed for a quarter of an hour. The refrigerator, lights, and everything else they didn't have in the eighteenth century captured his attention. By the time they sat down for dinner, he gave all his attention to her parents and laughter resounded throughout the night.

Now, he looked up and caught Aria's eye. The amused smile he was aiming at her mother changed into something that misted his eyes and then crinkled his nose until one eye closed, as if he was winking.

Aria's heart melted over her ribs.

"What puts such a smile on your beautiful face?" he asked, leaving the table to go to her.

Gray's deep, husky voice resonated through her and made

her sigh dreamily when she looked at him.

"You," she answered. "You seem to be a hit with my parents," she told him while he took her hand in his.

"A hit?" he asked with a furrow in his brow.

"They like you," she explained, loving him for worrying over it.

"Oh." His smile returned as he lifted her hand to his lips. "I like them too. Do you think they might like to go back with us?"

Her heart pounded like a drum, making her sick and queasy. He wanted to go back.

"Do *you* want to go back?" she asked in a whisper-soft voice.

His smile remained intact, but Aria had admired it too many times to know when it wasn't genuine.

She spotted her mother approaching and smiled along with him.

"Let me get the coffee, dear," her mother offered. "Go sit with Gray."

"No, Mom, you go sit," Aria insisted. "Gray will help me."

She waited until her mother returned to the table. Rather than try to question Gray about going back and risk one of them brooding for the rest of the night, she'd just have to make certain he didn't want to go back. She would do that by showing him how much the world had to offer in the twenty-first century. She'd start tomorrow, though. Even though it had been just two weeks since she'd seen her family, it felt as though a lifetime had passed. She didn't want to be away from them again so soon.

"What would you say is your favorite thing about our country, so far?" asked Aria's father.

Aria smiled at him for the millionth time since her poor eyes had found him walking toward her earlier. Her father wasn't a slowly dying paraplegic. He looked healthy, twenty years younger. She felt her eyes begin to burn and looked at her hands so she wouldn't start crying and they all thought she was crazy.

Then she heard Gray's reply, and she quickly swiped her cheek.

"The intimacy of your meals," Gray said, without thinking about it long—as if he'd already contemplated his reply. "Here, in this small homey room, at this small table, surrounded by people you love and eating food your wife cooked with her own hands, is my favorite thing. It's what I've always wanted."

"Were you raised away from your parents?" Aria's mother asked him in a soft voice.

"Yes," he told her. "I lost my mother as a young boy. My father soon remarried a woman who saw me as nothing but an obstacle for her own son."

"Well," Aria's mother declared, "As long as you are a part of Aria's life, we'll always do our best to make you feel like a treasured part of our family."

Surely, Aria thought smiling at her mother and then at Gray, he would choose this life over his previous one.

She didn't have a chance to speak to him in private again after that. Her mother assigned him to sleep on the sofa, then ushered Aria into her bedroom.

After counting sheep...and foxes and ravens, she tossed and turned for another hour.

Finally, and as quietly as she could, she slipped out of bed and tiptoed to her door. She really had no idea why she left her room, except that she couldn't sleep thinking about Gray with nothing to separate them but a thin door.

She wouldn't climb onto the couch with him. She wouldn't do anything disrespectful in her parents' house. She just wanted to see him, maybe talk to him. She liked talking with him. His voice calmed her, his words encouraged her, his heart revealed itself to her.

When she entered the living room, he sat up on her mother's sofa and whispered her name in the dim light.

"I couldn't sleep," she said, going to him.

"I couldn't sleep either," he told her, then pulled her closer when she sat next to him.

"Why couldn't you sleep?" she asked first.

He was quiet for a moment, and she thought she heard his slow heartbeat in the silence. Then the horn of a car blared from outside and his arm came around her tighter.

"Thoughts of you kept me awake," he admitted. "I finally found you. I don't want to spend the rest of my days without you."

She closed her eyes, wanting to tell him that she didn't want to be apart from him either.

"I haven't felt like Dartmouth was home since I can remember."

She believed him, but still, she heard a wistful longing in his voice. Was the longing for the time before his mother left? Or for something he wished he'd received from his father?

"Does that mean you'll stay here in the twenty-first century?" she asked him.

Instead of answering her right away, he leaned his temple on her head and breathed, in and out. Once, twice, three times…

"I know that after living amongst such fantastic wonders like little devices that play the most beautiful music upon request—" he laughed softly, then muttered almost too low for her to hear, despite her closeness—"I think I would miss that the most."

Her heart stopped. She stopped hearing what else he was saying and let his previous statement reign supreme. *I think I would miss that the most.* He would miss her Echo the most because he wouldn't be here.

She felt sick. She might faint. He hadn't answered her when she asked him if he would stay here. He was going to return. He was going to ask her to go with him. Words echoed between her ears, resounding like drums.

*I'll never forget this.* Her words at first, speaking of her father when she saw him walking. *He was given a death sentence and now he's alive and well.*

And his tender reply. *It sounds a bit how life left me until I met you.*

And then her thoughts ended as she finally fell asleep sitting up in his arms.

**>>>><<<<**

"WHAT DID YOU say this behemoth was called?" Gray asked her with wonder giving music to his voice.

"A train."

"And what powers it?"

"Electricity, I think," Aria told him, smiling at his face as he stared, astounded, out the window.

The train came to the next stop at Ocean Parkway and Aria grasped Gray's wrist and they hurried off.

They walked toward Coney Island though Aria thought they might never get there with the number of times Gray stopped to "talk" to leashed dogs on the way. Thankfully, they all told Gray they were happy and loved their humans. A few, like a terrier here and a setter there would rather be hunting rats or staring down birds...namely pigeons.

Aria thought, for the first time since knowing Gray, that it might be a terrible burden to be able to communicate with animals. Going to animal shelters would be so difficult to leave without adopting everything in them. What would zoos be like? Pet shops? She shivered thinking of it.

Today, they would forget the past and have fun. And what was more fun than an amusement park?

The Cyclone roller coaster in the Coney Island Amusement Park to be exact?

After a quick stop at an ATM, Aria paid for the tickets for the Cyclone and hurried to get them seats in the lead car. The ride started with all its rickety crackling, metal scraping against metal as the cars rolled across the track. One second into the first incline, a woman began to scream and hardly stopped after that. Not Gray. His hands were lifted high above his head and his laughter gave music to the air.

Aria knew he would enjoy the daring rides. She hoped he was getting a taste of how fast this life was. That night she took him to see a movie. He seemed happy enough, especially when her father gave them his blessing the next night at dinner.

By the time the weekend was over, they had been on the Circle Line around the Hudson and on a helicopter ride at the pier, and every night, no matter how tired they were, they visited the school and danced together. But Aria still couldn't jump. Though she'd done it leaving Dartmouth and Gray had caught her, she wasn't ready yet. Gray didn't push.

On those nights when they danced at the school, Mrs. B. didn't show up. But on the third night, Harper did.

"Grandmother was right," she said to Gray when she opened the door and stepped into the studio from the hallway. "How did you do it? How did you travel on your own?"

He shrugged a shoulder. "Ask Thoren Ashmore."

"But you did it on your first try," Harper continued. "And you didn't lose Miss Darling."

Aria coiled her arm through his in an almost instinctive gesture. She never wanted to let him go. "He also brought us to twenty-twenty-two, before—"

"We know. That's why it took our grandmother a little longer to find you," she told them, then turned back to Gray. "She's the only one who can locate others, and she can only find certain people. You're one of them."

Because Aria was holding onto him, she felt him go as taut of an overwound guitar string.

"Why are you doing her bidding, Harper?" he asked with a note of sadness tainting his voice. "Why did she send you, without bothering to come herself?"

"I wanted to come," the woman who'd raised him confessed. "I begged her to let me see you again, and to let me be the one who tells you."

"Tell me what? Tell me what, Harper?" he demanded.

She slipped her gaze to Aria. "He's fine. Grandmother is watching over him."

"Who?" Gray asked her.

"Connall Darling," Harper told him. "He's safe! I swear it!" she insisted when Aria swooned like one about to faint.

"You both didn't know he saw his sister and ran through the rift?"

"He...ran," Aria echoed, closing her teary eyes. "Yes, that's exactly what he would do."

"Remember, Aria," Harper said. "It's two years before the accident."

Aria nodded, her heart threatening to burst with joy for Conn and fear for his life. "We have to bring him back to 2022, Gray!"

"No, Gray you can't go back," Harper advised. "Grandmother will send Mr. Darling back. With all the time jumping, the Blagdens are being watched. We will all be separated by time if Grandmother is caught. Please, trust her to protect Mr. Darling until it's safe to send him back."

"How is she going to protect my brother?" Aria demanded, interrupting the topic.

"Aria," Harper said earnestly. "Grandmother loves your brother. She's known him since he was a little boy. I'd even venture to say there are things she knows about him that you aren't aware of."

"Impossible, I know—"

"In 2024, he never registered for his classes for next semester."

Aria blinked and her eyes filled with tears. "What?"

"He had no intention of letting you sweat and slave to pay for his courses. He'd gotten a minimum paying online job and was paying for his night courses."

Aria swiped her cheeks and shook her head. "That doesn't mean he can handle it back there."

"He is what he once was, Aria. He *will* handle it, just as you did." Harper said, smiling with Aria and wiping her tears. Then she turned to Gray. "You can't go back. Don't go back. Even if Timothy is given your title and plans to rule over the people. Don't go back, no matter what happens."

PAULA QUINN

"What about Will?" Aria asked. "I think he was shot by Mr. Cavendish—" She stopped speaking when Harper looked down.

"As far as I know, the young Mr. Gable didn't make it." Harper still didn't look up at either of them. "He was shot by Mr. Cavendish, who stumbled into the ballroom and saw William trying to help you. Harry Gable also perished when his brother collapsed to the floor before his eyes. Distraught, he leaped for Mr. Cavendish and reached him an instant before his sister did. He was struck down by your father's men. Sarah was almost killed as well. Mr. Darling saved her."

"My brother?" Aria cried and tugged on Gray's sleeve. "I'm thankful he saved Sarah, but they'll be after Conn now!"

"Grandmother won't let anyone harm him," Harper did her best to reassure her again.

She turned her attention back to Gray. "Listen to me, Grayson. Your father saw the manner in which you left. When you disappeared into thin air, the Cavendishes jumped on the opportunity to call you a warlock. They begged your father not to allow you to return and to imprison you if you do. They would no doubt request the high council to burn you at the stake." At this, Harper paused to wipe her eyes.

Aria didn't really know what she expected Gray to say. Maybe, 'That's okay, Harper. I'm not going back.' Something of that nature. But he remained silent, breaking Aria's heart with each second that passed.

Harper looked at her. The older woman's teary eyes made Aria want to cry with her. But she didn't. Why would she when she wouldn't let him go back? His enemies wanted to set him on fire and watch him burn! The more she thought about it, the more sickened she became. How could men be so heartless? She didn't blame Gray's mother for dragging the men who tried to burn her into the chaotic future.

"I plan on forgetting the past," Gray finally said.

Aria slipped her hands down his forearm and entwined her fingers with his.

268

He looked down at her and smiled. She tried to remember a time when he didn't smile upon seeing her. A fire came to life in her belly, warming her insides.

"I'm glad to hear that, Grayson. Of course, you're already wealthy here. Grandmother made sure to secure your inheritance and invest it." She pulled a thick envelope out of her oversized purse and handed it to Gray. "You own a safe deposit box at the bank. I noted the name of the bank on the documents inside the envelope. The key is inside with the rest of what you need, I.D. and all that. Miss Darling will help you go through all of it. You have different types of accounts with savings. There's a debit card in the envelope, as well as three credit cards. Money is at your disposal. You don't need to go back.

"Aria," Harper finally gave Aria her full attention. "Thank you for whatever you've done to his heart. I always feared he would walk straight into the flames. Before I knew about my sister, I knew that if his enemies found out that he could communicate with animals, they'd try to accuse him of practicing magic. I was glad he'd forgotten for so long."

She looked at him with shame in her loving gaze. But Aria didn't think Gray saw. His gaze was fixed on somewhere she couldn't see.

"Grayson?" Harper's voice broke through and pulled him back from wherever he was. "I'm so sorry I didn't do better."

His lips slanted upward. "You did better than my own mother. Better than Grandmother. You stayed by my side when everyone else left. You sheltered me in the forest and played your violin for me while I disobeyed my father and danced. There's no way to repay you for that."

She smiled and nodded, wiping her cheeks. Watching, Aria wiped hers, as well. Harper deserved all the love and respect that any good mother deserved. "Repay me by never going back."

He paused and then nodded.

# CHAPTER TWENTY-FOUR

G RAY LAY IN the dark on Mrs. Darling's sofa thinking about the last few days with Aria in the twenty-first century. He tried to decide which had been more thrilling, the cyclone roller coaster with its slow, rumbling climb toward the heavens perhaps to meet an extraordinary "plane" soaring through the clouds, only to tip over the top and descend with heart-stopping speed.

Or perhaps watching a movie in a theater was the most thrilling. His ears weren't used to the extremely loud volume of the various happenings on the "screen", and even the music bursting forth, but he'd already felt half-deaf from being in the front seat on the roller coaster with someone screaming behind him. He also never thought it possible for people to appear so large that their heads were as tall as his body. And how did the soldiers fly through the skies in their giant contraptions that resembled birds? His multitude of questions had to remain a mystery until after the movie, when Aria could explain it all to him. Ten breaths into the movie he'd found out not to speak when everyone, including Aria, shushed him. He still wasn't sure how he had felt as if he were there with the "pilot" beyond the clouds in his "jet fighter", breathing into a mask, and wondering if there would be anything left of him if he fell from the stars.

But lying there in her parents' living room, Gray knew what thrilled him most. Dancing with Aria in her proper attire of tiny "shorts" that were short alright. They very pleasingly fit her like her own skin, and with her matching lavender colored "crop top", she danced with more freedom of movement. Gray had believed each time he saw her that he surely had died and gone to heaven. He remembered thinking there was no way his darling could be so beautiful, but there she had been, tempting him beyond reason to reach out and touch her as she told stories with her movement to the hauntingly beautiful music coming from the small box she called a speaker...touch her before she faded away like some fevered dream. Breaking his heart when he let himself think clearly without her on his mind. But she was always there, making him selfishly want more.

When they were escaping Harry Gable, Aria had leaped into his arms. Then, her spine and shoulders were stiff with fear of falling. She hadn't made the leap again since, even though, now, her bones were unbroken. She had two years of fear to erase. Gray wanted to help her forget. He wanted to dance with her for the rest of his life. But there wasn't any more time.

He wanted to say that he knew things might end with Aria since last night's dream, but he'd known before that. It was not by a seer's power; though that particular "gift" was prevalent on the Blagden side of his family, he, thankfully, did not possess it. He knew he had to leave Aria because he had to go back for the animals—perhaps even for Beatrice, if she wanted to travel to the future with him. He couldn't leave them all to Cavendish. No matter how much he loved, and lived and breathed for Aria, he couldn't abandon them again.

There was the risk of being caught and tried and found guilty. Gray didn't want Aria there if that happened. If he had to leap out of 1795 fast, he might not be close enough to grab hold of her. He'd rather burn than leave her to his enemies.

He didn't sleep. He doubted if he ever would again, especially after the dream he'd had last night of his friends burning in the forest flames all around them. Kit and his fox mate, Maple, yelped and cried out as they tried to escape the fire with their pups. Matilda the raven and Onyx the alpha wolf from the north tried to escape but Matilda's wings smoldered, and she scrambled as she fell to the earth. Ash snapped at the embers falling into his fur. *Where is Grayson?* He heard a red squirrel squeak.

*How did this happen?*

*Where is Grayson? Has he left us again?*

Even now, wide awake as the sun began its ascent, Gray cringed and writhed as one in pain at the memory of the dream and finally sat up. He looked toward Aria's bedroom door. He wanted to wake her, promise to return to her.

Harper had begged him not to return to the past. She'd never come to him with news of worsening conditions under Cavendish's rule. He couldn't wait. What if Cavendish was going to set fire to the forest in the morning?

He squeezed his eyes shut. He should have told Aria yesterday. He could have tried to explain to her that he had to save the animals. They were the only family he'd had for a long time. But she would insist on coming with him—and he had to keep her away.

So, as dawn seeped through the curtained windows and bathed the room in a soft rosy glow, he left the sofa, got dressed in his eighteenth-century clothes, and without looking back at her bedroom door, focused all his thoughts on the forest around Dartmouth castle. Just this one last time, he swore in his heart.

This was no cause for a broken heart or tears. He would be back. Or he would die trying.

THE PHONE RANG in her ear, along with her pumping heart. The person on the other end picked up.

"Hello, Harper? It's Aria. He's gone." As the words left her mouth and settled on her ears, Aria brought her shaking hand to her nose to wipe it. She wanted to cry, to scream, to swear. "I saw him. I woke up and went to him. I saw the forest where my living room wall was supposed to be. He had stepped over and ...and he didn't even look back. Then the wall returned, and he was gone. Did he leave me? I think I'm going to be hysterical. Please find him and send him back, Harper."

Aria hung up and looked around. She couldn't stay here and fall apart in front of her parents.

She could barely think straight. He left. He left. He went back without her.

She pulled on a pair of jeans and a lightweight sweatshirt. Slipped on a pair of sandals and grabbed her sorely missed favorite bag. But not even the ease of dressing without the help of a servant made her happy to be in the twenty-first century without him.

She walked the streets painted amber in the morning sun, wiping tears from her cheeks. He was long dead in her time. So was her brother. The idea of it made her burst into a fit of tears. She thought these last few days of visiting the amusement park, the Empire State Building, the movies, would make Gray want to stay. She had so much more to show him, but he hadn't even given her the chance. Why? Why had he run home? Why hadn't he said goodbye? It wasn't like him. He wasn't a coward. Had he gone back for Conn?

"Gray," she said softly, hoping, praying that he could somehow hear her. "Just send me word that you're coming back to me. Come back to me."

But no word came.

She remained in bed the next day and refused to eat or speak to anyone when they tried to ask her where Gray had gone. What could she tell them, that Gray had abandoned—?

No. He wouldn't. How could she have doubted him? Wherever or whenever he was, he would return to her. She'd wasted enough time crying and upsetting her mother.

Resigned to trust that he hadn't dumped her and left to go century hopping, she got out of bed. The first thing she did was check her phone. She hadn't missed it. She'd never received good news on it. No missed calls. 8pm. What happened to Harper? Aria was tempted to call her. Had she heard anything from Gray? Was he okay? Was Conn okay? Soon, she'd have to tell her parents something about their son. Had they been caught and accused of being witches? Was Harper and Mrs. B. trying to save them, or was it too late and they didn't want to tell her? Time did not flow smoothly from century to century. Gray could have returned to Dartmouth a year before he left it.

She put her phone down and wrung her hands, then picked it up again, tapped her pathetically short list of contacts. She was about to tap Harper's name when the front doorbell rang. She heard her mother walk by her bedroom door to answer it.

She almost rushed out, hoping it was Gray, but she heard Harper's voice and nearly passed out instead. Why was Harper here? Why hadn't she called? Did she have news she would only give face to face?

Aria's eyes stung. She couldn't go out there. She didn't want to hear.

Someone knocked. She stared at the door, breath stilled.

"Aria, sweetheart. There's a woman here named Harper Black to see you."

Aria wanted to cry for her mother to send their visitor away, but she wouldn't put her mother in such an awkward situation.

She walked to the door. Had her heart stopped beating? Was she breathing? Her mind had forgotten how to continue living.

Closing her eyes, she closed her hand around the doorknob, turned it, and opened the door.

She saw Harper. Her eyes didn't appear swollen and red. Their visitor looked toward Aria's mother, who took the hint and excused herself to make some coffee.

When they were alone, Aria stared at her, waiting for her to speak.

*Please. Please. Please.*

"Forgive me for making you wait. I wanted to make sure what I was telling you was accurate."

Aria could feel a thick fog settling over her. "Tell me," she managed.

"Yes," Harper breathed out, making Aria sway on her feet. "Alright, well, he returned to his father and things got ugly."

"Ugly?"

Harper nodded and sighed. "According to my grandmother, Gray warned him not to touch his title or his castle and lands or he would go on a warpath and kill Timothy and his mother—and then he'd come for the duke. I don't think he meant it. Grayson hated killing in the king's army, but I don't know what he will do if the duke tries to give everything to Cavendish."

"Why did he go back?" Aria asked. "Did something happen?"

"Grandmother didn't say."

"You haven't seen him then or Connall?"

Harper shook her head.

Aria was about to ask her how exactly they stayed in contact and could Aria contact Gray in the same way? But she didn't want to just speak with him. She wanted to fill her senses with him. To see him smile at her the instant he saw her, to hear him say her name in his soft, resonating voice, to smell his scent—that faint scent of forest and fresh air, to touch him, and taste him while he kissed her senseless. If she didn't do so soon, she'd go out of her mind.

"Tell your grandmother...tell Mrs. B. to take me to him," she demanded. Then added a softer, "Please."

Harper gave her a regretful look and shook her head. "She can't."

"Why not? I thought she could do—"

"He doesn't want you there," Harper cut her off. "He expressly forbade her from contacting you."

If he appeared and ran her through with his sword, it would have felt the same for Aria. She staggered against the wall, then turned and clutched it to keep her upright. What had she done to make him just completely cut her off like this? Nothing! She'd done nothing for him to have a change of heart. And even if she had done the most heinous thing, she didn't believe he would leave in the night without a word.

He didn't want her to go back in case his enemies hurt her. Here in the future, they were powerless against her.

"I don't know what his plans are," Harper continued. "But he requested that my grandmother transfer all his assets to you."

"He doesn't plan on coming back," Aria murmured in a whisper. It was all she could manage.

"Right," Harper agreed, "and there's a good chance he'll die there. The Cavendishes have friends on the council. If Grayson's caught and charged with witchcraft, they'll try to burn him. That's why I've disobeyed my grandmother and come here. And that's why I'll bring you back to convince him to live here with you. I know he loves you, Aria. This isn't what he really wants."

"You'll bring me to him? Really?"

Harper nodded, and then gave a short, soft laugh when Aria threw herself in her arms and hugged her.

"When should we go? Right now?" The sooner the better for Aria. She couldn't wait to set her eyes on him. It felt as if a year had passed since she had.

"Alright, go tell your family you'll be back in a day or two."

Aria agreed and hurried off to tell her parents she'd be staying with Mrs. B's granddaughter Harper for a few days. Before they left, she changed into a pair of leggings, a bustier-style top that was most similar to her eighteenth-century bodice, and a cropped hoodie.

She'd agreed to meet Harper outside in front of the building, but Harper wasn't there when Aria arrived. At first, Aria thought she'd changed her mind and left without her, but then she saw Harper running toward her.

"We have to hurry," Harper breathed, reaching her. "There's trouble. A fire."

Fire? Aria nearly fainted at the thought of them burning Gray...no. Please, God. "Wait!" She hurried to the door. "I have to go back up!"

"What for?" Harper asked impatiently.

"A fire extinguisher. If there's a fire, we'll need it. My brother bought one for my father the Christmas of 2021. It should still be in the kitchen. I'll be right back!"

Aria sweated waiting for the elevator. She tapped her foot while it ascended, then burst out when it reached her floor, and the doors opened. She made up a ridiculous excuse about seeing one of the neighbors who asked to borrow the fire extinguisher. Without explaining further, she procured the extinguisher, kissed her mother on the way out and raced back to Harper.

"My key!" Aria gasped when Harper pulled the gold key from her pocket. "You had it all this time?"

"I couldn't let you leave him," Harper explained quickly while she pulled Aria back to the building's front doors. "I wanted to give you both a few more days together. I knew he was losing his heart to you."

She moved to insert the key, but Aria stopped her. "The key won't fit that door—"

"It will fit any door," Harper said, then turned the inserted key and pushed the door open.

Aria immediately smelled smoke in the air. It was midday and the sun still shone, but a mammoth charcoal cloud was slowly approaching. They stood atop the roof between the parapets of Dartmouth castle. The roof where she'd seen him dance for the first time. From their vantage point, they could see the smoke rising from the treetops in the north.

"Is that a forest fire?" Aria asked, her words snatched away on the wind.

But Harper caught them and pulled her gaze away from the smoke to turn to her.

They both knew in the same instant that if there was a fire that threatened his friends, that's where Gray would be. Aria also knew that her measly fire extinguisher was no match against a forest fire.

Together they raced out of the castle not stopping to speak to anyone. Harper led her to the stables and helped her mount a strong young stallion. Harper leaped up in back of her and gave the horse a gentle kick with her heels.

It didn't take them long to reach the tree line north of the castle, and the billowing smoke rising from the center.

Dismounting, Aria pulled the pin on the extinguisher, unlocking the lever. She'd be ready if they came upon flames.

They were about to enter the forest when they saw three men carrying fiery torches and walking along the tree line ahead of them. They were lighting more of the trees on fire! Aria raced forward with Harper close behind. When Aria reached the backs of the men, she lifted her fire extinguisher high over her head and brought the metal canister back across the man's head. He went down almost instantly. She hoped she hadn't killed him, but there was no time to check. The second and third men were coming for her. As the third grew closer first, she spun in a pirouette and smashed her foot into his face. When he paused and swooned, she brought the bottom of the metal extinguisher down into his jaw and knocked him out.

The second brute had Harper by the throat, her punches having no effect on him.

"Harper!" Aria called out. When Harper looked at her, Aria motioned for her to duck.

Sinking her teeth into her captor's arm worked at loosening his grip. Harper was able to lower her head. It was enough for Aria to pull the lever and shoot a quick blast of extinguishing agent into the arsonist thug's face.

They heard a cry in the air as the second man screamed and coughed and gasped for air.

Aria looked up. Toric! And then she saw movement within the trees.

She ran forward with Harper hot on her heels. She didn't see many flames, but the underbrush was burning. It would be almost impossible for the animals to run on the ground.

She pulled the lever again and fired the agent onto the ground while she ran forward.

She almost fell over Gray's body.

"Gray! "Gray!" She screamed falling to her knees to lift his head in her arms. She didn't wait for Harper to catch up, but quickly checked to see if he was breathing. He was! She felt dizzy with relief.

His eyes fluttered open and he smiled when he saw her. "I dreamed..." He coughed and began again, his voice weak. "I dreamed this. I couldn't abandon my friends to the fire. I came back to save them, Aria."

"Ssh, don't speak, my love," she whispered gently, holding him.

"I would have found a way back to you," he breathed out, his eyes closing again. "I love you..." He was quiet. Aria feared he had passed out again. But then, she heard him. ..."most."

Harper appeared beside her and together they hoisted him up and dragged him beyond the trees. She heard Toric cawing overhead and felt as if she could understand him. The others. She turned to look behind her and saw a line of forest critters and a few deer following on the cooling ground.

When they broke through the trees, Aria and Harper collapsed with an unconscious Gray between them.

Aria was no nurse, but she knew Gray could be suffering from smoke inhalation. When she suggested they return to the twenty-first century to get him to a hospital, Harper insisted they bring him to their grandmother first.

"Where's my brother? Aria pleaded the instant she reached Mrs. B.

"There now," Mrs. B. said, patting her hand. "He's well at the Gable holding. He's been sent for so that he can go home with you.

Aria smiled with great relief, but Mrs. B. wasn't done. "You disobeyed me," she admonished her great, great...many times removed granddaughter.

"I know," Harper said as he was carried away to a sickbed. "I love him."

Mrs. B. gave Harper a scowl that didn't reach her eyes and

then shifted her gaze to Aria.

"I love him too."

Mrs. B. broke into a smile. "I'm glad my Gray is so well-loved.

"Our Gray," Aria corrected, then followed her up the stairs to Gray's room, where he was being put into bed.

Mrs. B's gaze warmed on Aria. "He didn't want to be separated from you, Aria, dear. But he was afraid that if they caught you, they would do the same thing to you that they did to his mother. He told me if that happened, he would step into the flames with you. There would be no point in him escaping."

Aria felt like bursting into tears. He'd risked his life and their life together to come back and save his friends and she loved him all the more for it. She wouldn't lose him now that she'd willingly returned to the past for him.

They were quiet while Tessa Blagden examined him. When she stood over him, quiet for a long time, Aria went to her. Was she a healer? Was she healing her grandson?

"What are you doing?" she asked the older woman.

"I'm praying, dear."

Aria nodded and joined her, taking Gray's hand while she bowed her head. She prayed first to God, and then,

*Gray, my darling love, if you can hear me in that thick beautiful skull of yours, I need you. I need to be by your side as your wife with your seven children around our knees, loving you enough to have seven more. Come back to me, Gray. Come back and dance with me again. Come back and touch me again.*

His finger moved over hers, startling her and making her look at his hand. He tightened his grip as she held his hand and then moved his pinkie over hers again.

Tears filled her vision, and she swiped them away to see him. His eyes were still closed, but his touch promised her a lifetime.

# EPILOGUE

*Upstate, New York*
*2033*

G RAY PACED THE outside of the birth room, sweating, pushing back his hair, staring at the door.

His wife was inside suffering her first labor, despite the six boys they had playing outside. He would have been in the birth room with her if he could have done it without getting in the way, to the extent of bumping into the doctor, almost knocking him out when he hit his head on a stool.

They could have gone to the hospital, but his darling wanted to have their child at home. They had enough money to get a doctor and a small team of nurses to come to the house Gray had built for her when they first came to live in the twenty-first century eleven years ago.

He was much like his mother in that he preferred the future over the restrictive past. There was medicine here to help with the pain of childbirth and a myriad of other things.

By now, he was well-used to the wonders of the time. Technology was indeed a powerful thing. He was able to change his name legally to Grayson Ashmore without leaving his home more than once. Pity, he liked driving his jaguar with the roof down. The jaguar was for Caleb, his third son, who liked everything his father liked. The Lamborghini was for his oldest son Sebastian, the Ferrari for William, a pair of Aston Martins for his twin boys, Finn and Scout. The Koenigsegg Gemera was, of course, for the youngest. Well, not the youngest for long. Gray had collected the cars over the years and four out of the six were in his private garage, away for the boys until they each reached their twenty-first birthdays. The Rolls Royce Ghost he bought for his seventh child being born today was with the rest.

"Dad," ten-year-old Sebastian called out in a whiny pitch, "tell Caleb to give me my phone!"

Gray stopped pacing and looked around the hall. He saw his third son's mane of golden curls, the only one of the six with such a color, peeping out from behind his ajar bedroom door. "Caleb, do you have your brother's phone?"

"Yes, Daddy. It's one-fifteen."

Gray checked his antique watch—not that he doubted his brainy son. For a seven-year-old, Caleb was ahead of the other students in his school. He wore his thick, black rimmed glasses as shamelessly as his high grades. He astounded Gray every time Gray saw him. Caleb was his little fighter. Born to a mother addicted to drugs. He was given up at birth—also addicted.

After Gray and Aria had successfully adopted their first two sons, the adoption agency contacted them about tiny, lion-hearted Caleb.

"Give the phone to me, Caleb."

Caleb came out of his room and hurried to his father, keeping his eyes off Sebastian.

Gray gave his oldest a stern look. "You know the rules. You're to be off your phone at one o'clock. Don't make your little brother have to tell on you again. Do you think he enjoys it? He was there, hiding. You should be setting an example." Gray told him and placed his hand on Sebastian's head. "We have a new babe coming today. What kind of brother will you be?"

Finn and Scout came barreling around a corner and crashed into their father before they could stop. "Is it a baby yet?" they asked in unison.

Gray sighed then smiled for the twin's sakes. "It will be soon."

"Nothing yet?" Another voice asked, following the twins and carrying a two-year-old baby girl in his arms. Connall and Sarah

Darling's third child. Sarah was in the birthing room with Aria, Harper, and his mother-in-law, Rose Darling, along with four nurses.

"Are William and Cody still with Mrs. Gable?"

"Yes, relax. I know it's technically your first time, but my sister is strong."

"I know she is, but I won't relax until she's smiling at me, alive and well." He added the last in a low voice so the boys wouldn't hear. Though one time, many years ago, he'd had a vision of six sons and a daughter, he wasn't a seer. Even though sometimes images of his daughter would flash across his mind. She was the only one he shared the gift with. Even his grandmother had no idea why. As far as she knew, no one in the family line had ever communicated with the unborn. But Gray couldn't see the future.

He didn't know how long he had on this earth with his wife, so he cherished every moment with her.

The bedroom door opened, stopping everyone from speaking another word. Gray's heart stopped, as well. He waited for Harper to say something.

"Gray, you have a daughter."

His daughter. The words echoed in his head over and over. He didn't think anything could make him as happy as the thought of his wife and sons, and his peaceful life on land vast enough and with a forest to the east to house all his animal friends, but he was wrong. Having a daughter was better than all of it.

He took a step into the room, but Harper stopped him. "Aria's uterus is weak, Gray. She probably won't go to term again. The doctor thinks for her safety, she should make an appointment at the hospital to get her tubes tied. This baby will be your last. We're not sure why we didn't see it. The prophecy is still unfulfilled."

Gray looked at her and smiled. "The prophecy is fulfilled, Harper. I knew I'd have a daughter. I know her name. I've spoken to her already. And do you think it really matters that my sons were not born to me and Aria? We raise them in love, as we will raise their baby sister. She'll lead her brothers, and the curse will be broken."

Without another word, he stepped into the room. When he saw his wife lying in bed, the nurses cleaning up after her while she nursed their daughter, he felt his eyes burn. He went to her and smiled when she looked up from the baby and saw him.

"Oh, Gray," she said with a tender smile for the tiny babe in her arms. "We have a daughter. Isn't she beautiful?"

He let his worshipful gaze rove over his wife. "Yes, just as beautiful as her mother."

"We never discussed a name for a daughter—" Aria said, handing the swaddled baby to him. "I can't think of a single thing."

"Kaia," Gray said. "She told me her name is Kaia. It means pure and innocent."

Aria stared at him, her face flushed. "She told you?"

He nodded and smiled at his daughter's pink face and mop of black fuzzy hair. "Do you like the name, darling?"

"Yes," Aria said with a sudden bright smile. "I love it."

Sitting on a chair close to the bed, Gray held his daughter in the crook of one arm and took Aria's hand in his free hand. "Have I told you how much I love you?"

She nodded and smiled at him. "You tell me every time you look at me."

He laughed softly and then beckoned his sons, who were crowded by the door, to come in. As they took turns meeting their new baby sister, Gray noticed another figure by the door.

He gave his wife back the baby and went to the visitor.

"I wasn't sure you'd come."

"How could I miss the birth of Kaia Ashmore?" his grandmother asked, smiling into the room.

"You knew about her, then?" Gray asked her, wondering what role his daughter would play in the Ashmore saga.

"I just recently learned of her. She kept herself hidden. She's powerful."

"I know. But I want her to have a regular life."

His grandmother nodded, and then she laughed a little, making him squirm. What did she know about Kaia's future?

When the baby began to cry, Gray rushed into the room and sent everyone away. They could all see the baby later. His wife was tired.

Alone, Gray climbed into the bed with Aria and the babe between them.

"It's been a while since I've seen you dance," he said in a quiet voice.

She laughed a soft little laugh that flipped his belly over and made his heart accelerate. "Well, it will be a little while before I can."

"I know," he told her, smoothing her hair from her eyes. "I want the rest of our days to be filled with dancing, and lots of lovemaking, but no more children."

"I have to have surgery," she told him with a nervous catch in her voice.

"I'll be right by your side when you wake up and take care of you until you're well."

She gave him a loving smile, then, "Are you happy here, Gray?"

He chuckled. "Darling, I've been here for over a decade now. Can't you tell that I'm happy?"

She nodded. "Yes. But it's not because you smile all the time and laugh at the silly things the boys do. I believe you're finally happy because of the way you dance now. There's joy and freedom in your movement."

He gazed at her, as lovely as she was the first time he saw her. "You brought those things to me, Aria, and helped me fulfill my purpose."

"Your purpose is to love me?" she teased lightly. Her lids drooped over her eyes.

"Yes," he whispered lovingly, "my purpose is to love you, and I will for all time."

## The End

# About the Author

Paula Quinn is a New York Times bestselling author and a sappy romantic moved by music, beautiful words, and the sight of a really nice pen. She lives in New York with her three beautiful children, six over-protective chihuahuas, and three adorable parrots. She loves to read romance and science fiction and has been writing since she was eleven. She's a faithful believer in God and thanks Him daily for all the blessings in her life. She loves all things medieval, but it is her love for Scotland that pulls at her heartstrings.

To date, four of her books have garnered Starred reviews from Publishers Weekly. She has been nominated as Historical Storyteller of the Year by RT Book Reviews, and all the books in her MacGregor and Children of the Mist series have received Top Picks from RT Book Reviews. Her work has also been honored as Amazons Best of the Year in Romance, and in 2008 she won the Gayle Wilson Award of Excellence for Historical Romance.

Website:
pa0854.wixsite.com/paulaquinn

www.ingramcontent.com/pod-product-compliance
Ingram Content Group UK Ltd.
Pitfield, Milton Keynes, MK11 3LW, UK
UKHW021505140525
5885UKWH00105B/893